FRACTURED ORBITS

Encoded Orbits Book 1

JEANNETTE BEDARD

Cover design by Rook Books Designs (rookbookdesigns.com)

Edited by Charlie Knight (cknightwrites.com)

Chapter One

The girl with the liquorice-coloured curls sat at a desk in the second row. She chewed on the end of her pencil with her side teeth as her adult front teeth hadn't grown in yet. Her 3D printed clothes marked her as a refugee from New Haven— someone who had fled when the bombs fell.

She shifted her datapad on her desk as the teacher brought up a hologram depicting a figure-eight dotted with cyan points of light. The shimmering image extended until it filled the area above the students, forcing them all to tilt their chins up to see it.

"The Loop is the reason our ancestors on the generation ships chose this system almost two-hundred and fifty years ago," the teacher said, pointing at the hologram. "Each cyan dot represents a wormhole. All together, they form a network connecting a series of solar systems."

Molly pulled the pencil from her mouth and used it to scratch behind an ear, her glossy black hair bouncing with each movement. She frowned as she studied the loop of wormholes stretched through the air above her head.

"But there's a catch." The teacher pointed at the line joining the dots. "The network is one way. If you don't get off at the system you want, you need to go all the way around."

Molly put up her hand.

"Yes, Molly," said the teacher as he stopped in front of her desk.

Her brows pulled together before she spoke. "But what about the wormholes that don't fall on the figure eight?"

"Good observation." He strode back to the front of the class. "There are a few gates that we know of off the main loop. For example, Indigo Station and Rokan both sit at the end of off-Loop links."

Molly nodded and resumed chewing her pencil.

"Is that the one?" Greer asked as he looked away from the video feed and at Major Zane, Rock 13-A5's head of security. Her mono-brow and meaty hands suggested an unflattering throwback to Cro-Magnon genes. Zane lacked refinement—unlike Greer's new boss, General Swa.

"Molly Oswiu has displayed unexpected skills," Zane said.

The woman sat way too close to him, but her office was tiny, leaving no other option. Greer shuttered. He could even smell the coffee on her breath.

"You need to be more specific. The skills I'm looking for only manifest in less than one in a billion children." Greer studied the classroom. Could that little girl really be what he was looking for? From his current point of view, Molly Oswiu seemed ordinary.

The colourful artwork plastered across the wall didn't hide the fact that the room had been repurposed from an adult space. Children were never supposed to be on the Protectorate's secret base—yet here they were.

"We've detected vibrations through the ground that originate from the girl's quarters. She's also had a few disagreements with classmates that have resulted in objects being moved."

Greer cocked his head. "What kind of objects?"

"Stationary, shoes, food. Nothing big. And no one has gotten hurt."

"Have you sequenced her genetics?" Greer asked as he returned his attention to the feed.

Zane frowned. "Her mother has not authorized us to. We can't just do that to a civilian, let alone a child."

Greer pursed his lips as he focused the video feed on the little girl. According to the files, she had just turned seven— younger than he was hoping for. That could be a problem.

"The girl's mother...tell me about her."

"Veena Oswiu was a professor of mathematics at New Haven University. After the bombing our cryptography department recruited her."

"And the father?"

"Hwicce Oswiu. He's a soldier, currently deployed on Candy Cane Lane."

"Hmm." Candy Cane Lane was the last active battlefield in the Protectorate's war against the Nadar Alliance.

He zoomed the video tighter onto Molly.

The latest intelligence reports suggested the Nadar Alliance had figured out how to take people with abilities like Molly's— that is, telekinetic tendencies—and turn them into super soldiers. Molly was the first person within the Protectorate who they'd found with even a hint of this kind of potential.

Why did she have to be so young?

"Have you seen enough?" Zane's gaze bored into him.

Greer shifted his focus back to the screen. After months of hunting, Molly Oswiu was the best human candidate he'd found to be the Protectorate's first super-soldier; he needed to overlook the fact she was a child, push away his misgivings and focus on the task he'd been assigned. If he accomplished it, the reward would be great, and his name would go down in the history books.

"Does anyone know how the gates work?" the teacher asked.

The little girl in the classroom raised her hand once again.

"Yes, Molly?"

"A rock world holds each gate in its place. My mom says these worlds are extra heavy; she also says no one really knows how the system works or who built them."

Greer turned off the video feed and turned to Zane. "I need to take the girl with me."

The edges of Zane's mouth pulled down. "Absolutely not. The Protectorate doesn't kidnap children."

"General Swa ordered me to reproduce the work the Nadar Alliance is doing on super soldiers. This girl is the key to that." Greer shifted in his seat under Zane's continued gaze.

"Molly is too young to consent to being your lab experiment, and I'm certain her mother won't on her daughter's behalf."

"It's for the good of us all," Greer said. "According to the intel reports, the Nadar Alliance already has dozens of super soldiers. If they attacked here, there wouldn't be a thing you and your team could do to stop it. We need to defend ourselves."

"The Rock is safe." She leaned back and smoothed the indigo fabric of her uniform. "I've done as General Swa has ordered and shown you the girl, but I won't condone you getting closer."

"My work cannot be completed without taking that girl to my lab." Greer shifted in his seat, surprised a mere security chief seemed willing to contravene her commanding officer's orders.

Zane pointed to the door. "Get the hell out, and if I catch you going anywhere near that child, I'll throw your ass in a cell."

Greer stood and left the office without a word. Zane wasn't going to help him get what he needed; the woman was more of a goon than a strategic thinker. But if he didn't produce a super-soldier for the Protectorate, General Swa would fire him and condemn him to obscurity. He couldn't let that happen, even if it meant kidnaping a little girl.

He strode through the hallways heading towards the tram

station. The mostly empty utilitarian grey corridors gave him the space he needed to think. With the introduction of the GenEn protocols shortly after humans arrived in the area, no one was openly tweaking human genetics, yet Molly clearly had abilities beyond a normal human, and the Nadar Alliance had found dozens of others like her.

As he arrived at the tram station, he paused. Swa was going to expect him to have a plan. He took inventory of what he knew.

Millions of humans passed through the gate systems each year, yet no one understood how the wormholes worked. On the surface, the radiation inside the gates appeared harmless to humans, yet both plants and insects showed rare mutations after passing through. If only their ancestors had thought to bring higher animals with them when they left Earth, he'd have better lab animals.

As the tram rolled into the station, his thoughts went to Subject 33. He licked his lips; that specimen would be in his possession soon. Then there was the writing found carved into walls in caves on the anchor worlds. Most likely, the Gate Makers wrote those words before they vanished. Would decoding them give him the insight he needed to reproduce and augment the gates effects? Everything had to be related—he was sure of it.

Without Molly Oswiu, his project couldn't progress. But how would he get her? Zane was right on one point: kidnapping a child was distasteful. So he needed that little girl to show her true colours. Then for her safety and that of everyone on the Rock, she would be handed over to him and become Subject 34.

Chapter Two

Hwicce hit the ground, the servos in his battle armour groaning from the impact. He sprinted behind a ticket booth made of simulated sandstone and dropped to one knee. Whirring fans whisked away the stench of his exertion as he paused to get his bearings.

A flashing green line showed him in his helmet's heads-up display where he needed to go. Blue call signs marked the locations of all his platoon members. As his team landed around him, they spread out in the pre-planned formation, heading towards their objectives.

Creating a billow of dust, Baker landed off to his right. The brassy metallic coating to her armour glinted in the bright light. She raised her weapon and scanned their target: the gaudy casino in front of them.

"You good?" he asked.

Keeping her gaze focused on their objective, she gave him a thumbs up. "I don't see any movement, sir," she said over a private channel.

"Even though this is a routine sweep, stay sharp," he broadcasted to his team. "I expect everyone to make it home in one piece." Raising his pulse rifle, he shifted to get a view of the casino. "Sound off."

"Alpha squad is in place," Dogan's voice came over the comms.

"Bravo squad's got the rear," Fin said.

"Charlie's to the south," Chang answered.

Hwicce confirmed their locations before he stood. Their cruisers above had already won the space battle, but a lot of work remained for ground troops like his platoon. Intel said to expect resistance from the multiple groups of Nader Alliance soldiers hiding in the area.

"Stick to the plan, everyone," he transmitted. "Let me know the instant you spot enemy movement."

As he started moving forward, he glanced to his right. Baker stayed right with him—as always. He'd never admit it, but her presence was a relief. Even in the chaos of battle, she remained predictable and solid. Confident she had his back, Hwicce let his eyes follow the green line of his projected path.

Dead ahead, the Pharaoh Casino rose from the ground in the shape of a pyramid. The travel brochures declared it as true to the original down to the simulated sandstone blocks covered with glittering gold decorations. Staring at the monument to gambling, Hwicce remained sceptical that the people of Old Earth had ever built anything that tacky. Fortunately, his display didn't show any enemy forces in view.

He and Baker passed two bird-headed, human-bodied statues constructed from the same simulated sandstone as the ticket booth. His head didn't reach past their shins. He could've just stepped into one of the historical vids his daughter loved—except for the flashing neon lights visible even in the midday sun advising massive jackpots.

"I thought they shut this place down," Baker said on their private channel.

"If it's this tacky under minimal power, I can't imagine how awful it'd look on full." He paused to confirm his platoon was in position.

Baker snorted. "Maybe the bright lights are to dazzle the patrons into parting with more cash."

With a chuckle, Hwicce continued forward, his eyes on their target.

The bright sunlight made the oversized entrance to the casino appear dark. He did a quick IR scan to make sure no one waited for them inside.

"Sir." It was Chang. Hwicce checked, and she was off to his left around the side of the structure. "There's movement at the west door. We spotted a group of Rokan soldiers entering."

Hwicce paused. The Rokan were among the plethora of groups that loosely made up the Nader Alliance military. Rokan soldiers didn't wear combat armour, instead hiding their faces behind goggles and respirators. They moved unnervingly fast, showing up when least expected.

"How many?"

"Five." Chang spoke with the certainty of someone who'd survived many battles.

"Roger that," Hwicce replied. "Everyone, stay alert. We now know for sure there are enemy troops inside."

"Covering." Baker dropped to one knee.

Hwicce sprinted as fast as his suit would go until he reached the gaping entrance. Up close, the building loomed overhead, nearly blotting out the sun, but his suit quickly adjusted to the lower light levels. He reminded himself the mission was just a routine sweep—the enemy had already surrendered; their goal was to just round up the few remaining soldiers who hadn't gotten the message.

He kept his body relaxed as he dropped to one knee beside a pillar of faux stone. Keeping his rifle sights on the dark interior, he said, "Covering."

Baker darted forward and behind the pillar on the other side of the entrance.

Resetting his display filters for the interior lighting, Hwicce rose and made his way around the pillar. Inside, the ornate atrium complete with palm trees and rectangular pond appeared empty. Further in, rows of old-school slot machines extended in multiple lines. The metal machines blocked his IR scanner, creating infinite hiding spaces. The enemy could be anywhere.

"They're on the run," he reminded himself without activating his comms. He kept his thoughts from descending into the worst-case scenarios and forced himself to stay focused on the moment.

"Contact!" Fin shouted into the comms link. "The bloody Rokan got behind us. Fucking mutants!"

Weapon fire sounded from the drop zone.

"Dammit." Hwicce turned away from the casino's entrance and started sprinting towards Fin. Baker followed close behind.

The bird-headed statue on the right disintegrated. A millisecond later, the concussion hit him, tossing him backwards and against the casino's wall. For a moment, his heads-up display shorted out. His mind raced through possibilities. Was it an unexploded bomb? A mine? Grenade? After a glitch, his display of tactical information returned. Red dots indicated some of his soldiers were down.

"Crap!" Hwicce pushed the rubble off and started moving towards the firefight. "Baker," he called as he lifted his rifle and looked down the sights. "Where are you?"

The air thirty metres in front of him seemed to swirl as though heat was rising off the pavers. Then a woman appeared squinting in the bright sunlight without goggles and a respirator. Her pale face was exposed—meaning she wasn't Rokan. A web of some sort covered her shaved head like a cap. Dark cloth cloaked the rest of her, and she didn't appear armed.

Hwicce didn't see her move, but suddenly, she stood directly in front of him. Her movement seemed impossible, but she didn't seem threatening. Hwicce decided she wasn't a combatant and lowered his weapon.

"Get down." He gestured towards the ground. He ran a diagnostic routine on his display. The visual band seemed to be glitching; maybe that's how he missed seeing her move. "It's not safe out here."

She ignored his instruction. Instead, she cocked her head, but her expression remained blank. She'd clearly heard him. Maybe she was shell-shocked.

"Are you lost?" Hwicce took a step closer to her. She would be in the line of fire if she stayed out here. "It's dangerous—"

With her palm, she struck the chest plate of his armour. He flew backwards with enough force to send him through the casino's wall.

As Hwicce scrambled to his feet, the alarms in his armour started sounding. Chest plate integrity down 13%, right rear proximity sensor off-line, servos in both knees near failure. He'd owe the suit techs when he got back to base, but he couldn't worry about that right now.

"Baker?" His heads-up display flickered, then went dark, leaving him with no idea where anyone was. At least he could still see through the clear surface of his visor. "Baker?"

He was inside the casino now. Other than a Hwicce-in-full-battle-armour-sized hole in the wall, his surroundings were pristine. He glanced back towards the entrance, hoping to see Baker. Instead, the un-armoured woman stood silhouetted in the light.

"Dammit." He pulled up his rifle and fired, this time without hesitation. Bolts of light flew towards his adversary.

She shimmered and vanished; he'd missed her. Intel had said there would be a new group of super-soldiers on the field. They failed to mention anything about teleportation. How was that even possible? Her bare face confirmed she wasn't Rokan, and even though Rokan were reported to move fast, it was not like this. Other than the cap, the woman didn't appear to be carrying much technology.

"Crap!" The woman was gone before he'd managed to get many sensor readings off her.

With a squelch, Hwicce's comms link returned to life.

"We've beaten them back," Fin transmitted.

"Everyone okay?" He turned to look for either Baker or the mystery woman.

"Just some dented armour," Fin responded.

"Good. Be warned: there's at least one super soldier in the area. She appears unarmed, but she's still dangerous." Hwicce swallowed. He seemed to be all alone in the casino's foyer. Where was Baker? "Can you pick up my location?"

"Got you, sir."

"I can't locate Baker. I need backup."

"We're on our way." Fin sounded confident.

"Stay sharp. The super soldier I encountered can teleport."

Hwicce re-booted his battle computer, but the heads-up display didn't fully come on, just the IR. At least he was no longer as blind.

Turning, he surveyed the casino. The slot machines limited what he could pick up, but a heat signature shone from deeper inside. He couldn't tell if it was Baker or the enemy. Using the cover of slot machines, he advanced. He knew he should wait for backup, but he kept going anyway, worried that Baker needed his help.

With his pulse-rifle at the ready, he circled around slot machine after slot machine. More heat signatures came into view up ahead, but he maintained his slow and steady advance.

"Baker," he called again on the comms.

The now-familiar shimmer materialized ten metres ahead. He aimed and squeezed the trigger just as the woman appeared. She vanished before being struck.

"Crap!"

His left-rear proximity alarm went off. He swung around,

but his failing armour slowed him. With bare hands, the woman struck his left side, sending him flying a second time.

He skidded into a row of slot machines, causing them to cascade like dominos as he tumbled over top of them. On the other side, he rolled across the floor, only stopping when he slammed into the base of a bar. The power to his armour failed, and its weight made him slump to the side. He re-booted the armour, and to his surprise, it powered back up. But another blow like that, and he might not get lucky a second time.

Swallowing, he tried to focus on the world beyond his display. Who was that woman? And where was she now? As though summoned, the woman appeared in front of him.

"Captain Oswiu." His comms link to command crackled to life. "We have reports of super soldiers in your area. It's imperative that you capture one of them."

He frowned. As usual, the staff officers working in command had no idea what it was like on the ground. The super-soldier before him remained where she was, staring at him—but she hadn't resumed her attack.

"Acknowledged," he said before cutting the line.

His rifle had broken free of his armour, and he didn't know where it was. He was unarmed and uncertain how long until backup would arrive. He gulped, trying to force his fear down. With his eyes fixed on the woman standing a few paces in front of him, he pushed himself up to his feet, expecting his armour to fail at any moment.

She took a step back and just stared at him.

"I won't hurt you. I just want to talk," he said. "Who are you?"

She froze, then cocked her head. "I don't know," she whispered. She scratched her cheek and squished her eyebrows together.

"I'm Hwicce." He opened the faceplate to his helmet, and the warm air of the casino dried the sweat on his brow almost instantly.

The woman met his gaze, her dark eyes boring into him. She said nothing. On the surface, she appeared to be an ordinary human—but clearly, she was much more.

"Where are you from?" he asked, keeping his tone as friendly as he could. Maybe her origin would give him some clues—the rumoured Nadar super soldiers had to be from somewhere. Intel said they were most likely a further tweak on people whose ancestors had already been genetically altered.

When the generation ships arrived, some people colonized hostile worlds where tweaking their descendant's genes made sense. Only later did they discover how wrong that idea was. If the super soldier wasn't a descendent of one of those strains, maybe she was a throwback like Molly...

He pushed the thought of his daughter away and focused on the woman in front of him.

After staring up at the ceiling for a moment, she glanced around at her surroundings. It was almost as though she was genuinely surprised to be where she was. "Where am I?"

"In the Pharaoh Casino on Candy Cane Lane." Hwicce took in a deep breath. Maybe he could talk her into coming with him.

Her eyes fixed on him again. "I don't understand." She gestured at the toppled slot machines and once opulent Egyptian-themed space. "None of this makes any sense."

"You're right. None of this makes sense." Keeping his empty palms in sight, he stepped closer, stopping an arm's length away. "Why don't you come with me? I can take you somewhere safe."

Baker popped out from behind a nearby slot machine and fired two blasts at the woman. Before Hwicce could react, the woman vanished.

"Dammit, Baker!" He spun around to see if the woman would reappear. "I'd almost convinced her to come peacefully."

"Can't you even be slightly happy I just saved your life?" Baker walked closer and tossed him his weapon. "Sir."

"Well, I'm glad you aren't dead—that has to count for something." Hwicce closed his faceplate and scanned the area on IR. The human heat signatures he'd spotted earlier were still there. "Seriously, I'm glad you're okay."

Baker shrugged, a gesture made comical by the combat armour. "Just a minor setback."

"Our orders are to bring in that woman." Hwicce continued surveying the casino, expecting the mysterious woman to materialize at any moment.

"How are we going to imprison someone who can teleport?"

It was Hwicce's turn to shrug. "If we catch her, I vote we hand her off to intel as quick as we can." He focused on the IR reading deeper in the building. It was the best lead he had. "Follow me."

"Hell, sir, I'm always willing to follow you." Baker's words dripped with her usual sarcasm.

Hwicce groaned and led the way to the back of the casino. They passed through a series of corridors lined with faux hieroglyphics before reaching a ballroom filled with gilded tables and chairs. No windows meant the only illumination came from the emergency lighting.

Sticking close to the walls, the two of them circled the room —their IR sensors said it was empty.

"Where did she go?" Hwicce muttered under his breath.

"Don't know, sir." Baker continued to follow close behind. "That monster had skills."

Hwicce glanced up at the dark ceiling, then back where they came from. "I'm not convinced she's a monster."

"She threw you through a wall." Baker's tone was flat.

"Keep moving, soldier," he grumbled as they reached the doors that could only lead to the kitchen. The IR signature wasn't far now.

"Yes, sir."

He paused and checked in with the rest of his troops. Everyone was okay, and they weren't far behind.

"Moving," he said as he hit the door release.

"Covering." Baker took up position beside the doorframe, pointing the barrel of her weapon at the door.

As the door slid open, an automatic light came on in the room beyond. It was a kitchen—a massive industrial one. His armour's augmented hearing picked up a click from a far door closing.

"They're running for it." He broke into a sprint.

"Wait up, sir." Baker fell in behind him. "Blindly storming a building is normally my thing."

"I trust you'll cover me," Hwicce said as he continued through the doorway, hoping to glimpse the augmented woman from before. They entered a service hallway, the overdone decor now replaced by beige walls and dim overhead lights.

Someone far ahead darted into a side room.

"Stop!" His voice boomed in the confined space as he stormed after his quarry.

With a crunch, his armoured shoulder smashed the doorframe as he rushed through. As pieces of doorframe tumbled to the ground, he pulled up his weapon and activated the sights. Then his breath caught in his throat.

His wife and daughter cowered before him. Veena held Molly tight as if her flesh could protect their daughter. She looked up at her husband with accusation in her eyes. Hwicce's hands trembled, and he lowered his rifle.

"Huh, some non-combatants." Baker followed him into the storeroom.

"They...." His words trailed off as he squeezed his eyes shut, knowing what he just saw was impossible.

"Good thing you didn't shoot first." Baker's tone edged on inappropriate humour.

Hwicce opened his eyes; it wasn't his family. Instead, a greenie woman dressed like a hotel attendant stood before him. She pushed her child behind her. Light from the hallway illuminated her green-hued skin. She said nothing, just stared at them.

"I'm sorry if I scared you," he said to her. "You two need to go to the refugee camp; you'll be safe there. I can arrange an escort for you."

The mother shook her head but said nothing as she took her child by the hand and filed out of the storeroom. The two of them looked nothing like his family—but they were someone's family and deserved to be safe.

"Baker, let the rest of the platoon know some non-combatants are on their way out.

"Yes, sir."

He bit his lip as he watched the mother and child go. He'd been away fighting when the bombs fell on New Haven. Had Veena and Molly been forced to hide like those two? What had they gone through? He should've been there to help or at least been there to comfort them after. He swallowed a lump in his throat. In the five months since the bombing, he hadn't even managed to get enough leave to see them in person.

Baker slapped his armour on the shoulder. "Yo, sir! You zoning out or something? Chang's calling you."

"Right." Hwicce shook his head. He needed to focus. "Chang, go ahead."

"We bagged three Rokan," she said with an edge of excitement in her voice. "Including one of the purple cloaks."

They weren't super-soldiers, but the Rokan might have useful intel. "Right, package them up. Take care with the purple cloak; they can twist your thoughts."

"On it. Chang out."

Chapter Three

Orin Akton wrung his hands together as he stood before the massive desk. The pounding behind his left eye suggested an impending migraine. He struggled to keep a grimace from his face as he stared at General Swa, the Coordinator of Information for the Protectorate's military.

He hadn't been invited to sit and knew better than to assume he could. The military facility within the hollowed-out asteroid of Rock 13-A5 was her domain, and she made sure no one forgot it. The gold trim on her indigo uniform glinted in the low light of her office, casting sinister reflections on her skin. He swallowed. Even though he'd been the head of the decryption department for almost a year, coming into his boss' office still intimidated him.

"Dr. Oswiu's analysis turned out to be correct." Swa leaned back in her chair behind the desk.

Orin shifted his weight as her gaze fell on him. He said nothing.

"You might as well call it for what it is," Dr. Greer said from his seat beside the wall of windows. He adjusted his jacket as he spoke as though he wanted everyone to notice the expensive garment. Orin wondered why Greer was in the room—or even on the Rock. Although he reported to Swa, Greer ran a top-secret research lab in a different system, a location so classified, Orin had no idea where it was.

Swa shifted her attention and scowled at Greer. "Remember, you're only an observer here."

"Dr. Veena Oswiu's analysis won us the war," Greer said, ignoring Swa's warning. He leaned forward and focused on Orin. "I'm curious how she broke the code."

"The messages were double encrypted. Veena used—"

Swa cut Orin off with a wave of her hand. "I don't need the details." She stood and walked over to the floor-to-ceiling windows that filled one entire wall of the oversized room. Outside, the shield gate aperture glinted under the system's far-off sun. The shield gate sealed the entrance to the cavern, keeping them safe from intruders—like the bombers that struck his home on New Haven. A small aperture allowed in autho-rized shuttles. Bigger ships docked outside.

"Do you trust Dr. Oswiu's analysis?" Swa's gaze bore into him.

Orin took a moment to compose himself. Even though the circumstances behind bringing Veena into his department had been difficult on her, she remained the best codebreaker he'd ever worked with. His gut feeling was to trust her.

"Absolutely," he said.

"She has given me reason for concern." General Swa returned to her seat behind her oversized desk. She projected Veena's file into the air between the two of them. He'd seen it before. Her past contained nothing shocking. She'd been an ordinary mathematician working at an ordinary university, married to a military officer with whom she had a daughter.

Orin shifted his weight from foot to foot. "I've been through her file."

"Well, it seems you didn't dig deep enough." With her left hand, Swa swiped another page of information, replacing what was there. "Here's her communication with her husband."

The sight of Veena's personal letters made Orin's stomach roll. The fact Swa had them wasn't right. "That should be private."

"The Overwatch AIs check everything that passes to our troops on the front line." She pursed her lips and stared at him with her dark eyes. "The two of them exchange ridiculously long love letters filled with cumbersome passages that leave me wanting to vomit."

Orin shrugged. "Perhaps they're just terrible poets."

"Or perhaps they're sending encrypted messages back and forth."

He said nothing. Swa was probably right, but he still believed he could trust Veena. What couple wouldn't want to ensure their conversations were private? It wasn't a sign of anything nefarious.

"My people can't break the code." She frowned.

Orin shifted on his feet. Up until that moment, he'd thought his team contained the only codebreakers around.

Swa leaned back in her chair. "It seems your best code breaker also excels at cryptography."

"That was her research focus at New Haven university." Orin grimaced; he'd gone too far—Swa hated when anyone talked back at her.

A scowl spread across her face. "What information could she possibly be sending to her husband?"

Orin opened his mouth to answer, then closed it again. What would she send? His mind raced as he tried to come up with what they might be sending that needed to be secret. Swa's tapping of her fingernail on the desk surface brought him back to the moment.

"Both her record and her husband's record are beyond repute. They're an honourable pair."

Swa raised an eyebrow. "Is that so?"

Orin swallowed. He'd fallen into her trap.

"She has an encrypted account on the DeepNet."

"What?" That didn't sound like the Veena he knew. The DeepNet was for illicit activities and wacko conspiracists. "That can't be right."

"She accessed it last night." Swa leaned back in her chair and crossed her arms. Her gaze continued to bore into Orin.

He took a deep breath. As intimidating as Swa was, she wasn't all-powerful. He could steer the conversation back onto familiar ground.

"Veena walked me through how she decrypted the messages," he said to turn the conversation back to the message contents. "Since her husband's unit is at Candy Cane Lane, I believe she was highly motivated to ensure her decryption was correct."

"Fine." Swa leaned forward and scrolled through the message again. "But did she pass on all the information in the messages?"

"I want to know more about the 'lab subjects' referred to in the correspondence from Vortex View," Greer cut in.

"Can you clarify what these 'lab subjects' are?" Orin asked. The tactical information in the messages had made sense, but the references to 'lab subjects' had seemed out of place—almost another level of encryption.

"That's well above your pay grade." Swa steepled her fingers together. "What Dr. Greer is asking is if all the information on these subjects was included in the report."

"Yes," Orin said. "I double-checked all of Veena's work."

Swa fixed her gaze on Greer. "Does that answer your question?" She raised an eyebrow as though daring the scientist to ask more.

"I expect there'll be firsthand reports from the soldiers on Candy Cane Lane." Greer stood and paced over to Orin but kept his gaze on Swa. "About that task…"

"I'm getting there," she said, waving Greer back to the seat by the windows.

Greer clasped his hands behind his back and stayed where he was. Swa narrowed her eyes at him, then focused on Orin.

"Due to Veena's DeepNet activity, I have no choice but to shut down all personal net access for your team until further notice."

Orin pursed his lips. His people were going to hate that; they were already far away from their homes, for those whose homes still existed.

"Give them until the morning. With the news of victory, everyone is going to want to reach out to their loved ones." Orin swallowed. Everyone except him. He didn't have anyone to reach out to. The woman he loved more than anything was gone.

Swa cocked her head as she studied him. "At midnight, personal net access will be cut."

"Thank you," Orin said.

"You need to keep better tabs on your people," Swa continued, oblivious to Orin's pain.

"Of course."

"Now, to Dr. Greer's task…" Swa stood and paced over to the windows. "We found some encoded data. I want Veena to work on decrypting it. I'll need you to prioritize it over all her other work."

"What kind of data?"

"It's highly classified."

Orin sighed. Declaring things classified seemed a common tactic Swa followed when more information would be useful. "I'll advise Veena that a new assignment is coming her way."

"Good." She turned her attention to the view out the window. "You're both dismissed."

Without another word, Orin left the office, and Greer followed close behind.

"Akton," Greer called, and Orin turned. The two of them

were alone in the foyer outside Swa's office. "I'll send the files directly to Dr. Oswiu in the morning. I suspect victory celebrations will fill up everyone's evening."

"I'm sure she'll be ready," Orin said.

Greer paced forward. In the bright light, his meticulous attention to his own grooming and attire seemed out of place for a military scientist. "I hear she has a young daughter."

"Yes." Orin raised an eyebrow as he stared at the other man. "Many of the staff here have children with them. It does not impact their work."

"Of course it doesn't." Greer moved closer than Orin was comfortable and leaned in, lowering his voice. "Now, have you met Veena's girl? What did you notice about her?"

Orin took a step away. "I've seen her playing with the other kids in the barrack module. She's just an ordinary kid."

"Hmmm..." Greer turned and strode off down the corridor.Orin waited until Greer was out of sight, then headed the opposite way to the tram station.

On the tram back to his office, Orin sat alone in a row at the back of the car. A handful of staff officers boarded after him, but they clustered around the door, chatting in excited tones about the victory party to come. No one even glanced Orin's way.

Picking up speed, the tram circled the command module—a place he could only go when invited. On the other side, Orin got the full view of the hollowed-out rock's interior landscape. Nestled on the inside of an asteroid, Rock 13-A5 contained several well-separated facilities—some so secret, Orin had no idea what went on inside. Biometric codes controlled access everywhere except the barrack module, keeping everyone in their place. Even when he was exactly where he was supposed to be, the Overwatch AI still kept tabs.

Only the vertical farm that kept them fed stood out from the series of low grey modules. It was a multi-story structure set off to one side of the great cavern. Full-spectrum lights, too bright to look directly at, cascaded out of all the windows, casting a blue glow on the rock surrounding it.

Grateful for a few moments of solitude, he stared at the beacon of light from the vertical farm.

He'd been open about most of his background with his department, how he'd once been a shuttle pilot before he'd gone back for an advanced mathematics degree. How after that, he'd taken a post working for the Protectorate military at the Rock. But what he hadn't said was that he also had had family on New Haven when the bombing began. Just his wife, Mary. She'd been in her studio behind their house when a bomb hit the roof. A crater now marked what had once been a warm and welcoming home. He wasn't even left with a body to cremate. A lump formed in his throat as he thought about the last conversation he'd had with the woman he loved. They'd argued.

He took another deep breath and fought to keep his expression composed—he couldn't afford to show his people too much emotion. Outside, the grey landscape mirrored his general internal state.

No one looked his way when he entered Blackview Hall Room B, the cryptology department he ran. His team remained focused on their consoles, decrypting the near-endless number of messages that came their way. News of the declaration of victory clearly hadn't made its way here yet, and he couldn't muster enough energy to tell his people the good news. Without making eye contact with anyone, he continued on toward his office.

At his door, he paused and glanced towards Veena's cubicle. Her dark hair shadowed her face as she worked. She didn't deserve the scrutiny Swa directed her way—four months after they'd seconded Veena to the job. There had to be more to the story, but he had no idea where to even start looking for the answer. Besides, his head was pounding.

He sighed and entered his office, closing the door behind him. The bottle of generic rum in his bottom desk drawer beckoned, promising a few hours of numbness.

Chapter Four

Hwicce stepped out of the command module and into the evening light. He paused and gazed up. Glinting reflections from the Protectorate's armada flashed as they circled the planet. The only stationary object in orbit was Candy Cane Lane's spaceport tethered above. He let out a sigh.

"Hey, sir. Coming out for some generations dice?" Baker asked. She'd already showered after the days' mission and was back in her standard evening wear of a ratty, black tracksuit.

"Thanks, but not tonight. I've got to hit the showers, then I'm going to write my wife before hitting the rack," he said.

Even though his commanding officer had chastised him for not capturing the super solder they encountered, he did receive praise for bringing in Rokan prisoners, so the day wasn't a total loss. More importantly, none of his soldiers got injured in the day's fighting, and he didn't have to write anyone's family tonight with bad news. He let out a long exhale.

Eighteen months of fighting had left him skeptical whether the war made any kind of sense. Yes, his homeworld had been bombed back to a pre-terraformed state, and only luck had kept his wife and daughter safe. But the enemy hadn't struck first— they had. He'd arrived after bombs had dropped on at least five worlds now. Candy Cane Lane was unique in that it hadn't been levelled with explosives before he'd arrived.

Unaware of his inner turmoil, Baker shrugged. "I'll have to swindle you out of credits some other night then." She strode off towards the mess hall.

Relief swept over him as she vanished out of view. He wouldn't be forced to put on a happy face for the evening, but he didn't want to let his troops know how worn out he felt. They deserved a focused leader—not one who'd begun questioning everything.

The hot water did wonders, leaving him feeling near human again. Looking forward to some time alone, he slid open the door to his pod and stepped inside. The glossy white walls of his tiny quarters greeted him. The pod followed him wherever he deployed, giving him a sense of normalcy. The room's compact configuration left him barely enough space to move around, but he didn't have to share.

After hanging up his towel, he sat on the built-in bunk and tucked his shower sandals away. Sleep tempted him, as he'd have to be up sooner than he liked—he hadn't had a chance to sleep in since his last visit home. Leaning his elbows onto his knees, he buried his face in his hands. He knew sleep wouldn't come easy.

The super soldier bothered him. She fought with a vacant expression, almost as though a puppet master pulled her strings, controlling her. He doubted she'd consented to being used that way.

When angry, Molly shook things without touching them. Would a skill like that grow into what he saw in the super soldier? He and Veena worked to keep Molly's skills secret, but it was only a matter of time until she got angry and her parents couldn't cover it up. He swallowed. Being away meant Veena had to deal with Molly on her own.

From the alcove at the head of his bed, he pulled out his datapad and projected his favourite hologram of Veena and Molly.

Molly's grinning face appeared on the swing at the park near his home on New Haven. Her black hair shone under the bright sunlight; the curls bounced chaotically as the swing moved. Her dimples made his heart melt like they did every time.

"Higher, Mommy," she said as she tightened her grip on the swing's chains.

From out of the hologram, Veena laughed, her voice rich and almost musical. "Are you sure?" She stepped into view behind Molly. Her smile created the same dimples as Molly, and her curls were only slightly more contained.

Molly kicked her feet. "Higher, higher."

Veena placed her hands on Molly's back and gave a big push. Molly screeched as the swing accelerated.

"You'll have to take a turn," Veena said as she stepped to the side of the swing and came towards him.

"I want to capture this," his own voice came from the recording. "I have to ship out in the morning."

"A big tough army guy like you surely has the muscle to push her even higher." Veena flashed him a mischievous smile. "Besides, I need to save some energy for later…"

The recording ended, and the smiling faces of his family blinked away. For a moment, he stared at the spot where they'd been.

"I miss you two."

After taking a deep breath, Hwicce pulled out a thin comic and turned it over in his hands. A brightly coloured view of the interior of one of the old generation ships covered both the front and back. Splashes of pinks and blues marked the walls, contrasting the black view out a window. A little girl, her dark brown skin highlighted by a yellow dress, held a tentacle of an octopus-like alien in one hand. The alien's tentacles undulated around its body like the old earth-bound cephalopods, and purple dots covered its white skin. The girl's name was Bubble, while the alien was Click.

He felt the pulp paper, studying the gaudy-over-the-top cover. The *Bubble and Click* comic was volume 21 second edition. It wasn't his kind of thing, but Molly loved these comics, and she had the same edition with her.

Opening the comic to page 6, he put his finger on the text in the box in the bottom right corner. Veena had taught him the simple substitution cypher he was about to use. Easy to break if one had the key—in this case, the same edition of this comic—but pulp books were rare. Veena felt it was safe enough to use in passing messages back and forth.

He began transcribing the letters into a message for his wife, continuing to the point he felt he'd begun rambling. He signed off as Bear—her pet name for him—and sent the message to one of Veena's secret accounts. This time, he'd said nothing secret, yet he liked keeping his personal thoughts out of the hands of the Overwatch AI censors. Besides, sometimes they had to discuss Molly, not a state secret, but one that had to be kept.

With a sigh, he put the comic away, then buried his face in his hands. His family needed him; he needed to reunite with them soon.

A sharp crack sounded outside his pod. His heart began to race as he shoved his bare feet into his boots. More cracks sounded like a volley. Were they under attack? With laces flopping around his ankles, he grabbed his rifle out of its rack and sprinted outside. Two paces from the door, he stopped, and his jaw dropped.

Glittering lights bust in the sky above him. As each pinpoint of light descended in a plume of sparks, new lights burst above them. Fireworks. Cheering erupted from the mess hall, and soldiers began pouring outside.

Hwicce let out the breath he'd been holding and lowered his weapon.

"Did you hear?" Baker stopped beside him. "Sir?"

"Command finally called it," he said, watching the cascading lights above. "The Protectorate declared victory over the Nader Alliance."

"Fuck yeah! We've won." She let out a cheer of her own, then darted off into the mass of celebrating soldiers.

A weight lifted off Hwicce's shoulders. The war was officially over. He'd be able to go home. Soon, he'd be back with Veena and Molly, and they could be a family again. A slow smile spread across his face.

Things were finally looking up.

Chapter Five

"And they all lived happily ever after." Veena stifled a yawn. She'd read the story aloud at least a dozen times now. She let the comic rest on her lap and squeezed Molly in tight for a hug.

Molly stirred. "That's not what it says." She pointed to the pulp page, sounding more awake than Veena. "It says 'The End.'"

Veena smiled and ran her hand over the soft curls on Molly's head. Her little girl smelled like peanut butter with hints of bubblegum like she always did. A little piece of normal in their up-ended world.

"I stand corrected." Veena closed the well-worn comic and put it back into Molly's pink backpack with her other comics. "It's time to sleep." She tried not to notice the institution-white sheets on the narrow bed.

"But Mom…" Molly sat up straight and reached for the next comic in the series. "I want to know what Bubble does next. She's trapped and needs help."

Tired after a long day at work, Veena smiled. "Click will rescue her like they always do." She couldn't help thinking about the illustrated characters currently in peril—Bubble, a girl about Molly's age, and Click, an alien that looked like an octopus. She and Molly had read the stories so many times, Mol knew exactly what would happen next.

Molly set the comic down and activated her bucket-o-stuff. The nanites emerged as a flock of tiny blue and red birds from the mug-sized container. The little birds flew around Molly's head. She grinned, exposing her two missing front teeth.

"It's late." Veena stood and put the backpack on a shelf beside the few belongings they'd had on them when the bombing had begun.

That day, Molly's pink backpack carried her Click stuffy, the comics, and her bucket-o-stuff while Veena's messenger bag held a datapad and a pair of black satin slippers that Hwicce had given her. Other than the clothing on their backs, that was all they owned; everything else, from their toiletries to the small room they now lived in, had been issued to them by the military.

"The bucket-o-stuff, too."

Molly stuck out her lower lip.

"Mol..."

"Fine." Molly sent the nanites back to their container. "Can you get a Click pattern?"

"Huh?" Veena raised an eyebrow.

Molly held up her bucket. "For this."

Veena sighed. Molly had a near endless list of patterns she wanted for the nanites. "Add it to your birthday list. We'll be taking a trip to Jupiter Station then."

"Can't you just hack in and download it?" Molly put the bucket on the small shelf at the head of her bed.

"That's illegal."

"Please?" Molly clasped her hands together under her chin and made her cute face. "I just want to play with Click."

Sitting on the edge of the bed, Veena took a deep breath. They'd been over why hacking was wrong multiple times, yet Molly kept asking her to do it. "First of all, it would be stealing, and that's wrong. Second, the Overwatch AIs would catch me.

Then I'd be put in prison, and you'd get sent to Aunt Selene. Got it?"

Molly groaned and leaned back against her pillow. "Got it."

Veena handed Molly her Click stuffy and pulled the blanket up under her chin. "Now, you need to get to sleep."

She yawned. "How will Daddy find us here?"

Veena sighed. Molly asked the same question every night. The biggest worry in her world was that her dad wouldn't find her. Veena dimmed the lights and sank down onto the single chair that filled the narrow space between the two beds. She wished she could tell Molly it would all be over soon, and her dad was on his way to join them. Being stuck in a holding pattern until they could be a proper family again was tiring for both of them.

"The army told him where we are."

Molly's wide eyes glimmered in the low light like pools of liquid. "So, he won't forget about us?"

"Of course not, silly." Veena smiled as she reached over and poked Molly's belly. "He'll come back to us soon."

"When?"

"I don't know. But he loves us so much, he'll come as soon as he can."

Seeming to accept Veena's explanation, Molly nodded before rolling onto her side and snuggling up against her Click stuffy. The eight arms of the pink octopus seemed to wrap themselves around the little girl.

"Goodnight, love."

Molly mumbled something in response, and a few moments later, she started snoring softly.

Veena resisted the urge to curl up beside her daughter and go to sleep herself. Ever since the Protectorate assigned her to the code-breaking unit on Rock 13-A5, she never got enough time to hang out with Molly. Fortunately, there were plenty of other kids around, so Mol had lots of playmates.

She took a few minutes to watch her girl sleep. Part of her

regretted not telling Molly that she had been in contact with her dad through non-official channels. But Molly wasn't one to keep secrets—and Veena had a few that needed keeping.

Turning to the narrow desk, she opened her datapad. Even though she now lived in a secret military facility, she could still access the DeepNet with the protocols she'd set up on her personal drive. Hopefully, the ubiquitous Overwatch AIs remained unaware of her activities.

A dancing bear twirled across her inbox, causing her to grin. It was her lucky night; Hwicce had written her less than an hour earlier. Her world was suddenly a little bit brighter. She smiled. From Molly's backpack, she found *Bubble and Click* volume 21, second edition, and she opened it to page six. Using the comic, Veena decoded the message.

His unit was currently on Candy Cane Lane—the most contested spot in the system. He expressed concern about the way the war was being fought, how even their side now resorted to tactics that resulted in excessive civilian casualties.

"Oh, please stay safe," Veena whispered as she placed a hand on her heart. She'd decoded enemy traffic in the area. Hopefully, her efforts had kept him safe. The war had ripped her family apart, and she had no idea when they'd all be back together again. She couldn't even remember why war had been declared in the first place.

Taking her time, she composed a response and encoded it. Using physical comics made their cypher nearly impossible to break—a decoding AI would never have the information it needed to do it. She told him about how she and Molly were settling in and how Gloria Norton, an old colleague from New Haven, had become a friend as well as co-worker.

Veena sent her message just as a message from Theo65, an old DeepNet contact, popped up. Theo65 wanted her help deciphering a newly discovered code. She opened it and stared at the strange symbols. Even though this set was new, these symbols were found when the first generation ships arrived in the system. Official channels said it wasn't writing at all, just random mineral crystallization found in caves on the worlds next to the gates. Theo65 remained convinced it was alien writing that could be decoded, and Veena suspected they were right.

These codes used to be a fun problem, a great distraction. But Orin would expect her to perform in the morning. Military-grade codes needed breaking—work that could keep her husband safe. She sighed as she kept staring at her datapad. Yet, she wanted to work on it. She'd helped before, back when she had a stable job at the university. Now, she'd sworn an oath to keep state secrets. She glanced again to Molly and knew she couldn't afford to dabble with them anymore.

Rubbing the back of her neck, Veena put her datapad away. Maybe she should get some sleep.

"No!" Molly shouted, and the room began to shake. Eyes still closed, she thrashed back and forth, throwing her stuffy and most of the covers to the floor. "No!" Her bucket-o-stuff flew off the shelf.

Veena's heart began hammering in her chest. Molly was still asleep; it had to be another nightmare. Veena stood, knocking her chair over in the process. It skittered across the vibrating floor. She swallowed.

"Mol." She sat on the bed beside Molly and put a hand on her shoulder. "Molly?" she said as calmly as she could and gathered Molly into her arms.

Rocking back and forth, Veena hummed the only lullaby she knew. Molly didn't wake, but the shaking slowly subsided. After several more minutes, Veena set her back down onto her pillow and brushed a curl away from her face. Molly's face relaxed, and she looked peaceful once again.

Biting her lip, Veena's mind began to churn. Maybe the military didn't have the capacity to detect such movement, or maybe they'd think it an earthquake? But how could there be an earthquake on a hollowed-out asteroid? She swallowed. If they had the right sensors, it would be no problem to triangulate back to their quarters.

"They won't pinpoint you," she whispered to Molly's sleeping form. "I need to not worry myself silly."

Veena needed a distraction for a few moments—a friendly voice just to chat with. She got up and went to the door. With one last glance at Molly, Veena went out into the hall, closing the door behind herself.

Gloria happened to be passing by Veena's door. She stopped and smiled. Her blonde hair and lilac dress contrasted against the grey of the walls around them. "Veena! Did you hear the news?"

Before the bombing, she and Gloria both had jobs at the university, though they'd only become friends since arriving at Rock 13-A5. It was nice to confide in a familiar face, even if Gloria relished sharing gossip—and was constantly on the lookout for more.

"What news?" Veena ran her hands down her 3D-printed khaki pants, grateful she'd found someone to chat with. Somehow, Gloria managed to escape the bombing with a significant wardrobe. Veena didn't envy her friend's wardrobe exactly; she just wished she had more than one option.

"We won the war!" Gloria grinned. "People are partying so hard, even the floor's been shaking."

Veena blinked. "It's really over?"

A ball of hope welled up within her. Soon, she could get Molly away from here. Hwicce would come back to them. She swallowed. Soon, they could be a family again.

With a grin, Gloria pulled Veena in for a hug. "It's over."

Veena pulled away and leaned against the wall next to her door. She bit her lip and met her friend's gaze. "We'll be able to leave this place, move on with our lives."

"Where do you guys plan on settling?" Gloria leaned against the wall on the other side of the hall.

Exhaling, Veena let her head tip back until hit rested against the wall. "I'd like to go somewhere with open skies like we had on New Haven."

"There's not a lot of worlds with breathable atmospheres, even less where our plants can grow."

Veena sighed. "I know. Maybe we'll make one of the space stations our home."

Further down the hall, a group exited one of the common rooms and loudly headed the other way.

Gloria grinned. "Looks like there's going to be an epic party tonight. Let's go join in, unwind and have some fun."

Veena turned and looked at the door to her room.

"Mol will be fine, and we won't be far."

"Ever since the bombing, Molly fears being alone. I can't risk her waking up and not find her mom nearby." She sighed and met Gloria's gaze.

Gloria smiled. "I get it."

"I'll catch you in the morning, though, and you can tell me all about the fun I missed."

"Oh, I'll fill you in—it'll be like you were there." Gloria took a step, then she turned back to Veena. "Seriously though, some-time soon, I'm dragging you out to unwind."

Veena smiled. "That would be great." There was no way she and Gloria would have ever become friends back on New Haven, but here, Gloria was the friendly face Veena needed right now.

Chapter Six

Hwicce stepped out of the mess tent and into the blinding sunrise light. The morning was still cool, but the blazing orange ball peeking over the horizon would soon change that. Yawning, he turned his back on the sun and faced the camp.

Even with last night's declaration of victory, the sense of unease from the battlefield the previous day still hung over him like a storm cloud. Breakfast hadn't appealed to him—nor had conversation with his peers. Instead, he opted for a travel mug of coffee and a few moments alone.

He'd woken to a message from Veena detailing another of Molly's nightmares that shook the ground. Although Veena didn't come out and say it, she was clearly afraid. He debated calling his sister to see if Veena and Molly could stay on her ship for a while. The two of them needed to get away from the Rock before anyone caught on to Molly's abilities.

Before he got two steps from the mess hall, Baker sprinted his way. "Hey, sir." She waved as though she thought he hadn't seen her.

He turned towards her. "Morning, Baker. You look awfully spry for the morning after the victory party."

Baker skidded to a stop next to him and buried her hands in

her pockets. Even out of combat armour, Baker would make a formidable enemy. She was as tall as him and solid. He wouldn't dare accept an arm-wrestling challenge from her as he might not win.

"We only shared a few pitchers," she said. "And I cleaned out Fin and Chang at dice."

Hwicce took a sip of his coffee; it wasn't good, but that was to be expected of army coffee. "What I could hear from my bunk sounded wilder than that."

"I'm not ratting anyone out, sir."

"Right." He surveyed the debris of the previous night's party that littered the ground before looking back to Baker. "So, what's gotten you up so early? Today is a scheduled down day."

"I didn't feel like being a lazy ass." She took a hand out of her pocket and ran it over her shaved scalp. "Besides, I heard they're moving the Rokan prisoners this morning."

"That's true. The entire group of them are going to be taken off-world later this morning. I'm going to see the purple cloak while I still can."

"An interrogation?" Her eyes lit up, and she raised an eyebrow. "Is it true the purple cloaks can read minds?"

Hwicce shrugged and started walking. He knew Baker's real reason for intercepting him was her curiosity about the purple cloak. He could use having an ally in the room—and sometimes, she saw things in a way he never considered.

Baker fell into step beside him as they reached the prison compound circled in razor wire. Instead of soldier pods, old-fashioned canvas tents filled the enclosed space. Guards patrolled both inside and outside the wire, but from what he'd heard, none of the prisoners were making any attempt at escape. Besides, where would they go? The Nader Alliance had abandoned them.

"What if he reads your every thought?"

"I doubt he'll find me that interesting." Hwicce showed his credentials to the on-duty guard. The guard waved them through. "I assume you're coming with me?" he asked Baker once they were past the gate.

"Hell yeah," she said with a grin. The white of her teeth flashed in contrast to her dark skin. "I've never seen a Rokan up close."

"They're just people, but I'm always happy to have you as backup." Hwicce opened the door to the interrogation tent. "And if he does read minds, the blank slate between your ears might prove a distraction."

Baker grunted but didn't retort.

Inside, the Rokan sat at a table in the centre of the space. Above, a bright light shone with more lumens than seemed necessary. Four guards kept watch, one in each corner of the tent. The Rokan's traditional clothing were all gone, replaced with the standard grey jumpsuit given to all prisoners. He kept his head bowed as though he was studying his manacled hands resting on the table, yet his form dominated the room.

Hwicce nodded to the sergeant next to the door and took a seat at the table. Baker remained standing one pace behind him.

"I'm Captain Oswiu," Hwicce said as he studied the man. He didn't appear injured, and he was clean. At least his side was still treating enemy combatants with dignity.

The Rokan's dark hair and skin seemed ordinary—not what Hwicce had expected from their obscure warrior clan. Hwicce shook his head. He'd never even seen a Rokan's face before, so expecting them to be different was a bit ridiculous. However, the Rokan was muscular enough, Hwicce wondered if Baker should challenge him to an arm-wrestling match.

"Hank Temple." Hank's voice was deep with an accent Hwicce hadn't heard before. He kept his head bowed.

"How many Rokan were with you?"

Hank snorted. "Only those of us who survived your previous assaults."

"Look at me when I'm speaking to you," Hwicce said in an even tone. It was disconcerting to be talking to the top of the man's head.

"What do you know about my people?" Hank didn't look up. On the bare skin of his forearms, swirls were etched into his skin—a backward initiation rite, no doubt.

"I know your home world is independent, so it doesn't make sense for you to be fighting for the Nader Alliance." Hwicce pushed his spine into the back of the chair and crossed his arms over his chest.

"Hmphf."

"You need to start answering questions," Hwicce said.

The sergeant in charge of the guards leaned down to whisper in Hwicce's ear. "You want us to rough him up a bit, sir?"

Hwicce let out a long exhale. Even though he knew it regularly happened, violence against prisoners wasn't something he wanted any part of. He waved the sergeant away.

"I know what you really want to know about," Hank said, still looking down.

Hwicce frowned. "And what's that?"

"Turn down the lights."

The sergeant whispered in his ear again. "Sir, Rokan eyes are modified for low light. If we keep it bright in here, that dickwad is basically blind."

"Lower the lights, Sergeant." Hwicce made sure his words sounded like the order they were. The overhead light blinked out, leaving only a dim glow coming through the tent walls.

Hank raised his head and stared Hwicce in the eye. The Rokan's eyes glinted golden in the low light.

"What do I really want to know about?" Hwicce hid how unnerving the reflective eyes made him. A piece of trivia surfaced in his head about how the Rokan home world was on a moon circling a rogue planet—a world that would always be dim. The early settlers engineered their children's eyes to see in the low light.

"The woman." Hank spoke slowly, as though he had all day to explain. "The one who can teleport."

Hwicce couldn't stop himself from leaning forward. "Is she one of the super-soldiers?"

"A group of eight of them arrived about a week ago. She was the only one who lasted."

"What happened to the others?"

"It's the net on their head that controls them. It's still in the experimental stages. On the others, it failed." Hank paused and rubbed his face in his hands. "They went berserk, killing everyone in range. We had no choice but to put them down." His voice trailed away as though laced with regret.

"The one I saw was the only one who lived?"

"Yeah."

"What happened to her after she vanished?"

Hank shrugged. "Your soldiers had me by then. I assume the brass got her out of here. Unlike ordinary soldiers like us, *they* wouldn't leave an asset like her behind."

"I assume *they* is the Nader Alliance." Hwicce cocked his head, and Hank nodded. "So the Nader Alliance created these super soldiers?"

"That's what I understand."

"Who within your alliance is doing this kind of work?" Hwicce leaned forward again.

Hank leaned back. "Genetically engineering monsters, you mean?"

"Yes." Hwicce felt an additional worry well up in him. The woman he'd faced had alternated between being confused and being a stone-cold killer. What made her suitable to be formed into super-soldier? Did she consent? Or was she just born with a genetic mutation that someone found out about? He shivered. He and Veena needed to double down and keep Molly safe.

Hank looked Hwicce in the eye. A shiver ran through Hwicce along with Baker's earlier comment about purple cloaks having the ability to read minds. After a moment, Hank frowned. "I don't know. The fact that the Nader Alliance might be experimenting on people doesn't sit well with me."

Hwicce nodded in agreement. "Is there anything at all you can tell me?"

"One of the handlers mentioned Vortex View."

Vortex View was a private space station deep in Nader territory. Rumour had it that it an entertainment centre just like Candy Cane Lane—and twice as gaudy. News that Vortex View engaged in genetic research was new, though.

"They also mentioned that the Protectorate is running a similar program."

"That's impossible. Our GenEn laws prevent anything like that." Hwicce clenched his jaw. His side would never do anything like that. *Or would they?*

Hank shrugged. "That's just what I overheard."

"Right." A new urgency around getting a message to Veena was all he could think about.

Hank leaned in until his head was centimetres from Hwicce. "Keep your girl safe," he said in a whisper.

Hwicce's breath caught in his throat as he met Hank's gaze. Without another word, Hwicce stood and strode out of the interrogation tent.

Chapter Seven

Hwicce had only been on patrol a few hours, but already the inside of his battle armour stank from his exertion. His head's-up display listed the outside temperature at over thirty-five degrees Celsius—hot enough to challenge his air conditioning. He let out a long exhale and glanced up the steep path ahead. At least he was almost to the top.

As the suit techs had pointed out when he went to the armoury to pick up his armour, they had worked all night to fix the damage from the day before, but the air handling system still needed work. He pondered sending a flat of beer to the armoury as thanks for the new servos in his armour; no one wanted to climb steep slopes without servo assist.

That morning, he'd seen a new sense of relief in the eyes of his troops, but plenty of work remained. Intel expected there would be pockets of resistance as they continued clearing the city. Mopping up could take months yet. The knot of worry in his gut continued to tighten—he needed to find a way to return to Veena and Molly much sooner than that.

Fifty metres on, he reached the top of the ridge. On the crest, he stopped and focused on the panoramic view. The entertainment zone of Candy Cane Lane sat on a planet of the same name, a world barely terraformed. Breathable air and a few scraggly plants were the only nods to humanity's manipulations. No farms, no mines, nothing of much use except a city built around a single purpose: entertainment.

"Fuck, sir." Baker stopped at his side, holding her rifle at the ready. "This place sure is a shit hole now."

Hwicce didn't say it out loud, but he agreed.

On the valley floor, a thick layer of dust coated the few remaining buildings. Rubble and military checkpoints blocked the roads. Only a few gaudy hints remained of the city's hay day. The hotels and casinos that once housed and entertained the millions of visitors each year were now destroyed or put to use as barracks and prisons. The only exception was the pyramid of the Pharaoh Casino that rose at the far end of the city; it remained nearly pristine and seemed to taunt him from a distance.

"I can't wait until we rotate off this hell hole. I'd prefer to hit the gym on the *Defiant* over marching across this dust bowl," she said.

"I suspect what you really want is to clear those sailors out of their credits by decimating them at generations dice."

Hwicce looked up at the glinting outline of the spaceport above. Somehow, despite the carnage, the line of the space elevator remained intact. The fact that both sides needed it likely saved it from being a target.

"Hell yeah," Baker said.

Hwicce checked his display to confirm the location of the rest of his platoon, but the augmented hearing in his helmet alerted him of a rubbing sound from behind. He swung his rifle around, pointing the sights on the source.

"Come out with your hands up," he ordered.

Keeping her hands held high above her head, a little girl emerged from the other side of a boulder. She trembled as she stared at the barrel of his rifle. The girl had to be close to the same age as Molly.

Hwicce blinked, and the girl's features changed to those of Molly. She winced as she stared up from the rifle to the faceplate of his armour. It's not Molly, he told himself as he lowered his weapon. He swallowed. That was twice he'd hallucinated his family.

"Where's your family?" he asked, knowing his voice sounded harsh through the helmet speakers.

She wrapped her arms around herself. "Gone." Her voice was tiny.

This girl was alone in a war zone. He couldn't in good conscience leave her out here. "Come with me; I'll take you to the refugee centre."

She stared at him and shook her head.

"I got this, sir," Baker said over their private channel as she slung her weapon.

Baker knelt down to the girl's level and opened her faceplate as Hwicce backed away a few paces.

"He looks pretty scary." Baker gestured to Hwicce. "Kinda like a bear, right?"

The girl nodded and bit her lip. Then she shifted her gaze to Baker.

"Tell you what," Baker continued. "I've got a stash of Space Chews back at camp. Would you like to share some?"

The girl's face brightened at the mention of candy.

"While we do that, we can send the bear off to make sure there's a cozy bunk for you at the refugee centre." She smiled. "Maybe he'll even find your family. Would you like that?"

"Yeah," the girl said.

Baker held out a hand. The girl took it, and she and Baker started back down the ridge towards the camp. Hwicce held back and watched them for a moment. Baker's ability to relate to a kid was unexpected. There was more to her than he'd realized.

With one hand full of glittery candy wrappers and the other holding onto Baker, the girl let herself be led to the refugee compound. As Baker took her inside, Hwicce studied the sea of humanity on the other side of the fence. The hundreds of people inside were more diverse than he'd ever seen in one place. Cybernetic implants, green skin, and even goggled Rokan hiding their altered eyes from the bright light, entertainers with tentacles for fingers, dancers with tails for balance. The variety of modifications was astounding.

What would the founders think of what humanity had become? He sighed. It didn't really matter.

Veena's latest message about Molly's nightmares was what mattered. They needed him. The army didn't—not anymore, not now that the war was over. The remaining work could be done by others.

He turned and walked away from the refugee camp gate without waiting for Baker. There was too much to think about. He needed a few moments alone.

Major Tong looked up from his desk when Hwicce knocked at the door just before lunch. The small man smiled and waved Hwicce in before gesturing to the seat across his desk.

"Good job on capturing those Rokan," Tong said as he put away his datapad.

"The credit goes to my troops. I'll pass on your compliment." Hwicce sunk down onto the folding chair. It groaned as it took his weight.

Tong leaned back and looked Hwicce in the eye. "But that's not why you're here."

"No, sir. I'd like to request a transfer to Rock 13-5A to work as part of their security detail." He'd hate that kind of work, but at least it would get him closer to Veena and Molly.

"Your platoon here needs you. Especially now that victory

has been declared. We still have months of work ahead of us. Keeping morale up is going to be critical."

The two men locked gazes. Major Tong was right; Hwicce had an important role to play here—but how could he stay?

"I understand that my contract allows me to terminate it early once a victory has been declared." Hwicce's skin crawled at what he was saying. He hated doing this, but it seemed his only option.

Major Tong's body language and facial expression changed. No longer did Hwicce's commander seem open. It was as though Hwicce had shut a door.

"You are correct; you could just walk away from this." He gestured around as though meaning the world. "But there will be administrative ramifications."

A sour taste filled Hwicce's mouth. "I understand."

"You will be listed as having broken your contract—which is one small step away from a dishonourable discharge." Tong's face was taking on a reddish hue.

"I understand."

"You will be expected to leave this base immediately, and the army will be no longer responsible for getting you home."

Hwicce nodded—there had to be a ship heading the right way from the spaceport above. Getting to the Rock wouldn't be impossible. He wouldn't be allowed access to the base, but Veena and Molly could leave. His sister would hate it, but she would shelter them for a while.

"A review committee will be called to examine your departure. Until they complete your investigation, your veteran benefits will be frozen."

A knot formed in Hwicce's gut. Was this the right path? Would a few more months apart really matter? Maybe Veena could hold on for a while longer.

Tong leaned forward. "I think the best thing you can do for both your family and your soldiers is stay."

Hwicce nodded again. "You might be right, sir. I'll need to think on this."

"Leaving now would cost you in unexpected ways. Besides, we should talk about that super-soldier you encountered yesterday."

"I included all my observations about her in my report."

"Yes, of course." Tong pulled out his datapad and put it in front of himself again.

Hwicce assumed Tong was reading the report and settled into to wait. Scents of frying foods wafted into the office from the nearby kitchen, turning Hwicce's stomach. The piling uncertainty was getting to him. He needed to make his mind up soon and act.

Tong looked up. "My superiors have a couple of questions. First, you reported that she didn't seem aware of what she was doing."

"That's correct. I spoke with the purple cloak this morning. He confirmed that the net on her head controlled her actions."

Tong paused to take a few notes.

Hwicce's gut twisted further as he saw his chance. "I heard a rumour that our side is planning on creating super-soldiers as well."

"That's classified." Tong met his gaze. "But peace may not last, and we need to be able to defend ourselves against super-soldiers like the one you encountered."

Hwicce's mind began to churn. If the Protectorate launched a program to create super-soldiers, would they be looking for subjects? On the Rock, Molly would be an easy target. He didn't have months to get to her. All his other responsibilities had to be pushed aside. Getting back to his family was the course he had to take.

By dusk, Hwicce's resignation was official. He was walking away from everything, including a free ride home. So far, his sister hadn't responded to his messages, meaning he was on his own to get back to Veena and Molly.

On purpose, he arrived at the supply hut while the rest of the base was at dinner. He didn't want to end up justifying himself to either his peers or subordinates. Standing there in civilian attire seemed wrong, but it was what he had to do.

"I'm checking out," he said to the corporal manning the counter. Hwicce had seen him before around camp. Higgs, his name tag said.

He put his issued datapad on the counter, then backed a pace away and put his hands in his pockets.

Higgs projected the list of Hwicce's issued kit into the air between them. "Right. Let's start with your armour."

Hwicce opened the armour case and stood back as Corporal Higgs went through the parts, checking items off the kit list as he went. The armour looked worn. It had done its job by keeping him alive in some pretty dodgy situations. Part of him felt naked now that he was handing it over to someone else.

"Rifle," Higgs said as he closed the case.

Hwicce set his rifle on the counter, followed by his uniforms, rucksack, and electronics. With each piece of kit he handed over, Hwicce questioned his choice to leave until finally, he was left empty-handed, and all items on his kit list had been checked off. Uncertain how he should feel, he returned to his quarters and picked up the small civilian pattern backpack containing a change of clothes and his toiletries.

The only thing left was to find a berth on a ship heading towards Veena and Molly.

"Sir, where in the fucking hell are you going?" Baker blocked his way out of the camp. She wore her full battle armour, but her faceplate was open, allowing him to see her expression of betrayal.

"I just gotta go," he said, his shoulders slumping forward under her glare. He started walking away from her down the dusty path towards the city.

She raced to block his way. "Higgs told me you handed in your gear. Did you think you could just sneak out of here without saying anything?"

"There's blood on my hands." Hwicce stopped and faced Baker. They stared at each other in silence for a few moments.

Baker ran a hand over her face, then bit her lip—a very uncharacteristic gesture from her. "Hell, sir, there's blood on all our hands."

He sighed. He'd hoped to avoid conversations like this, and he wasn't sure he should tell her the truth about needing to get back to Molly. "Maybe, but I can't do this anymore."

"But we fucking won." She paused for a moment and glanced back into their base. "Right?"

"They say we did." A knot formed in Hwicce's gut as the names of the soldiers he'd lost ran through his mind. But the remaining ones didn't need him anymore.

"You went and resigned, didn't you?"

Hwicce's mouth went dry, and he said nothing.

"You fucking quit, and now you're sneaking out of here without a word to anyone. It's a dick move." She clenched her jaw and glared at him for a moment. Then her demeanour changed as she looked down on the tally of kills scribed into the armour on her left forearm. Even though they'd been through several recent battles, it had been months since she'd updated the count.

"You're an outstanding soldier," Hwicce said.

Silence fell between them as they both stared at the marks on her armour. After a moment, her brow wrinkled, and her eyes went wide. "Fuck it. I'm coming with you…sir."

Hwicce stared at her for a moment. He didn't know much

about her background, but he knew she loved being a soldier. At least she'd used to love it. But he knew that after one of the missions a few months ago, something in her had changed. He should have asked what was going on with her, but there never seemed to be a good time. Nevertheless, she shouldn't just quit because he did.

"I order you to stay. Be a soldier. You're awesome at it, and I know you love it."

"You're a god damn civi; you don't get to order me around."

Another silence fell between them as Hwicce tried to find the words to convince Baker to stay.

"If you resign here, you cease to exist to the army. They'll expect you to leave right away and find your own way. They won't even give you access to veteran benefits until a 'review committee' goes through everything."

She stared at him, her dark eyes boring into his. She seemed to be thinking through the ramifications. Finally, she licked her lips. "I'm with you. The army can go fuck itself."

"You can't take your armour," he said.

"Well... shit." Baker ran her hands down the smooth surface of her armour. "I love my hard shell."

Hwicce met Baker's gaze. "The army's not going to let you walk off with their fancy battle armour."

"Fine." She started stripping out of her armour and dropping the pieces on the ground. "But I'm buying a black-market version as soon as I can."

He nodded, uncertain if he wanted the responsibility of having her tag along but out of reasons to convince her to stay behind. Being a soldier seemed to be her world; who would she be without that? But it was her choice to make—even if it seemed so sudden.

Baker ran her hands down her black track pants. "So, where the hell are we going to go?"

"I need to get back to my family. They need me." He

debated telling Baker everything—if she really was coming with him, she deserved to know.

"And they were on New Haven?" Baker asked.

"They were."

She looked down at her feet. "Shit! I'm sorry. You must feel awful."

"They made it out okay. After the bombing, Veena was recruited to work at the army base nearby."

"So we're headed to the fucking Alpha System." Baker tilted her face up towards the sky, her soldier persona back in full force. "Step one: get on a ship. We're gonna have to get up to the spaceport."

Hwicce looked up, letting his gaze follow the long line of the space elevator down to where it reached the planet's surface. In that moment, Hwicce was grateful for her company. She'd keep him focused and not allow him to wallow in self-pity.

"Turn in your armour, and then we'll get going."

Chapter Eight

Rows of symbols filled Veena's screen—one hundred and one symbols, to be exact. Way more than needed to encode their human language but not enough to be a pictogram representation of actions.

What she hadn't admitted to Orin when he assigned her this decoding project was that she recognized the code; it was the same as the one Theo65 had been working on for years. Just before the military shut down their off-Rock links, Theo65 contacted her about new writing in the same code. It couldn't be a coincidence.

She ran a hand over her head and down her ponytail. Her notes from her previous decoding attempts were safely stowed on a civilian server—one she could no longer access. She was starting from scratch. Scrolling through the encoded message, she pondered her options. She started one of her brute force decoding algorithms, then headed for a cup of coffee.

As Veena filled her mug, Gloria burst into the break room. "Veena, you're here!" She tossed her blond hair over her shoulder and smoothed her hands down her cherry-red dress. "Orin's asking for you; he seems to be in a bit of a tizzy too. He wants you to go to his office."

Veena nodded. "I'll go see what he wants." She started towards the door. "You still haven't filled me in on last night's fun."

"Ohhh! I have stories. Ted from the comptroller's office..." Gloria shook her head. "We'll talk after you find out what Orin wants."

"Right." Veena took a sip of coffee before looking out the door.

"Oh, wait."

Veena turned and met Gloria's gaze.

"General Swa's in his office too."

Veena's breath caught in her throat. Swa's presence meant this had to be about Hwicce. Did something happen to him? But the war was over... Leaving her full mug of coffee on the counter, she headed for Orin's office. She counted her steps in an effort to remain calm—it didn't work.

Orin's office door stood open. From behind his desk, Orin gestured for her to enter as soon as he saw her. Swallowing, she went inside.

"You'll need to sit for this," Swa said. Even though Swa was tiny, her presence filled the small office.

Struggling to keep a veneer of calm, Veena swallowed and sank into the single chair in front of Orin's desk. Behind the piles of paperwork and dirty mugs, her boss sat bolt upright with his gaze fixed on the far wall.

Swa leaned against the side of Orin's desk. "I came down because I felt it was important I deliver this news in person."

"It's about Hwicce, isn't it?" Veena clenched her hands together to keep them from trembling. Hwicce had promised to stay safe.

"Hmmm." The general crossed her arms over her chest. "Yes. Lieutenant Oswiu has been reported absent in the aftermath of the Battle of Candy Cane Lane."

Veena's jaw dropped. She'd been afraid of something like

this happening ever since the war began. The weight of the news pulled on her, and she struggled to take a breath.

"He's okay," Orin jumped in. "He just submitted his resignation." He glanced at Swa then back to Veena. "He's okay."

Veena bit her lip. "He's okay? All he did was resign?" It wasn't like him to just take off—there had to be a good reason.

"Yes. However, your husband was last seen traveling with one of his subordinates." Swa cocked her head and smirked. "A woman."

"What are you implying?" Veena fixed her gaze on the general.

"You need to know the facts." Swa pressed her lips together.

Veena cocked her head. Swa's rush to tell her Hwicce ran off with someone seemed odd. "You have given me few facts. Why the innuendo?"

Swa glared at her in return. Just as she opened her mouth to speak, an alert flashed on Orin's display, and he leaned in to read it.

"Oh, no." Orin glanced at Veena. "You need to get to the school right now. Something's happened."

———

Veena didn't remember the tram ride or even the walk to the makeshift school. One moment she was in Orin's office; the next, she was running along the corridors towards the school office.

Major Zane, the head of the Rock's security, was the only person around. The big woman pursed her lips together as Veena approached. Her indigo and gold uniform seemed out of place in the school office.

"Where's Molly?" Veena asked. Why was the head of security waiting for her in a school's office?

"Dr. Oswiu," Zane started, stepping in Veena's way.

"I just need to see Molly."

Zane pulled herself up to her full height. The square set to her jaw made her an intimidating barrier. Then she sighed. "Your daughter is in there." She pointed to the door labelled 'Infirmary.'

Veena rushed inside. Sitting on a cheap printed cot on the far wall, Molly had her arms wrapped around her knees. Glistening tears streaked down her cheeks, and her nose was red. Her eyes widened when Veena entered.

"Please don't be mad. I didn't mean it." Molly sniffed as a fresh tear cascaded down her face. "It was an accident."

"What happened?" Veena sank down onto the cot next to Molly. She had never gotten in trouble before.

"Amber said Dad deserted. She said he isn't coming back to us." Another wave of tears started to flow.

Veena felt tears of her own start to well up. She wrapped an arm around Molly and pulled her in tight. She didn't know what the news about Hwicce meant or why another child had known about it, but she was sure that neither of them had heard the full story.

"What happened next?" The head of security wouldn't be there if it weren't for bad news.

"I... I..." Molly's voice trailed off, and she sniffed again.

"I'll make sure you are safe, no matter what."

Molly nodded. "I got mad at Amber."

"Did you hurt her?"

"I wanted to," Molly said. "But I didn't." She buried her face into Veena's shoulder. "I...I made all the desks move."

Veena forced herself to inhale slowly. This was bad news.

"The other kids were sitting in the desks. Once it started, I couldn't stop it. All the desks moved to the walls." Molly swallowed. "The teacher saw it."

Molly's secret was out. A whole room full of kids and their teacher saw what she could do. It wouldn't be long until an investigation would be called. Questions would be asked. A breath caught in Veena's throat.

"Mommy?"

To be safe, Veena needed to get Molly off the Rock—the sooner, the better. She hugged Molly tight. "It's okay."

Molly wrapped her arms around Veena's neck. "Are you mad at me?"

"No, love, I'm not. I should never have brought you here." She released her daughter and stood. "It'll be okay. Let's go back to our room."

Veena reached a hand out. Molly nodded and took it.

Out in the main part of the office, Zane was waiting. She glanced at Molly and frowned. Then she met Veena's gaze.

"I don't understand what happened," she said. "There's going to be an inquiry."

Veena nodded. "I expected that. Is Molly expelled from school?"

"If this were a normal school, probably." Zane shrugged. "Kids aren't really my area of expertise. But they need you to work, so Molly gets to stay in class."

Molly pulled Veena's hand. "I don't want to go back."

Veena swallowed and knelt down. "I'm sorry, but you'll have to."

"I will need you to keep Molly in your quarters outside of school hours," Zane said.

"Okay." Veena stood again. It would take a day or two for her to come up with an exit plan. She needed to play normal until then.

"I'm worried about everyone's safety." Zane's brow wrinkled as she glanced at Molly. "Especially yours."

Molly's face took on a somber expression.

"Can you try to avoid doing that again?"

Molly nodded and squeezed Veena's hand. "Can we go home?"

Veena glanced at Zane. The head of security gave a curt nod before turning and walking away.

Once inside their quarters, Veena sank down onto her bed and put her face in her hands.

"You okay?" Molly asked in a tiny voice as she sat on the bed beside her.

Veena sighed and looked at her girl. "What happened to the desks in the classroom?"

"I don't know." She turned away and shrugged. "I got mad, but I knew it wasn't okay to hurt Amber. The desks just moved."

Uncertain what else to do, Veena nodded.

Molly balled her hands into fists. "Why doesn't Dad want to come back to us?"

Veena shifted to face Molly as she ran through the facts in her head. Hwicce had left the army with another soldier—that much she believed. Swa's implication of a romantic tryst didn't sit right. He'd never do that. He was always clear in his messages that he loved her and Mol.

"Mom?" Molly's dark eyes were wide.

"Sorry, Mol, I was just thinking." Veena ran her hands down the fabric of her pants. "Your dad loves us. I'm sure he'll get in touch soon and explain everything."

Molly went silent for a few moments. She reached for her Click stuffy and cuddled it against her chest. She yawned and snuggled into Veena's side. It wasn't yet dinner time, yet Molly was acting like it was late.

"Are you okay?"

"I'm tired," Molly said before yawning again—and Molly never admitted to being tired.

"Why don't you lay down and get some sleep?" Veena smiled while wishing she knew how better to support Molly. Maybe moving desks with only her mind had wiped her out.

"Will you read to me first? I want to know how Click helps Bubble escape."

"Sure." Veena leaned over and pulled a comic off the narrow desk between the beds. The paper felt soft under her fingers, and the cheery colours on the cover appealed to her right then.

Molly snuggled up beside Veena as soon as she leaned back on the bed. Molly's warmth and scent seemed so right. Veena flipped to the first page and started reading.

Chapter Nine

Although no fighting occurred in this part of the city, a thick layer of dust and grime coated everything. Beneath, the cheap materials and decades of decay were a far cry from the luxury a few streets over. Even in its heyday, this area of Candy Cane Lane had been rough.

A vehicle passed and kicked up billows of dust in its wake. Hwicce wrapped his scarf over his face to keep from breathing in the fine particles. It didn't work, and he coughed.

Baker glanced over her shoulder at him, her expression unreadable. "The sooner we're off this fucking world, the better."

"Yeah." He coughed again.

Even out of uniform, the two of them made an intimidating pair. Both stood taller than most of the crowd; that combined with abundant army food and regular exercise meant they moved with physicality the locals couldn't match. Baker's glare cleared them a path through the surging crowds. For the first time, Hwicce followed his former subordinate as she marched towards the base of the space elevator.

As they got closer, more people lurked crammed into every doorway and alley. Blank stares met him wherever he looked. A shiver ran up his back. He didn't feel threatened, just uncomfortable and even guilty. He had the means to get off-world, while the surrounding crowds did not.

Small clusters of private security people lingered in the street starting about fifty metres out from the elevator. On the other side of them, the street was clear of anyone who didn't look like they had the means to buy a ticket. Keeping his chin up, he followed Baker right past security.

Baker stopped a pace away from the ticket kiosk. Turning to him, she raised an eyebrow. There wasn't a line—probably because the cost of a one-way ride had inflated to three times the price it had been two days ago.

"Right. Wait here, and I'll get us tickets." He stepped forward to the window.

Only after buying tickets did he think about his credits. His brow wrinkled as he did a quick calculation in his head. The two tickets had cost way more than he'd expected—he'd just spent most of what he had. And there was no guarantee of finding a ride off the spaceport above.

Ignoring his dry mouth, he tilted his head back and stared up. A speck of glittering metal marked the elevator car making its descent. He licked his lips and vowed to continue on. He would get back to Veena and Molly even if he had to stow away on a manure ship.

At his side, Baker cleared her throat. "We've got a half-hour, and I'm bloody famished." She jerked her head towards a food cart a few metres away. Bold lime green letters on a black background advertised fresh, spicy cricket tacos.

"Go grab something to eat. I wouldn't want you to faint like some sort of delicate civi princess." Hwicce leaned against the wall next to the ticket kiosk.

"Princess my ass." Baker snorted and walked off. She shouted back from the line, "Hey, sir, you hungry?"

"No, thanks." He was hungry, but he'd have to ration what he spent his credits on. Pulling out his personal datapad, he logged into his bank account. Just as he brought it up, a red bar appeared and cut him off. They had shut his link access down. "What the..." He turned the machine off, then back on again.

"What's up, sir?" Baker leaned against the wall beside him, holding a carton with three tacos in it. Pungent scents of hot pepper, cumin, and something burnt wafted his way.

"I'm cut off." He rebooted the machine. It still wouldn't connect to the link. The army had moved faster than he'd expected—his account on the army system had been shut down, meaning he'd have to sign up with a civi link company—none of which were currently operating in the area. "Boot up your datapad and see if you can access the link."

Baker chuckled. "Grunts like me don't own tech shit like that." She began stuffing the first cricket taco into her mouth. Pieces of antenna and legs fell like crumbs with each bite.

"How many credits do you have access to?"

She wiped her mouth with the back of her hand, smudging the red sauce across her dark skin. "I dunno, maybe enough for a fun night out."

A knot formed in his gut. He ran a hand over his face, ignoring all the grit. "Well...crap."

"We doomed?" Baker started in on her next taco. "Sir."

"We'll figure it out."

"Just so you're clear, you're the brains of this operation."

"I'll figure it out then." Hwicce sighed and mentally chastised himself for being so hasty in leaving the army. He ran a hand down his beard. If only he'd waited a day and gotten a message out to Veena.

"Good. I've got your back." Baker shoved her final taco into her mouth.

He stared up at the descending space elevator again. In the bright light, the carriage shone all fresh and pretty as if it had been exempt from the carnage that occurred on the ground. The orange logo of the private consortium who operated the spaceport was now visible—the same logo as on the shoulders of the security on the ground.

Hwicce did some mental calculations. With what he had on hand, he could feed the two of them for a day, maybe two—but he couldn't justify spending credits on link access, assuming it was even available on the spaceport. He wouldn't be able to message Veena. What would she think when she found out he'd vanished without a word? The knot in his gut tightened.

"What's up, boss?" Baker said, tilting her chin up to follow his gaze.

"The spaceport is as far as our credits will take us." He swallowed. "We don't have enough to book passage out of here."

She nodded, then fell silent for a moment. "Sir, where in the Alpha System are we headed?" Her dark eyes bored into him. "My family back on New Haven are all gone. I have a brother, but..." Her words trailed off.

She had followed him out of a secure job away from the world she knew, but there was no clear destination for her. She didn't have a family to get to. All that was left was the bombed-out remnants of the world she grew up on. Why did she rush to follow him? She loved army life, even loved combat—yet she'd left that all behind on a moment's notice.

The responsibility of having Baker with him weighed heavily; she was like another little sister. But it wasn't too late to send her back.

"I'm sure they haven't finished filing your paperwork. You could go back and continue being a soldier."

"I'm fucking with you, sir—to the end."

He swallowed, reminding himself she'd made her own choice. "Veena and Molly are on Rock 13-A5—a hollowed-out rock in the asteroid belt. But we won't get access there, so Jupiter Station seems our best bet."

"So, how are we gonna get there?"

"Right..." Hwicce let his voice trail off. Veena was good at planning; he wished he could talk to her. She'd come up with a solution that would get them back together sooner rather than later.

"Hey, Space Case." Baker jabbed him in the ribs. "What's the plan?"

"We're going to have to get jobs."

The elevator's brakes squealed, slowing it to a gentle stop at the ground station.

"Soldiering is the only skill I have." She shoved the last of her third taco into her mouth.

"Yeah, me too." He looked up. The spaceport was just visible—just a tiny speck in the yellow sky. "I'm sure there's a ship up there in need of a couple deckhands," he said, not wanting to tell Baker about his backup plan to stow away.

"Deckhand..." She wiped her mouth with the back of her hands. "Sure, I could do that. But you're gonna have to brief me on what deckhands do."

Hwicce titled his head slightly and focused on Baker as she licked the last of the taco sauce off her fingers.

"Why d'you follow me?"

Baker shrugged. "I'm just curious what you might do."

"No, really."

"Because..." Her words trailed off, and wrinkles formed across her forehead. "I like soldering a lot...too much. Without you making sure I don't get carried away, I could do something truly terrible. Something that would make me into a monster. It was time for me to get out."

Hwicce opened his mouth to respond, then closed it. His assumption that she was happy being a career grunt now seemed off the mark. Baker was turning out to be way more complicated than he expected, and she'd given him no hint this was how she felt. But now wasn't the time to interrogate her further on her motives.

"Well... I'm glad you're with me."

"You are fucking lucky to have me," she said with a grin.

"True."

The gate to the elevator opened. It was time to board.

Chapter Ten

For the second time in two days, Orin found himself on the tram heading to General Swa's office. Her aide said the general urgently needed to see him, forcing him to drop everything and rush her way. What the aide didn't say was why she wanted to see him. He hated Swa's head games.

As he watched the grey landscape outside the tram window go by, he tried to figure out why he'd been summoned. His team had been doing routine work since Veena's breakthrough on the enemy's activity around Candy Cane Lane—hell, the Protectorate had even declared victory over the Nader Alliance. The war was supposed to be over.

With a gentle thud, the tram stopped at the command module, and Orin set off on autopilot towards his boss' office.

"You sure took your time," the aide said as soon as Orin stepped into the expansive lobby outside Swa's office. "Wait here. I'll let the general know you've arrived."

As Orin watched the aide disappear into the other office, he realized there was nothing worth calling him in for. He clenched his hands into fists to keep from trembling as he regretted leaving his flask back in his office. Too agitated to sit, he strolled to the far wall where floor-to-ceiling windows brought the grey rock of the hollowed-out asteroid into view. Maybe Swa planned to disband his unit. Send everyone home.

At the thought of home, his kitchen back on New Haven came to mind. He'd hated the lemon yellow walls at first. Mary had painted them while he'd been away for work—the scent of the paint still lingered. When he walked into the room, the bold walls almost glowed. The overwhelming colour was too much. Just as he opened his mouth to say he hated the walls, Mary came in with her divine grin, and he'd told her he loved them. And in time, he had grown to love the walls. But that world was all gone now—ashes and memories were all that remained.

Standing an arm's length from the clear metal wall, he rocked back and forth as he stared out the window. The greyness suited this phase of his life. Without Mary, the colour had vanished from his world.

As he rubbed the back of his neck, he noticed something outside had changed. Trying to figure out what, he pushed his misery aside. The view from this end of the asteroid differed from the barrack module or the module his team worked in.

In the distance, the aperture of the shield gate separated the interior from the open space beyond. On the other side, a few military ships were visible, their matte hulls defined by sharp lines. To his left sat the barrack and work modules connected by the ribbon of tram line. To the right, the vertical farm producing their food rose as a shining beacon of light.

But nearly hidden by the massive farm sat a structure he hadn't noticed before. He scratched his head. No obvious tram line connected to it.

Before he could ponder too hard, General Swa's aide called him into her office.

Inside, Swa wasn't alone. Three civilians stood before her huge desk. The two women and single man all wore asteroid grey suits and cultured blank expressions. No introductions were made, but Orin recognized Dr. Greer from their earlier meeting.

Swa stood and put both hands on her desk and stared Orin in the eye. He swallowed before meeting her gaze.

"I saw security's report about the 'event' with Dr. Oswiu's daughter." Swa's harsh tone was matched by her freshly pressed indigo uniform.

"It's been taken care of. The girl has been through a difficult time—first surviving the bombing of New Haven, then having her father disappear..." His words trailed off as he realized Swa wouldn't care.

"I suspect Miss Oswiu will continue to have these 'events.' And they'll get more severe with time." Greer came forward. "I've been over her blood analysis. The girl has the XE-73 genetic marker—the same marker we found in the super-soldier corpses we recovered on Candy Cane Lane."

"The marker is not a natural mutation," the closest of the two women said. She held her nose high and looked down on Orin.

"What are you saying?" Orin asked. "Security combed through both Dr. Oswiu's and her husband's records. Both of them came up clean. And until she came here, Molly spent her entire life on New Haven. We even have all the little girl's medical records."

"Yet, she isn't who she seems." Greer's nasally voice grated on Orin's already frayed nerves.

The woman who'd spoken before took a step closer to Swa. "And she is a risk to this facility." The third one hadn't said a word yet.

Swa pulled herself up to her full height and crossed her arms over her chest. "I can't afford a wild card like her on this facility."

"Dr. Oswiu is a critical member of my team." Orin's anxiety crept in, amplifying his worry about where the meeting was going. "Don't forget she's the one who broke the code resulting in our victory at Candy Cane Lane. Her work has saved thousands of Protectorate soldier's lives."

"She broke a code that confirmed information we already knew. Not exactly worth decorating the woman for." Swa paused and pursed her lips. "However, we need her to keep working. Breaking the new codes is critical to our project."

All three of grey suits nodded in unison. A shiver ran up Orin's spine.

"The girl is sufficient for my part of the project." Greer turned to Swa. "You can keep the mother. However, those codes may contain important insights to my research. I need to be kept informed of her progress. Even partial results may accelerate my work."

Swa nodded. "Then we go ahead with removing just the girl. Best bet would be to pick her up at school."

Orin's eyes widened. Were they really planning to kidnap a child? He stepped forward between the general and Greer. "What are you talking about? I can't condone taking that girl away from her mother."

The woman who hadn't spoken yet cleared her throat. "That girl represents a deliberate human genetic mutation." She spoke to Orin like he was a child. "Deliberate mutations created the rift between human populations. The GenEn laws were supposed to prevent more of these...experiments."

A breath caught in Orin's chest. He couldn't believe what he was hearing. "Experiments?"

"It is unlikely the mother doesn't know—meaning she has played a role hiding the girl's mutation."

"But..." Orin scrambled to pull his thoughts together. "It can't be."

"I think we're done here." She nodded to her two colleagues. "You are authorized to proceed with your plan."

Greer and one of the women turned and walked out of the office. A sense of dread crept over Orin.

"We have a facility for people with these sorts of potentially dangerous mutations," the remaining woman said. "She will be well cared for."

"You can't just take a child!" Orin stared at the woman, but she wasn't intimidated. He turned to his superior. "General, you can't let this happen."

Swa sat on her chair and steepled her fingers together. "Don't forget your place in this organization. You will go back to your office and make sure Dr. Oswiu remains engaged in her work for the rest of the day. My people will take care of the rest."

"You're nuts. There's no way Veena will do anything for us if we take Molly." Orin's voice rose with each word, and heat started radiating from his face. "You can't kidnap a little girl!"

"Thank you, General." The woman smoothed the front of her blazer. "I'll keep you abreast of our progress." She turned and left.

"Dr. Oswiu will remain in your department. See that she continues her good work," Swa said.

"What the hell is going on here?" Orin's nostrils flared. "I thought we were moral people."

"You're dismissed, Dr. Akton." She swivelled towards the exterior view.

"You can't do this!"

"Do I need to call security?" Swa glanced over her shoulder at him and raised an eyebrow.

Pursing his lips, he tried to think of something to say that would change Swa's mind. He stared at her profile; her features appeared carved from stone. She wasn't going to budge.

A shiver ran up his spine. They'd called him here to make sure he was complacent in Molly's kidnapping. They wanted him to be as guilty as they were. They could use his guilt to manipulate him into doing more things he didn't approve of down the road. He swallowed and wished for a second time that he'd brought his flask with him.

70

He turned and left the office. Out in the waiting room, he went over to the window. A tram had just left the Command Module—no doubt containing Greer and the two women on their way to take Molly. There was nothing he could do to stop it.

Clenching his trembling hands at his side, he forced himself to turn away from the window. "I'm just a fucking pawn," he said under his breath.

General Swa's aid looked up from where he sat at his desk. "Can I help you?"

Orin's gaze went to the comms console in front of the aide. He could call Veena. Maybe it wasn't too late for her to get to Molly before Greer did. He bit his lip. No, there was no way Veena could escape with Molly in time.

"If the general is done with you, you need to move on," the aide said.

Orin nodded and starting trudging towards the tram station. With every step, he hated himself more and more. Swa had gotten her wish—his compliance in kidnapping a child. A cold wave washed over him as he considered what Swa might force him to do next.

Chapter Eleven

By the end of the day, Veena had made no progress on the encoded message. Staring at the jumbled mess of symbols vexed her. None of her normal tricks got her anywhere. One hundred and one distinct shapes seemed too many to represent an alphabet, but her attempts to combine resulted in dead ends.

She had enough for one day. Molly was waiting for her and needed her now more than ever. After saving her notes on her datapad, she headed out of the office.

A few minutes later, sitting on the tram, Veena yawned as she considered how she and Molly should spend the evening in their quarters—perhaps reading one of Molly's favourite comics.

Veena closed her eyes and let herself relax. She'd figure a way off the Rock soon. Soon, they'd be safe. Hwicce would message her and explain—maybe he was already on his way back to her.

Major Zane, the Rock's head of security, stood at the school's entrance when Veena arrived. The hard set to Zane's jaw suggested bad news.

"Dr. Oswiu," the big woman said as soon as Veena got close.

Veena's breath caught in her throat. Did Molly have another outburst?

"Umm...." The normally domineering woman's expression faltered, and wrinkles formed on her forehead.

"Is Molly okay?" Veena tried to get past Zane and into the class.

Blocking the way, Zane held her chin up and stared Veena in the eye. "They have directed me to inform you that they have taken Molly Oswiu from this facility."

Veena's jaw dropped. Her entire body quivered, and her heart started pounding.

"No!" She charged past Zane and into the classroom. Swivelling her head around, she hunted for Molly, refusing to believe her daughter wasn't there. The room looked the same as always —colourful artwork lined the walls, bins of supplies filled low shelves, and in the corner sat the ant farm the children cherished. The silent rows of empty desks taunted her. She'd missed her chance to protect Molly.

The guard followed her in and closed the door. "Look, I'm sorry. I couldn't stop them. General Swa signed the authorization order."

Veena rubbed the back of her neck as she focused on the little desk Molly usually sat at. It was already cleared of her daughter's belongings. Forcing her emotions away, she turned to the guard.

"Can you get me in to see General Swa? I need her to explain this to me."

Major Zane's usually stoic face softened. "I'll take you there, but the general isn't going to be happy to see you."

A chime sounded announcing dinner in the mess hall as Veena and Zane stepped onto the tram. The rigid meal hours meant the car was empty. Neither of them spoke until the tram's doors closed and it pulled away from the station.

Zane licked her lips and took a deep breath. "They said Molly was a risk to this station. They said she might blow our atmosphere or kill one of the other kids."

Veena sank down in a seat next to the window and stared out. The landscape passed without her really seeing it.

Zane sat across from her. "Look, I didn't want to do it."

"All she did was rattle a few desks after one of the other girls bullied her."

"I...." Zane's words trailed off.

Veena tapped her finger against her knee, counting out prime numbers with each series of taps. She needed to focus on what she could do; with each tap, she analyzed the situation, the rhythm helping her think. Maybe it wasn't too late. Maybe she could get Molly back. She gritted her teeth and stared at Zane.

"Do you know who took her?"

"A group of civilians—two women and a man. They aren't from here, but I've seen them around the last few days." Zane shifted in her seat. "The only one I've been introduced to is the man. His name is James Greer."

Veena leaned forward. "You have to know more than that."

"Rumour is General Swa recently took over a couple of other departments."

"What departments?"

"Secret stuff. Above my pay grade."

"Why would a secret department take Molly?"

"Again, I don't know."

Veena nodded and stared at the passing landscape. She closed her eyes and pictured Molly's face. She never liked being with strangers—how afraid she must be. An image of someone pulling Molly along by her upper arm came to mind.

Tears threatened to well up in Veena's eyes, and she forced

herself to push the thoughts away by tapping out more numbers —this time the Fibonacci sequence. By the time the tram arrived at the command module, she was ready to assume a veneer of calm. She would get Molly back.

Veena followed Zane onto the platform and down the corridor leading to General Swa's office. Zane used her access to get Veena through the checkpoint, and they continued to the suite of command offices.

"You can't go in there," the general's aide said when Veena charged towards the door.

Veena ignored him and marched into the office. Inside, Swa sat at her desk, scrolling through a holographic report. As soon as she spotted Veena, she shut down the display and stood.

"You don't have permission to be here." Swa pointed an index finger at Veena, then shifted her attention to the security chief. "Major Zane, remove her from this module."

"Ma'am..." Zane winced as she spoke. "I think Dr. Oswiu deserves an explanation."

Red patches bloomed across the general's face as she stared down the security chief. "You don't get to make demands here. Get her out of here, or you'll find yourself busted down to private and sent to the front lines."

"Ma'am—"

"That's enough out of you! Get her out of here."

Zane's shoulders slumped forward slightly as she turned towards Veena. "I'm sorry."

As she reached to grab onto Veena's arm, Veena twisted away and circled around the desk, coming face-to-face with the general.

"Where's Molly?" she demanded, staring the intimidating woman in the eye. "She needs to be with me. I demand you release her." Veena clenched her fists at her side.

"That girl poses an unacceptable risk," Swa said.

Veena's heart raced. "I'll take her away; we can go to a remote habitat. You never need to see us again."

"Dr. Akton said he can't afford to lose you. Your work here is vital to the war effort."

"The war is over. Hell, I can even work remotely if I must. Molly's well-being is more important than..." She gestured to the room around them. "This place."

Swa pursed her lips together. "If you resume your decoding responsibilities, I'll arrange for you to have weekly holo-chats with her."

"Weekly?" Veena put a hand on her heart and took a step back. "Weekly?! Molly needs me. She'll hate being alone. We need to be together."

"Nevertheless, she is now gone."

"With who?" Veena leaned in until her nose was a few centimetres from Swa's.

Swa met her gaze. "She is safe with my people. No harm will come to her."

"Bullshit! Ripping her away from me has already caused her harm."

"Your girl may provide the key we need to defeating the Nader Alliance for good."

With a gasp, Veena took a step backwards. "Wait a minute. You took Molly to be your lab rat?"

Swa snorted and crossed her arms across her chest.

"The war is over!"

"No, the war is only paused. We need to gain the upper hand before making our final assault."

"I don't want any part of this." Veena clenched her hands into fists. "Bring Molly back. She and I are leaving."

Swa pointed a finger at Veena. "You are not in the position to demand anything." She turned to Zane. "I told you to get her the hell out of here. I'm done listening to her whining about her spawn."

"Come on," Zane said, pulling Veena with her. Just as Veena was about to resist, the guard leaned close and whispered, "I have an idea."

Veena allowed herself to be guided out to the reception area and then into the hall. After the door slid shut behind them, Zane looked both ways to ensure they were alone, then released Veena's arm.

"I shouldn't tell you this," she said. "But the Rock has a secret spaceport for VIPs and top-secret shit. I bet that's where they took Molly."

"What?" She'd never heard of a second way off the Rock. She told herself not to be surprised; her paltry secret security clearance gave her access to only the bare minimum.

"You and the rest of the civilians aren't supposed to know. But I have access." Zane turned and led Veena in a different direction. "When they hollowed out the asteroid, they drilled an exit right through the rock."

"Where?"

"Behind the vertical farm. There's a separate tram line running there from here. Follow me." Zane turned down a corridor Veena had never used.

Veena tried to make sense of everything. From the school, it would have been closer to take Molly to the main spaceport. Was Zane going the right way? She released her ponytail and licked her lips—Molly needed her to make the right choice.

"Why would they take Molly that way?" Veena asked.

"They'll want to hide that they've stolen a child." Zane turned and met Veena's gaze. She frowned. "Most of us wouldn't condone that sort of thing. Hell, I shouldn't have let it happen in the first place."

"Thank you," Veena said. "For helping me."

Zane gave her a curt nod.

Around the next corner, they arrived at another tram station. It was smaller than the main station without any benches to wait on. Fortunately, no one was there.

After Zane waved her credentials at the gate, a light flashed green, and an automated car pulled up to the platform. It was smaller than the trams Veena normally took—a single car just big enough for a half-dozen passengers. The outside was painted the same dull grey as the Rock's landscape. From a distance, it would be almost impossible to see.

As soon as the doors slid open, Zane stepped inside. Veena followed, and the door closed behind her. The tram took them out the other side of the command module and looped towards the vertical farm. As soon as they were clear of the structure, another module came into view, tucked behind the farm. The low building was nondescript. Its most defining feature was that it was out of view from the modules Veena had access to.

The tram deposited them on another platform, again empty of people. The same military-grade cleaner scent as everywhere else on the base hung in the air. Veena's feet felt encased in concrete as she took a first step onto the platform. Racing after the people who'd taken Molly was what Hwicce was equipped to do, not her.

"This way." Zane gestured to the single door on the far side of the platform.

Zane led her deep inside to a waiting area with floor-to-ceiling windows overlooking a massive hangar cut right out of the rock. At the far end, a perfectly circular hole descended into the floor—presumably the exit.

An assortment of military spacecraft parked in neat rows filled the front half of the hangar. All were small ships ranging from sleek VIP shuttles to gate-rated personnel transport ships.

In the centre, one ship stood out. It was a make Veena didn't recognize. No markings graced the silver ship's hull, not even a call sign. Its bullet shape suggested it was rated to go through standard atmospheres, and the engines suggested it could travel long ranges.

"That must be them." Zane smiled at Veena. "We made it in time."

Veena put her hand on the clear surface and looked down at the waiting ship. Lights were on in the cockpit. "How do we get down there?"

"This way." Zane turned towards a door in the clear wall. Outside, a catwalk connected to a set of metal stairs leading down. The two of them ran down to the hangar floor, their footfalls echoing.

"Mom!" shrieked Molly.

Veena spun around and spotted her girl being held by a woman dressed in a grey suit. A man and woman, also in grey, stood beside her.

"Molly!"

Molly struggled with the woman who held her. "Mom! You found me." She twisted her arm out of the adult's grip and raced over to Veena.

"I'm here," Veena said as she knelt to hug her daughter.

Thirty metres away, three guards emerged from a side room. They pointed their rifles at Veena as they advanced, but Molly reached Veena first, and she wrapped her arms around the girl, lifting her.

"I thought you wouldn't come," Molly said as she squeezed Veena tightly. Molly still smelled exactly like she should, a combo of bubblegum-scented shampoo and peanut butter.

"I will always come for you." Veena forced her voice to sound calm as she swung around, hunting for her best escape route.

"She needs to come with us," said the man in a grey suit. Veena guessed he was the James Greer that Zane had mentioned. "Let her go, and everyone will be safe."

"No!" Veena gritted her teeth.

Her options were limited; the only place she might reasonably reach was the way she'd come in. Swallowing back the lump in her throat, she sprinted for the stairs.

"Stop!" yelled a guard, but Veena kept going, her feet pounding back up the stairs. She didn't let Molly's weight slow her down. Zane followed close behind.

"Keep going," Zane said as Veena reached the top.

Veena glanced down to see the security chief pull out her weapon and face the others.

"I order you to stand down," she yelled at the guards.

Two of them ran up the stairs. The third stayed on the ground and aimed his weapon at his boss.

"Don't make me fight you." Zane's tone suggested she expected her subordinate to follow her orders.

"Our orders are to secure that girl," the closest guard said as she continued her advance. "You're the one who is out of line."

Zane fired, hitting the guard on the stairs. She fell backward into the one behind her.

The guard on the ground fired his energy weapon, hitting Zane in the chest. Veena's unexpected ally collapsed to the deck. Zane's eyes remained open as smoke rose up from a charred hole in her chest. Her own people had killed her.

For a split second, Veena paused. Then she put a hand on the back of Molly's head and kept moving, hoping Molly hadn't seen what happened.

Running as fast as she could while holding a seven-year-old in her arms, Veena followed the corridor back to the tram station. Once there, she sighed in relief. The tram was still there.

Just as she stepped onto the tram, something hit her from behind. She lost her balance, falling sideways and losing her grip on Molly. Before she hit the floor, everything went black.

Chapter Twelve

With a jerk, Veena woke. The lumpy mattress beneath her barely hid the hard surface under it. Her mind raced, searching for the familiar scents of peanut butter and bubblegum that always followed Molly like a cloud. But only a musty scent filled the air—she wasn't in her own bed.

Memories of charging into the secret hangar to rescue Molly flooded back. She shivered, then ground her teeth together. She and Zane had been foolish to rush in like that. Zane's dead gaze haunted her. She swallowed.

"Mol?"

She rolled to her side and stared at her surroundings. The room was small, barely bigger than the size of her cot. The ubiquitous grey of the Rock covered the walls. Here and there, stains punctuated the surface. She stared at the abstract shapes as her mouth went dry.

"No!" She was in a cell—alone. Molly wasn't there. "No, no, no...."

As she jumped to her feet too fast, a wave of nausea swept over her. She reached up to the back of her head and found a swollen lump. Ignoring the throb, she went to the door and started pounding.

After a few moments, the little window set into the door slid open. A guard she didn't recognize wearing the standard indigo uniform peered inside.

"You're awake," he said in a tone laced with disappointment.

"Where's Molly?"

"Someone will be here to see you soon." He closed the window with a thud.

A breath caught in Veena's throat. Molly was gone. She'd failed her little girl.

"Mol, I'm so sorry," she whispered as she turned away from the door. She wished the floor would open and suck her out into the void.

She swallowed a lump in her throat and forced herself to take a deep breath. The thumping of her heart matched the pounding of her head. With a sigh, she slumped down onto the cot.

"I don't know how to get you back," she said as she put her face in her hands. She wanted to scream. Instead, she counted each breath she took.

Twenty minutes later, the door opened. With a slump to his shoulders, Orin stepped into view. He stood in the doorway for a moment, staring at her.

"I'm..." His voice cracked. "I'm sorry."

"Did you know about this?" She stood and stalked towards the shorter man. "Did you know 'they' were going to kidnap my little girl?"

Orin nodded.

The image of Molly struggling in a stranger's grip flooded her mind as she stared at her boss. He'd known what was going to happen and let her continue her efforts decoding that message. Heat rose across her skin until her cheeks burned.

She balled her hands into fists at her side. He was part of this.

Putting her body weight behind it, just as Hwicce had taught her, she launched an uppercut. Her fist connected with Orin's jaw. He stumbled back into the hallway, and the guard rushed to his side.

Veena staggered back, her fist throbbing as much as her head.

"No." Orin rubbed the side of his face as he blocked the guard from entering the cell. "Leave us."

"You sure?" The guard stared at Veena. "It's my ass if she beats the shit out of you."

Orin pushed his shoulders back as he made eye contact with Veena. His brow furrowed, and he appeared more present than Veena had ever seen him. "Yes, I'm sure."

With a shrug, the guard left. Orin stayed in the hallway.

"I tried to talk them out of it."

"You fucking asshole." Spit flew with every word. Veena flexed the fingers of her right hand, then clenched them into a fist. "How could you?"

Orin pressed his lips together into a grimace and said nothing for a moment. "I should've tried harder to stop them."

Veena's nostrils flared as she took a deep breath. What could she possibly say to him? She crossed her arms over her chest. "An apology won't fix this," she said through clenched teeth.

"Swa had no right to take Molly."

Veena said nothing, and the silence between them stretched out.

After a few minutes, Orin nodded. "You're free to go back to your quarters." He turned and walked away.

With a whoosh, Veena released the breath she'd been holding. As much as she wanted to race after Orin and kick him to the ground, it wouldn't bring Molly back. Although he deserved her anger, it was Swa who'd instigated Molly's kidnapping. And Zane had paid a steep price for trying to help.

She swallowed and stepped into the hall. All the lights in the halls were cycled to their nighttime levels. Mulling over everything that had happened, she walked until she stumbled upon a tram station. Too distracted to even sit, she rode the tram back to the barrack module, and from there, she headed directly to her room.

Veena was grateful she didn't encounter anyone on her way. Her head still throbbed, and there was a gaping hole in her heart. The walls seemed even duller somehow, like the colour had been drained from her world.

At her door, she stopped. A brown box sat on the floor just outside her room, her name written in bold script on the label. She wasn't expecting anything, and normally, packages went to the mailroom.

Biting her lip, she picked it up and turned it over in her hands. The box was slightly larger than a datapad but twice the depth. There was no return address; the only marking other than the label was a stamped octopus on the back. She ran a thumb over the tentacles rendered in indigo ink. Whoever sent it had a flair for old-fashioned packaging.

She glanced both ways down the hall. No one was there. With a sigh, she opened her door and went inside. As soon as the door closed behind her, she leaned her back against it. With the package still in her hands, she slid down to the floor.

Tears welled up, and this time, she let them drip down her face. Molly was gone. Even though Veena had tried her best, she hadn't been able to hold on to her little girl. She sobbed and clutched the package to her chest.

From its perch on Molly's pillow, the Click stuffy stared down at her. Its bright pink tentacles and shiny eyes were more out of place in the grey military decor of the room than ever. And its eyes seemed to be judging her.

A new round of tears came. Not only did she fail to rescue her daughter, Molly was alone among strangers without her favourite stuffy.

When she finally reached a state of numbness, Veena crawled over to her bunk. Unsure what else to do, she opened the package.

Inside was a *Bubble and Click* comic she hadn't seen before. The brightly coloured cover suggested the intrepid duo had taken a shuttle out for an adventure around a gas giant. She checked the box to confirm there was no return address.

Where did the package come from?

She bit her lip and shifted her gaze to Molly's Click stuffy. It was all too much. She shoved the package into Molly's backpack with the rest of the comics.

After picking up the soft toy, Veena lay down on Molly's bed. Within moments, she fell asleep.

Chapter Thirteen

With his back to the floor-to-ceiling windows in the captain's cabin, James Greer stared down at the little girl. She had her arms crossed over her chest as she frowned up at him.

"My mom is going to be mad at you," she said before jutting out her chin.

Greer sighed and looked over at Walker, his colleague, where she sat on the sofa against the wall. "I need you to take Subject 34 to the holding area."

Walker glanced up from her datapad. "Molly's right about her mom's anger."

Greer pursed his lips together. "The girl is called Subject 34."

"She's going to come for me," Subject 34 said.

Walker nodded. "I believe it."

"Enough talk of Subject 34's mother." He could still picture the anger on Veena's face when she almost succeeded in rescuing her daughter. But it was too late for her now; he was away, and there was no way she could follow.

Walker shrugged. "Did you conclude your negotiations with Long Enterprises for a more accessible facility on Hamber's Hole?"

"They got too greedy," Greer said. "They wanted—"

"I want my Click," Subject 34 said loudly, cutting into the conversation.

"What the hell is a 'Click'?" He met the girl's gaze for a moment. "Never mind." He gestured to Walker. "Just take her to the holding area."

Greer turned to the window. The grey surface of Rock 13-A5 was receding into the distance. He was glad to be off that lifeless facility and away from Swa. He still couldn't believe that woman was now his boss.

Walker grabbed the girl by the upper arm.

"I demand you take me back right now!" Subject 34 stomped her foot on the deck, and the entire ship shook.

"Come on," Walker said as she dragged the girl away. "I think I have a roll of Space Chews stashed somewhere."

Greer watched them go. It was unfortunate that the best subject he'd found happened to be a child, but his work was too important to let that stop him. If the Nader Alliance had super soldiers, the Protectorate needed them too—and he was the one who could deliver.

Swa had assigned him a military transport ship. Utilitarian was the best way he could describe the ship. The captain's cabin he'd commandeered was a prime example. He surveyed the grey room. It was neither refined nor aesthetically pleasing—he deserved better accommodations than this.

He sat down at the desk and composed himself. Then he called Swa.

"Yes?" she said as her head appeared above the desk.

"Subject 34 is secure." He pulled himself up as tall as he could. "Our extraction was a success."

"I hear a mathematician nearly stopped you." Swa kept her face neutral, yet her tone seemed mocking.

"Dr. Oswiu turned out to be more resourceful than you let on. She recruited one of your staff to help her."

Swa frowned. "Major Zane chose the wrong side and paid heavily for it. Dr. Oswiu is now in custody."

"Good," Greer said.

"Where are you going to take Molly?"

"Subject 34." Greer steepled his fingers. "My negotiations with Long Enterprises have stalled, so I'll keep her at my lab in the X-ray System for now."

Swa raised an eyebrow. "My understanding was that Long Enterprises already invested heavily in supporting your research."

"The greedy corporation wants to fill my lab with their own people. I won't have them spying on me. It's almost like they want to make a profit off my work on top of what we'd pay them for the facility."

"They have performed adequately on other top-secret projects," Swa said. "And cutting ties with them now will have consequences. They don't view contract breakers fondly."

Greer waved a hand as though brushing the issue away. "We're the government; they wouldn't dare touch us."

Swa frowned. "I expect you to provide me with results, not more problems."

"Well, my general, results take time."

Red bloomed across Swa's cheeks. "Don't forget that you aren't irreplaceable."

Greer shrugged but didn't say anything. He knew there wasn't anyone else in the Protectorate who could do his work.

"Now, what are your next steps?"

"I'll send Subject 34 directly to my lab. I have samples I need to collect on Jupiter Station, then I'll follow on a civilian transport."

He terminated the comms link then leaned back in his chair.

The *Garden Princess* would be leaving from Jupiter Station in a day; it would provide him the kind of luxury he deserved and a few days of relaxation before he was stuck once again on the ice world containing his lab. As much as he hated the remoteness of his current lab, he did prefer the privacy it provided. Only technicians he'd recruited were there—none were spies from Long Enterprises or from General Swa.

He massaged his temples with his fingertips. Swa expected him to deliver super soldiers, but it was turning out to be a more difficult problem than he'd expected. He opened his datapad and reviewed his progress so far. Swa had sent him several genetically engineered specimens, including several captured Rokan soldiers and three greenie women. The problem was that it was their ancestors who'd had their genetics tweaked as zygote's, not as fully formed humans. He could reproduce that kind of tweaking, but Swa wouldn't be happy waiting for her super soldiers to grow up.

With a sigh, he smoothed his hair down. To make a super soldier out of a more mature subject, he needed to activate genes they already had—and that was where his recent failures had been. And if he managed to get that working, he still had the issue of how he'd control the subject.

He activated the hologram image recorded on the helmet camera of one of the soldiers on Candy Cane Lane. A woman appeared in the centre of the room. The harsh mid-day light shone on her pale skin.

Standing, he walked over to the image. Her features were blank, and a web of some kind covered her shaved scalp. Zooming in, he studied the details of the headpiece. Electrodes appeared to be attached to her head, but there were no clues as to how it worked.

He let out a long exhale and returned the image to life-size. "Why didn't you capture her?" he grumbled to no one. "I can't get what I need from just an image."

The woman's blank expression intrigued him. The control over her had to be complete—her own will subjugated to whoever pulled her strings. The ideal super-soldier.

Now he needed to get to work and figure out how to create one of his own.

Chapter Fourteen

A soft tapping at her door woke Veena. For a second, she worried the sound would wake Molly. Then it all came back to her—Molly was gone. The thought left her sick to the stomach. Plus, Hwicce had left his army post and vanished. Was he on his way back to her? More than anything, she wanted to confide in him.

She realized she was in the wrong bed and still fully clothed from the day before. Pushing the escaped wisps of hair out of her face, she yawned and sat up.

On the floor, staring up at her with its oversized eyes, was Click, Molly's favourite stuffy. One of her few possessions that survived the bombing. The one thing she needed to fall asleep. Now, the toy looked discarded. New tears threatened to well up. Veena rubbed her face and swallowed. How was Molly doing? Did she get any sleep without Click?

More tapping came from the door.

"I'm coming." Veena picked up Click and placed it back on Molly's pillow before opening the door.

Gloria stood in the hall. "Hey." Her tone was uncharacteristically soft.

"Hey."

"How are you holding up?"

Veena sighed, then shrugged. She wanted to be alone but couldn't find the words to send Gloria away.

"Can I come in? I heard about what happened and did some digging."

With a nod, Veena moved out of the way. As she did, she caught another glimpse of the Click stuffy. Molly would miss it...

"Focus, Veena." Gloria put a hand on Veena's shoulder. "I found out where they took Molly."

Veena bit her lip as her mind cleared. There might be something she could do.

"It's a small military research facility only four jumps on from our gate." Gloria sat down on Molly's bed.

"In the Echo System?" Veena frowned as she tried to picture the figure eight loop of the main gate system.

"No, it's on a secret, off-loop link from the Delta System." Gloria licked her lips. "It's a supposedly 'dead' system—one of the few around here with no inhabited worlds."

Veena sat down on her bed and pressed her hands to her temples. Secret loops, uninhabited systems...what the hell was she supposed to do with that information? She swallowed. If only the Rock's link access hadn't been turned off—then she could get a message to Hwicce.

"What do I do?"

"Well, you go get Molly, of course." Gloria grinned. "Pack your shit. I've got a plan."

Veena nodded, stood, and looked around the spartan space. "I can't message Hwicce right now. What if he's on his way back to the Rock right now?"

"Right, he resigned." Gloria nodded, and for a split second, Veena wondered when she'd told her friend about her husband. "As a civilian, he won't get access to the Rock. Besides, as soon as you're on a civi station, you can get link access again."

"Of course." She would just send him a message en route. No doubt there were messages from him as well.

She grabbed Molly's backpack and shoved her datapad inside next to Molly's *Bubble and Click* comics and mysterious package she hadn't wanted to deal with the night before. Next went in Molly's bucket-o-stuff and the Click stuffy. In a daze, Veena looked around.

Gloria took the backpack from her and held it open. "Throw in a change of clothes and maybe a few extra pairs of underpants."

"What would I do without you?" Veena added a few more things, including the black satin slippers from Hwicce. The backpack itself was an over-the-top sparkly pink hue, the kind that would draw attention, but she didn't want to leave it behind.

"Okay, let's go." Gloria handed the bag back to Veena and led the way into the hall. It was still early, and the halls were quiet. "I've found you a way off this Rock."

Veena looked her friend in the eye. "Why are you helping me? You could get yourself into trouble just talking to me."

"Don't be silly. You're my friend; I couldn't not help."

A tiny bud of hope formed in Veena's mind. Maybe Gloria wasn't just a font of gossip, and maybe, just maybe, her help would result in getting Molly back. Veena wasn't going to question the only lead she had.

They took the tram to the mouth of the hollowed-out rock, where the spaceport linked to the interior. The team entered a tube to protect it from the electronic shield gate before arriving at the port.

"How?" Veena asked, trying to pull herself together. She'd need to focus to get Molly back.

"Last night, I ran into Sam," Gloria said.

Veena just stared at Gloria blankly.

"You know, Jerry's husband?"

Veena nodded. "Right." Jerry was another code breaker in their department.

"Well... Sam's ship leaves in an hour, and he can get you on board."

"Isn't he on a military ship?"

"Nope, it's a civilian freighter unimaginatively named *Freighter-51*." Gloria continued to lead the way. "He said he can get you to Jupiter Station. From there, you'll have to find another ride—plus you'll have full link access again."

"How in the hell will I get a ride to an uninhabited system?" Veena asked as they made their way through the port. A few people were moving about, but no one paid any attention to them.

"Take it one step at a time. I've got some leads—you know, people tell me things. Besides, I'm willing to help however I can." Gloria stopped and looked around. "We need berth 32-A."

A few minutes later, they found the ship. A man who had to be Sam waited at the mouth of the gangway. Short and barrel-chested with wide shoulders, he looked like he could take on anyone, yet he regarded Gloria with fear.

"We need to get going." He spoke to Gloria, barely glancing Veena's way.

"Right." Gloria turned to Veena. "The first thing you need to do on Jupiter Station is book passage."

Veena nodded even though she had no idea how she was going to find a ship headed to an unpopulated system at the end of a secret off-loop link. Her head spun at the thought—but she owed it to Molly to find a way. "The Delta System is where I need to go, right?"

"Anywhere on the way to Delta System will make a good first step. I hear that Jupiter Station is crammed full of refugees, so it'll be a challenge to find a spot on a ship going anywhere."

Veena nodded. Her worry piled onto her chest, keeping each breath shallow. How could she possibly do this?

"We need to keep in touch," Gloria said. "I'll do the best I can to help you, and maybe I'll be able to find out more information. Molly is such a sweet girl; you need to get her back."

"Thank you." Veena tried to smile. "You've been a great friend."

"You'd do the same for me." Gloria pulled Veena in for a hug. When they pulled apart, she said, "And take this." She held out a compact device.

"How do you even have that?" It was a military-grade comms device—the kind that required a security clearance she didn't have.

Gloria shrugged. "I'd rather not tell on my source. But I've hacked it. It'll now give you a direct link back to me."

"You have two?"

"Yep." Gloria held up a matching device in her other hand. "So don't forget to keep in touch."

Veena nodded as she took the device and slipped it into her pocket.

"I'll contact you as soon as I have more info," Gloria said. "Just get yourself to the Delta System. I'll reach out to my contacts and find you a ride the rest of the way."

Veena nodded a second time.

Gloria put a hand on Veena's arm. "You can do this."

"Come with me," Sam said. Leaving Gloria behind, he led Veena into the ship. The inside was clean and utilitarian—just how she expected a transport ship to look.

"It'll take us eight hours to reach Jupiter Station." He turned down a smaller corridor. "I've got a cabin set aside for you."

"Thank you." The thick scent of lemon cleaner in the air nearly caught in her throat.

"We don't normally take passengers. Stay in your cabin, or the crew will ask questions." At a door, he turned towards her. "I'll bring your meals, so you don't need to worry about going hungry."

"Thank you," Veena said again.

He opened the door, exposing a room even smaller than she'd had on the Rock. She forced a smile and stepped inside.

"I'll check on you in a few hours." Sam closed the door behind her.

Alone, Veena let out a long sigh. She dropped Molly's backpack beside the bunk before flopping on the thin mattress. She rolled onto her back and put her hands over her eyes.

"How am I going to get Mol back?" She sighed as tears threatened to well up. "Hwicce, why in the hell did you run off without a word? I need you." She swallowed. If he were there, Hwicce would know exactly what to do—hell, he wouldn't have let Molly get taken in the first place.

As she started churning through her worries, exhaustion caught up with her, and she soon fell asleep.

Chapter Fifteen

Sitting with his back against the wall, Hwicce stared out into the sea of people filling the concourse. Even after two days, his disappointment at finding the spaceport as crowded as the city down below hadn't lessened. As he pushed himself up to standing, his knees and hips groaned. Sleeping on the floor left him feeling like a decrepit old man. With a sigh, he rubbed the back of his neck.

Going from ship to ship hunting for work hadn't gotten them any closer to finding a job. Most ship crews wouldn't even speak to them. And those that would weren't hiring. Two ex-soldiers from a war no one really wanted weren't in high demand.

"I don't want to be a whiner." Baker stood beside him and rubbed her lower back. "But sleeping on the deck is doing a number on my back."

"You've slept on rocky ground for weeks at a time, and now you've gone soft after only two days as a civi. What would your peers say?"

"Pound salt. Sir."

Hwicce smiled. At least Baker was still herself. "How about another round of spicy tacos for breakfast?"

Baker scrunched up her face. "That crap is all we've eaten."

"You used to like them." Hwicce frowned as he glanced down the spaceport's main concourse.

"Once there were more options in my diet." Baker bent over and touched her toes before stretching her hands up towards the ceiling.

"Crickets are the cheapest protein source around." He watched as the taco cart proprietor started getting ready for the day. Although it was still early morning, shops were beginning to open up. All around, other travellers still slept on the floor—and would until security arrived to clear the area ·for daytime commerce.

"They'd be better with beer."

He turned to Baker. "For breakfast?"

She shrugged. "It wouldn't be the first time."

"Tell you what. When we get jobs, then paid, the first round of beers is on me."

She snorted and picked up her bag. Stepping around the other sleeping people, she headed to the taco cart. Hwicce retrieved his belongings and followed.

Halfway to the taco stand, Hwicce noticed a heavy-set man looking nearly as rough as they did approaching them from the opposite direction on the concourse.

"Can I help you?" Hwicce asked, stopping and waiting for the newcomer. Baker remained at his side.

"I heard you two are looking for work." Up close, the man stood at least a hand's width shorter than either of them. The exertion of walking left him red in the face. His shabby cargo pants and jacket labelled him as someone off a low-end transport ship.

Hwicce ran a hand over his beard and did his best not to yawn. His aching body needed a softer place to sleep—although he'd never admit that to Baker.

"You heard right." Hwicce met the shorter man's gaze. "Are you looking to fill some positions?"

"I need a couple of deckhands willing to do dirty work... and keep their mouths shut." As he spoke, his right eyelid drooped in a distracting way. "You two look like the right type."

Hwicce stiffened. Alarms went off in his head. He knew he should turn the man down...except no one else had even spoken to them about potential work. He glanced at Baker, and she shrugged.

"That might be us."

"Boris Long." Boris extended his hand to Hwicce. "Captain of the *Shimmer*."

Hwicce shook the other man's hand, forcing himself to ignore Boris' sweaty palm. "I'm Hwicce, and this is Baker." He pointed to where Baker stood scowling. "Where's the *Shimmer* headed?"

"We're going to do a run along the off-loop link to the Beta System." Boris shifted from foot to foot. "I'm scheduled to pick up cargo at Hamber's Hole. From there, we'll probably head to Indigo Station."

Hwicce nodded. Boris seemed very shifty; no doubt his ship was not on a legitimate job. Plus, heading to Beta System would take them further from Veena and Molly, but the *Shimmer* was a ticket off this spaceport. Other stations might provide them with better transport options. It wasn't like Boris would want them to sign a contract in blood—he and Baker could just leave at the next port.

"We might be interested."

Boris pursed his lips as though making a mental calculation. "Pay is forty credits a day for each of you."

Hwicce's swallowed. Everything about this job offer felt dodgy and potentially less than legal. Plus, the pay rate was abysmal. But it was better than nothing—a day's work would earn him enough to get a message to Veena. He glanced at Baker and raised an eyebrow; she shrugged again.

He turned to Baker. "What do you think?"

She shrugged. "You're the brains of this operation."

A knot twisted in Hwicce's gut as he looked Boris in the eye. Taking this job was probably a bad idea, but hanging around hoping for a legitimate job would get them nowhere.

"We accept your offer."

"Good." Boris bobbed his head. "Good. The *Shimmer* departs in an hour."

"Show us to your ship, Captain."

Baker turned her head to the taco cart. The scent of roasting chilies and crickets was filling the air. "But tacos...."

Hwicce ignored her and followed Boris. With a less-than-subtle snort, Baker fell into step behind him.

Berthed at the end of a rundown hall on the port's lowest level, the cargo ship *Shimmer* wasn't anything special. Viewed through the port's windows, the ship didn't come close to living up to its name. Nothing about it shimmered. Pockmarks and stains added dull highlights to the matte grey hull. The mid-sized hauler was decades past its prime—definitely due for an overhaul or the scrap yard.

"We'll be pulling out as soon as I get clearance," Boris said as he led them down the gangway tube and into the ship's cargo bay.

The reek of rotten algae hit them in a wave, suggesting a problem with the air filters. Baker put a hand to her face but said nothing.

"Are you picking up cargo before we go?" Hwicce asked, following Boris as he continued through the empty cargo hold. The same grey as the exterior coated the walls, ceiling, and decking, creating an exceptionally drab space. Boris continued straight through the empty cargo hold.

"Naw, we just dropped shit off for the army."

"The troops need their shit," Baker said in a flat tone.

Hwicce gave her a dark look to silence her.

As he crossed the deck, he felt heavier in some places than others. A squishy gravity field was a bad sign. At best, it pointed to poor maintenance; at worst... He stopped himself from thinking too hard about how a failing gravity field could rip a ship apart. He almost turned back to the spaceport. But then what? With a sigh, he told himself they wouldn't be on the ship long and continued on.

"There're no contracts to be had here unless I want to fill my hold with corpses. The job at Hamber Hole is next up." Boris continued into a corridor where escaped algae oozed along the inside of the lights.

"Uh-huh." Hwicce tried to sound non-committal. The *Shimmer* was worse than what he'd pictured.

"Hey, Emiko," Boris said as they entered the cavernous algae filtering room. The stench here was strong enough that the air seemed more liquid than gas.

A small woman wearing a cut-off wetsuit descended the ladder leading down from an algal tank. Contrasting with her pale skin, her dark hair was cropped into a pixie-style cut.

"Well then," Baker said from his side as she studied the other woman. "This place might not be that bad."

Hwicce glanced from Baker to the new woman—Emiko—then to Boris. The captain shrugged.

Emiko reached the ground. "What have you dragged on board?" Even though she stood a head shorter than both Hwicce and Baker, she looked them up and down.

"You said you needed help to clean this shit up." Boris pointed to where the algae grew on surfaces it shouldn't. "So I'm giving you these two." He turned to Hwicce. "Emiko will get you to work." He then walked out of the room.

Emiko crossed her arms over her chest and stared at them. Her eyes lingered on Baker's shaved scalp.

"You two look like grunts." She scowled.

Baker scowled right back at her. "Cuz we are."

"Peachy." With both hands, she brushed the moisture out of

her short hair. "At least I can expect you to know how to follow orders."

"What do you want us to do?" Hwicce asked as the ship lurched, and he nearly lost his footing. "What the hell?"

Emiko laughed. "It's just Boris pulling us out of dock the only way he knows how. We're on our way."

"Doesn't he have AI assist?" Hwicce already regretted coming on board.

"He disconnected that shit years ago. Said he didn't trust it."

"Brilliant." Baker's tone remained flat.

Hwicce glanced her way and raised an eyebrow before turning to face Emiko. "What's the crew compliment of the *Shimmer*?"

"Well, aren't you full of questions? How about we start by getting to work." She handed him a scrub brush with a broomstick handle. "The algae got out before they hired me. There's a hell of a lot of scrubbing you two need to do."

Hwicce took the brush without a word.

"Start here." She pointed through a door to a room thick with algae. "It's the crew common room. I've been itching to play some generations dice. I'll take the two of you for all your worth."

Baker laughed out loud. "Bring it on, algae girl. But be warned, if the two of us put our fortunes together, it's unlikely we could afford a peanut butter sandwich."

Hwicce smiled and grabbed a bucket.

"And since you asked," Emiko said. "The arrival of you two doubled the crew compliment."

———

It took three hours, but they scrubbed up the common room shiny and clean. Hwicce's fingers resembled prunes from being wet for so long. With a sigh, he sunk down onto one of the plastic chairs Emiko had found somewhere. Baker flopped down onto the one beside him.

"This is a shit ship." She crossed her arms over her chest in an overly dramatic move.

"Would you rather keep sleeping on the floor of Candy Cane Lane's spaceport? The best we could've afforded was another day's worth of tacos."

"Hmph." Baker stifled a yawn with her fist as Emiko entered the space. "I'm hoping our cots don't need scrubbing."

"You can take your pick of cots through here." Emiko pointed to a door leading off the common room.

It automatically opened, exposing a long room with a series of bed alcoves two high, running along both walls. Twenty people could sleep in there. But best of all, it appeared clean.

"Well, we won't be tripping over each other," Baker said. "Hell, I might find a bunk far enough away to not hear you snore."

Hwicce crossed his arms over his chest. "I do not snore."

"Of course not. Sir."

Emiko gestured inside. "There's a linen closet just inside the door. You'll have to make your own bed."

"One thing the army taught me was how to make a bed. So I'm calling it a night." Hwicce stood and grabbed his bag.

Baker's gaze rested on Emiko as the other woman went to the fridge and pulled out a drink. "I think I'll hang out here a bit."

Hwicce winked at her. "Right."

With a frown, Baker pushed him towards the cabin. "Dipshit. Now get some sleep. Sir."

When the door slid shut behind him, Hwicce nearly collapsed into the closest bunk. Instead, he forced himself to find the bedding and make the bed. After setting his bag on it, he rooted through it for a change of clothes.

He didn't have much, just a change of clothes, some underwear, and couple extra t-shirts. As he reached the bottom a knot twisted in his gut. He flipped the bag upside down and dumped the contents out onto his bunk. Something was missing. He went through the contents several more times, but Molly's *Bubble and Click* comic wasn't there. Volume 21, second edition, should be in his bag. He was certain he had packed it.

In his mind, he could see where the comic was in his pod—in the alcove at the head of his bunk. He swallowed; the comic was probably still there.

With a ragged exhale, he leaned against the wall beside the bunk. Then he slid down until he sat on the ground and buried his face in his hands.

Without the comic, he wouldn't be able to send an encoded message to Veena. Anything he sent her would be readable by the Overwatch AIs. Even worse, he wouldn't be able to decode what she sent him. He tilted his head back until it rested on the wall. The comic was his reminder of Molly. Every time he worked on a coded message using the brightly coloured pages, he couldn't help but think of his little girl.

"Bloody hell."

Chapter Sixteen

With a heavy sigh, Hwicce slumped into a seat at the galley table that now filled the centre of the crew's common area. Emiko and Baker's efforts made the space livable, but like everywhere else on the *Shimmer*, spartan remained the best way to describe the space.

Still shovelling food into her mouth, Baker glanced up from her plate of re-hydrated glop. "What's up, sir?"

"I can't get through to Veena."

"Who's she?" Emiko swung a leg over the back of the chair next to Baker while holding onto her own bowl of glop. In the day they'd been on board, Emiko had taken to sitting next to Baker at every opportunity.

"My wife." He stared down at his plate. "She works on Rock 13-A5."

"Huh. I've heard of that place. Secret shit goes on there." Emiko began eating her dinner.

Hwicce shifted in his chair, wondering if he'd said too much —he'd only just met Emiko and wasn't sure if he could trust her or not. "She does clerical stuff."

Baker raised an eyebrow at him but said nothing. She knew exactly what Veena did.

"Secret clerical shit." Emiko finished her food. "Sounds fun. So why can't you get ahold of her?"

Hwicce met Emiko's piercing stare. "I don't know." He scratched his head and stared down at his food.

Veena always answered. Maybe not immediately, but within a day. He was sure she would even answer his uncoded message —but she hadn't. A knot formed in his gut, and he tried to think of a reason she would remain silent. All the reasons that popped into his head weren't good.

He stirred the glop around in his bowl. It stuck to his spoon in a way that reminded him more of glue than food. Realizing his appetite was gone, he sighed.

"At least it isn't another spicy cricket taco." Baker smiled at him.

"True." He pushed his bowl towards her.

Baker slid the remains of his dinner in front of herself. Without comment, she finished it.

Emiko gathered up the now-empty bowls and stood. "I've got an idea." After dumping the plates into the sink, she opened a top cupboard and pulled out a worn box. "How about we take the evening off?" She set the box on the table and opened it.

Inside was a set of Generations Dice. Even though their sides were well worn, the eight colours remained obvious. They looked festive, a punch of colour in the utilitarian space.

"Ooo." Baker picked up one of the eight-sided dice. "These are vintage."

"I found them in the back of the food storage locker." Emiko smiled as she dumped the remaining dice onto the table. "But Boris refuses to play with me."

"That..." Baker's words trailed off as she rolled a standard fist of three dice. Green, orange, and black sides faced up. "My lucky day."

"You two play. I'm going to try to call Veena again," Hwicce said as he stood.

Baker glanced up at him. "She's probably just working late. You always say how she can get lost in her work."

"Yeah." Hwicce took a deep breath. "Sometimes she does." He walked away as the two women nattered on about their dice rolls.

He returned to the only comms terminal the captain allowed him to access—an old-fashion one located awkwardly at the door to the common room. After placing a hand on the screen, he paused.

Why wasn't Veena answering his calls? It wasn't like her to ignore him. Did something happen to her? As more fear welled up inside him, he told himself his line of thinking was ridiculous. A military compound well behind the fighting lines was the safest place she could be.

She'd mentioned a friend on Rock 13-A5. He closed his eyes and tried to remember the friend's name. Gloria....Gloria Norton. After a quick query, he found her link and called her.

He was almost ready to abandon the call when a sleepy face appeared. "Hello?"

His breath caught in his throat. "Um..."

"You must be Hwicce," she said with a smile. "Veena talks so much about you, I feel like I know you already."

He leaned against the wall and rubbed the back of his neck. "I can't get through to Veena."

"She's on a freighter headed to Jupiter Station. It's an older one without real-time link access," Gloria said.

Hwicce frowned. "Why are they on a freighter? They weren't planning on going to Jupiter Station until Mol's birthday."

"Oh!" Gloria put a hand over her mouth. "You don't know."

"Know what?"

She bit her lip. "Um...well... Molly's been taken."

"What?" Hwicce put a hand on the wall to steady himself as his gut twisted in a knot. "Who took Molly?"

"Molly had an..." She looked both ways as though she feared being overheard. "An episode. She shook things up—literally."

The knot in Hwicce's gut twisted. "But who took her?"

"Um... The military decided she should be removed from the Rock. Dr. James Greer took her."

Hwicce didn't know what to say as he tried to process Gloria's words. Behind him, Baker and Emiko's loud dice game made it difficult for him to concentrate. He did his best to focus on the face in the screen.

"Veena's on the freighter to go after Molly?"

Gloria nodded. "Yes."

His mouth went dry. They had taken his child. He was stuck on this algae-soaked freighter heading to some mining colony while his wife went after Molly alone. "But how is she going to find Mol?"

"Rumour is they're taking Molly to a secret military lab."

"Where is this lab?" Hwicce winced at how harsh his words sounded, but Gloria didn't flinch.

"There's a secret, off-loop gate in the Delta System."

Gloria seemed very free with information; she must have been a good friend of Veena's. Hwicce let a long pause draw out as he considered what this all meant.

"I'm planning on taking leave and heading to Jupiter Station," Gloria told him. "I'll find her and help where I can."

A sense of relief washed over him—Veena wouldn't have to carry on alone. "Thank you. When you see Veena, please tell her to message me."

Gloria nodded. "I'll let her know. Bye for now."

The comms link blinked off. Uncertain what to think, Hwicce returned to the table. He sunk down into his chair but said nothing. The two women remained focused on each other and gambling away their chores, which left him alone with his thoughts.

Rubbing his face, he ran through all the choices he'd made

that had kept him away from his family. Why hadn't he found some excuse to be sent to Rock 13-A5? After the bombing, his family had needed him more than the front lines did. He swallowed and hoped Gloria would find Veena and tell her to contact him. There was little else he could do.

"Hey," Baker said after a few rounds. "Don't you find it a little strange this freighter doesn't have any cargo?"

Emiko shrugged. "We often don't take on cargo."

Happy to have a fresh problem to think about, Hwicce forced himself to focus on it. "I assume Captain Long is the owner of the *Shimmer*."

"His family owns it—and they're rich too. I don't know where Boris fits in, but my guess is he did something wrong and being on this ship is his punishment." Emiko stretched her arms up over her head, then cracked her knuckles.

"Long Enterprises?" Hwicce asked, remembering the contractor the military often used.

"Yep, that's them. Let's play another round. I don't want to clean the shitters anytime soon." Emiko took up the dice and rolled them. The little metal octahedrons clanged across the table's surface.

Boris charged into the room. "You're gambling?" He stormed up to the table and stopped across from Emiko, nostrils flaring. "At a time like this?"

"Nothin's going on," she said as she took up the dice again.

"There's still algae everywhere. We need to sort this place out." A red flush rose across Boris' face. "We may be taking on important cargo."

Emiko frowned at her boss. "We can't scrub clean years' worth of growth in a day."

"You can at least put in a full day." He pointed at the dice. "I'm not paying you to gamble away your chores. Do that on your day off."

There was a long pause while Boris and Emiko stared at each other. Emiko gave in first and let out a long sigh. "Fine.

We'll scrub the walls outside engineering before hitting the sack."

"You two"—he gestured to Emiko and Baker—"can take care of that." He pointed at Hwicce. "You can start cleaning the grime on the bridge." Boris stormed off as fast as he'd appeared.

"What a party pooper," Emiko said as she put away the dice. "I'll bet he's just mad we didn't invite him to play."

After filling his bucket with diluted lemon cleaner, Hwicce headed up to the bridge.

Windows ran along the curve of the semi-circular room, exposing a panoramic view of the void beyond. Six workstations flanked the pilots, suggesting the ship should be flown by a much larger crew. The faux leather chair raised above the others highlighted where the ship's captain would sit—but Boris wasn't there.

Starting to the right of the door, Hwicce scrubbed the grime off the metal walls. It wasn't algae; instead, it was grey grunge that quickly turned his hands the same colour. It could've been the charred remains of a previous crew for all he knew.

His mind wandered back to Veena and Molly as he worked, trapping him in a mental loop of analyzing how things could have been different if only...

He shook his head. "This is foolish," he said to himself. "I'm doing everything I can to get back to them."

Dropping his scrub pad back into the bucket, he turned and surveyed the room. He needed something else to focus on, and Baker's comment about the lack of cargo resonated with him. Even if the *Shimmer* was a smuggling ship, taking on real cargo would be a logical plan. Wouldn't authorities ask questions if a cargo ship remained empty all the time?

He went to the first workstation and booted it up. Boris hadn't set a password, meaning it only took Hwicce a few moments to bring up previous cargo manifests. He opened the customs documentation from when the *Shimmer* arrived at the Candy Cane Lane's spaceport. The ship had been empty—Boris had lied about bringing in cargo. What did that mean?

Cleaning now forgotten, Hwicce sat down and scrolled through the documents, stopping when he found a message about their upcoming stop at Hamber's Hole. It was from Long Enterprises HQ and designated high priority. Hwicce opened it and scanned the contents.

Long Enterprises was building a new lab facility for the military in an abandoned mine at Hamber's Hole. The *Shimmer* was tasked to collect a senior Long Enterprises official from Hamber's Hole, then they would be shuttling equipment from the military's current facility to the new one.

"That's interesting," Hwicce muttered as he leaned back in his chair. Maybe Molly had been discovered and taken to a secret military lab. And maybe if the incoming Long Enterprises official knew where one military lab was, they just might know where they all were. If he stayed on the *Shimmer*, he might get the information he needed.

A clunk in the hallway leading to the bridge pulled his attention. Hwicce flicked the console off and resumed his scrubbing.

Chapter Seventeen

With her arms crossed over her chest, General Swa stood at the window staring out at the grey landscape of the interior of the Rock 13-A5. Her career trajectory should have put her on the front lines, winning battles—instead, she was here, stuck in charge of a shitty, backwater installation. Sure, running the code-breaking work had netted results, but it forced her to play nice with too many whining civies.

"General Swa?" her orderly, Corporal Higgins, asked from the doorway. His broad features held a hint of fear as he regarded her—a trait Swa approved of. This orderly was a good one, subservient in the right way. He should be promoted, but she'd rather keep him where he was than break in a replacement.

With a slow, smooth motion, she turned to face him and raised an eyebrow. "Yes, Corporal?"

"The civilian you requested has arrived," Higgins said, keeping his eyes on the ground.

She snorted. "They sure took their time. It's like they think military precision doesn't apply to them."

"They don't pay you the proper respect, ma'am."

"Corporal Higgins, you're a gem. And right as always. Send them in, and let's get this over with."

She turned back to the view and pretended to not hear the tentative steps of her mole entering the office. Unlike Higgins, she'd rather not work with her mole—but circumstances forced her to. She let a long silence draw out as she watched the trams shuttling people from module to module. Finally, she turned to her visitor.

"I hear Dr. Oswiu didn't take the news of her daughter being removed well."

"No," the mole said. They were smart enough to not even attempt to sit.

"It's unfortunate she convinced a decorated military officer to take up her cause." Swa thought of the message she'd composed to the late security chief's family. She'd crafted the right combination of praise and compassion to ensure the family wouldn't complain. Unfortunately, Major Zane would be difficult—but not impossible—to replace.

"Yes, very unfortunate."

"Did you get access to Dr. Oswiu's personal files? Specifically, her latest de-encryption work." Her people needed to know what was in the alien text, and Veena was her best opportunity to figure that out. Why did the first feasible Protectorate super soldier have to be Veena's daughter? It was a complication Swa didn't need.

The mole flinched. "I haven't hacked into her work files...yet."

"I don't think you understand what I need." Swa advanced on the mole. "I have access to Dr. Oswiu's work files. But intel tells me she's been working on the same code for some time. I need access to her personal files."

Swa let out a huff. The DeepNet decryption effort was a project that had been going on for years—yet her agents hadn't been able to break in. Now that the same codes had appeared on military channels, decoding them was urgent. Especially now that she'd taken command of the Alien Investigation Unit. Her AIU operatives were convinced this new set held alien secrets— secrets she needed to know before anyone else did.

"I... I..." The mole looked down at their hands. "I didn't realize that's what you'd asked me for."

"I hear Dr. Oswiu left the Rock," Swa said. "Fleeing on a freighter heading to Jupiter Station."

"Yes. She's under the foolish assumption she can rescue her daughter on her own."

Keeping her rod-straight posture, Swa sat in the black chair behind her massive desk and steepled her fingers together. "If Dr. Oswiu finds her husband, the two of them could rescue the girl—or at least cause us a lot of problems."

"Captain Hwicce Oswiu doesn't have the funds to book passage to anywhere near us."

"Former captain," Swa corrected. "My operatives reported he spent his last credits on the space elevator up to Candy Cane Lane's spaceport. He's probably still there, squatting in a corner somewhere."

"Why not put a bounty on his head?" her mole suggested.

Swa smiled. "I like how you think. It would be very convenient if that man had an accident. See to it." She leaned forward and put her hands on her desk. "Now, back to our code-breaker."

"While she travels, she'll have plenty of time to work on that code," the mole said.

"Is she going to?"

"I think so. She's always been one to turn to her work for solace." The mole glanced at the chair next to them for a moment but remained standing. "Had she stayed here, she would have put all her energy into planning her escape instead."

"True." Swa exhaled. This was her opportunity to become relevant once again.

Cracking the alien code might accelerate Greer's work—or maybe even provide more. What if the alien text provided her with secrets she could leverage? She rubbed a finger over the one star on her uniform's collar. Maybe another star was in her future. Maybe even a Field Marshal post.

She licked her lips. The top rank was one her mother would have been proud of—if she'd lived. Her mole better not screw this up. Swa deserved that promotion.

"Let her run loose for a few days, but I want you to follow her, then reel her in. Pretend like you're helping her out but make sure she's working on that code.

"As you wish."

"Remember, Dr. Oswiu is an asset I can't afford to lose. I will hold you accountable if she drops out of sight."

"I won't let you down."

Swa met the mole's gaze. "You better not. You're dismissed —but I expect regular reports."

"Of course." The mole turned and left her office.

Swa smiled—she now had two solid avenues she could use to advance her career. Both the mother and child presented themselves as opportunities. She activated her holocomms and called Dr. Greer.

Taking longer than he should have, the incorporeal form of Greer's head appeared out of her desk. The ungrateful putz pursed his lips together when he saw her.

"We're still 24 hours away from the gate," he said. "I won't have a proper update until I get back to my lab, and that'll take at least a week."

"I know your timeline." Swa kept her tone flat. Greer often overstepped his station, and she needed to keep him in check. "I wanted to warn you that the girl's mother has left my facility."

"I hardly think that poses a risk. She's just an analyst, right? Without Zane's might, what's she going to do? She doesn't have access to any resources."

"I agree; she isn't much of a threat. However, I wanted you to be aware." She leaned back. "How is the girl faring?"

Greer froze. Swa narrowed her eyes as she studied his hologram. Was he hiding something? She didn't trust the man, but she didn't have a suitable replacement.

"I'm not used to dealing with children." He ran a hand through his short hair. "This one is more difficult than I expected. Perhaps bringing the mother would've made the subject more cooperative."

Swa said nothing.

"The subject is distraught at being separated from both her mother and..." He paused and drew his eyebrows together. "What I understand is a stuffed octopus."

"Mythical creatures are a hit with that age group," Swa said, making a mental note to make more of an effort to find a replacement for Greer. His work was too important to be left with a man who struggled to deal with a mere child. "I expect you to remain in control of the situation."

"Of course," Greer said.

"I also expect regular reports on your progress when you get back to your lab. You saw the footage from outside the Pharaoh Casino on Candy Cane Lane." Swa could still picture that woman throwing a fully armoured soldier through a wall.

Greer licked his lips. "I've been studying it. I have some ideas on how to replicate that..." His words trailed off as though he was searching for words.

"The Protectorate needs a way to fight back against super soldiers like her, and you're going to give it to us."

Greer nodded. Before he could say anything further, Swa shut the link down. She returned her gaze to the grey landscape outside. The situation with the Oswiu's was too fluid—and she didn't fully trust her people in the field.

She stood and paced over to the windows.

"My mother always told me that if something's important, it's best to oversee it in person," Swa said to herself. Her mother had never been kind to her, but she had ingrained the qualities into her daughter than ensured continual success.

Striding back to her desk, Swa opened a line to Corporal Higgins. "Tell Captain Von to prepare for an immediate departure and that I'll be coming aboard the *Defiant* to supervise."

Chapter Eighteen

For a second time, Veena woke and didn't recognize where she was, the lumpy pillow unfamiliar against her cheek. Rubbing her eyes, she sat up, and the thin sheet covering her fell away. She shivered. Dim emergency lighting highlighted the floor, leaving the rest of the room in darkness. This wasn't her room on Rock 13-A5. Her heart raced.

When she hugged her arm around herself, she realized the well-worn form of Molly's Click stuffy remained tight against her chest. In a tsunami, it all came back to her—Hwicce's disappearance without a word, Molly's kidnapping, Gloria's help, and getting on Sam's ship. She swallowed and lay back down.

"It'll be okay," she told herself as she took slow, deep breaths. It was a lie, but panic wouldn't help her form a plan. After a few minutes, her heart rate slowed back to normal. She turned on the lights.

A crude drawing etched into the grey paint on the bulkhead beside her pillow caught her attention. Another piece of Bubble and Click graffiti—the kind that popped up everywhere. Their crudes shapes exuded emotion in a way that matched her daughter's drawing skill. At the unexpected reminder of Mol, a lump formed in her throat.

Molly must be so scared. All alone and somewhere strange. "Please don't hurt my little girl." Veena hugged Molly's Click stuffy tight against her chest. The soft toy still had a slight cherry scent from Molly's shampoo.

Rolling over, she pushed herself up to sitting and glanced down at Molly's pink backpack—the only glittery thing in the room. The way it glinted in the light beckoned her. She opened it up and took out the comic that had just arrived, the one Molly hadn't even seen yet.

On the cover, a pink and gold Click used six of their tentacles to hang from the ceiling while extending their last two down. In a silver spacesuit, Bubble hung onto Click's extended tentacles. As she hung there, the cartoon girl grinned against the starfield backdrop.

Veena ran a finger over Bubble's face. Her brown skin and dark hair were just like Molly's. Molly regularly pretended to be Bubble; the illustrated girl was her daughter's hero. She would race through the corridors of the barracks pretending to explore a new world with Click at her side. Veena smiled at the memory, and a single tear dripped down her cheek.

"I'm coming for you, my little love bug," Veena promised.

She swallowed and flipped open the comic. A piece of paper fell out and fluttered down to the floor. It was the size of her palm and so crisp and white, it stood out against the worn grey floor almost as much as the sparkly backpack. She tilted her head slightly and stared at it. The single piece of paper captured all her attention. Leaning forward, she scooped it up and flipped it over.

The paper felt solid in her hand, its pulpy surface a disposable luxury only available to the elite. She blinked a few times to ensure it was what she thought it was. Among the rich and famous, retro cruises had been all the rage the last few months —and in her hand was a ticket for one complete with gold embossed lettering.

The ticket was for a stateroom on the *Garden Princess*, a

luxury liner leaving Jupiter Station that evening and heading to Indigo Station. And it had her name on it.

"What the hell?" She turned it back over.

On the back, written by hand, it said: 'Come to Summer's End Thrift Shop, I have something to give you.' Veena assumed the shop was on Indigo Station. It was signed Theo65–a DeepNet contact she'd never met in person.

The *Garden Princess* would go through the gate to the Beta system then onto an off-loop link leading to the dead-end where Indigo Station sat. It wouldn't take her to the Delta System. She stashed the ticket in her pocket before continuing to flip through the comic.

Theo65 must have sent her the package—a new comic for Molly and a cruise ship ticket for her. A stateroom on the *Garden Princess* was beyond what she could afford.

"But why would you send this to me?"

She set the comic down on her lap and pulled out the packaging it came in. It was a simple brown envelope with her name on it. There was no return address, nothing to show where it had come from. She swallowed before flipping through the rest of the comic. But no other clues were hidden inside. After putting the comic down, she studied the ticket again. Delta System was where she needed to go, not Indigo Station.

A knock finally drew her attention from the ticket.

"Come in."

The door slid open, exposing Sam standing in the hall outside. He smiled and held out a tray of food. "Good morning. Jerry said you liked your coffee black."

Veena rose to her feet and accepted the food. A bowl of oatmeal peppered with raisins and, as promised, a mug of black coffee filled the tray. Her stomach rumbled.

"Thank you. For this"—Veena lifted the tray a few centimetres—"and for helping me out."

"We'll be docking in about four hours," he said. "Stay put.

I'll come get you when the coast is clear." He stepped back out of the doorway, and the door slid shut.

Alone again, Veena sat on the bed and tried the oatmeal. It tasted like glue, but it was food. As she ate, she opened up her datapad, hoping that Hwicce had finally contacted her—now that she was away from the Rock, she had net access again. There had to be a reasonable explanation for him running off.

Her heart sank when she saw he hadn't sent her a message. She needed to talk to him, and soon. She couldn't believe he'd abandoned her and Molly. It couldn't be true. He'd contact her and explain.

Pressing her lips together, she realized her inbox wasn't empty. A single new message blinked, taunting her. The return address told her it was from Theo65.

"What the hell?" She put the spoon down and picked up the mug. After taking a sip of the coffee, which was actually good, she opened the message, hoping for an explanation for the package.

Instead, lines and lines of unreadable symbols filled her screen—but she recognized them. The symbols were the same as the last military decoding job she'd been assigned and the same as the old codes she'd worked on for fun back on New Haven.

"Why now?" she whispered. It couldn't be a coincidence she'd gotten the same code from two sources over two days.

Scrolling down, she studied the code. There had to be ten thousand unique lines. Using her best frequency analysis algorithm, she allocated her tablet's full capacity to the job.

When she first got the code, what had to be two years ago now, Theo65 had told her it was linked to an ancient alien message found when humans first arrived in the region. Supposedly, it was etched into a cave wall on the Alpha System anchor world, but subsequent expeditions to the site didn't confirm that.

Even though Veena remained highly skeptical of the alien

angle to the code, it still made for an interesting puzzle. She sipped her coffee while staring at the symbols. The puzzle was a distraction to focus on.

"Maybe it's a map," she said as she overlaid the symbols on a projection of the nearby solar systems. The four hours flew by as she tried every orientation she could think of.

Chapter Nineteen

Orin stood in the doorway of his office and stared out over the sea of cubicles. Two hours into the work shift and Veena's desk remained empty. He wasn't surprised. She'd lost her daughter the same day her husband vanished; that would shake anyone.

Memories of the first few days after he lost Mary filled his mind. At first, he'd hoped his wife survived the bombing on New Haven. The report of her death had to be a mistake—her body hadn't been found, just a crater where their home once stood. As the reality of her death sunk in, he'd gone numb. Months later, he remained numb and worked hard to stay that way.

He swallowed, tempted to go back into his office, close the door, and open the bottle he kept in the bottom drawer. But he didn't. He debated going to the barrack module to talk to Veena, but after their last conversation, he suspected he wouldn't be welcome.

Why did he always blow it in conversations that mattered? His last call with Mary still haunted him. He needed to apologize... he needed to take back what he'd said. But he never got that chance.

He scratched the side of his neck and stared at Veena's empty chair. "Bloody hell. Why didn't I convince Swa to leave Molly alone?" he said in a low tone. "The little girl should be with her mother."

"What's that?" Jerry asked as he returned from the break room. In his left hand, he held a mug from the ship his husband worked on. Orin couldn't remember the ship's name, a freighter of some sort.

"Nothing," Orin said as he studied the other man. Jerry was almost as bad a gossip as Gloria; maybe he knew what was going on with Veena. "Hey, have you seen Veena?"

"Umm...." Jerry turned and looked back down the corridor he'd come from, then back to Orin.

"I just want to make sure she's okay. I think I might swing by her quarters to check on her since she didn't show up for work this morning."

Jerry licked his lips. "She won't be there."

"What do you know?" Orin knew Jerry never could keep a secret.

"Can we go into your office?"

"Sure." Orin retreated inside.

Jerry followed, closing the door behind himself. "I don't know if Gloria told you or not..." He paused.

"Told me what?" Orin sat at his desk and gestured for Jerry to take a seat.

Jerry nodded and sank down. "Sam smuggled Veena off this rock last night."

Orin stared at Jerry. "Who's Sam?"

"My husband. You know the navigator on..." Jerry lifted his mug and pointed at the crest embossed on it.

"Right." Orin ran a hand over his balding scalp. "Why would she leave?"

"Veena's going after her daughter. Gloria said she has a plan to get her girl back."

"By herself?" Orin thought about Veena's husband and how

he'd run off with one of his subordinates. If he was such a dud, she couldn't turn to him for help. It wouldn't be easy for Veena to accomplish her mission alone.

"Yeah, I think so." Jerry stood. "I gotta go."

"One last thing."

Jerry frowned as he turned back towards Orin.

"Where is Sam taking Veena?"

"Oh, just to Jupiter Station." Jerry turned and left, closing the door behind himself. "From there, she's on her own."

Once he was gone, Orin let out a long exhale. Out of habit, he took out the bottle of whiskey he kept in his bottom drawer. It was low-end stuff but the best he could get his hands on. Any alcohol on the Rock had to be smuggled in as the base was theoretically dry.

After he set the bottle on the desk in front of himself, he stopped and stared at it. He could half hear Mary scolding him from beyond the grave. She would've reminded him that Veena —and her daughter—were his responsibility. He'd recruited her, after all, and promised her Molly would be safe on the Rock.

"Dammit!" He put the bottle away. "I owe Veena, and she needs my help." He may not be the strapping warrior Veena's husband was, but he had connections.

He stood, bumping his desk as he did so. The glass bottle rattled in the bottom drawer calling him, reminding him he probably couldn't help Veena—he might fail, potentially making things worse. With a sigh, he slumped back down into his chair.

"What am I thinking? I can't just run off. It's not like Veena's some sort of damsel in distress."

With a sigh, he opened the drawer and pulled out the bottle.

"She doesn't want my help anyway."

The bottle glugged as he tipped it and filled his coffee mug. Picturing his now-destroyed kitchen back on New Haven, he drained his mug.

"You could go back to flying," Mary said as she arranged the flowers he'd brought. *The yellow of the kitchen walls added warmth to her skin.*

"It's been a long time since I've flown. I'd have to re-qualify." He shifted in his seat at the kitchen table. The dahl bubbling on the stove filled the room with a delicious aroma. None of the meals on the Rock smelled so good.

Mary came around the counter and set the vase full of yellow flowers down in the centre of the table. She took the seat across from him, then leaned forward and took his hand.

"I know you gave it up to be home more," she said. "And I love that you did that. But the army took you away from me. And working on the Rock isn't making you happy."

Orin swallowed. "There's a war on. I need to help how I can."

"According to Rosie, they desperately need transport pilots. You used to love flying—and you would be able to come home more often."

"I don't know," he said and squeezed her hand.

"Give up your job on the Rock. It will only leave you with regrets."

With a jerk, Orin woke and shivered. He was back in his tiny office. The whiskey bottle sat empty, and everything was quiet. The warmth of his kitchen and Mary's touch were gone.

His head pounded as he stood. After grabbing the bottle by the neck, he walked over to the door. In the open office space, the lights had cycled to their nighttime levels. How long had he passed out for?

"You can do better than this." Mary's words came to him. "Don't let yourself be defined by regret."

"But I can't just leave—it's my fault Veena lost her daughter," he said to the voice in his head.

"Then you need to help her before you regret letting her get away."

He stood still for a moment, letting the silence wash over him.

"Dammit, I have to do something." He raised the empty whisky bottle and threw it against the wall behind his desk. It shattered into a million pieces and fell to the floor.

It wasn't too late to help Veena be reunited with Molly. Turning his back on his office, he left his office the last time.

With each step, the fog lifted from his mind. Even the tram back to the residential module seemed shinier and more exciting.

After making a pit stop in his quarters to pack a few things, he sent a message to an old contact—one who owed him.

———

"Rosie," he said, finding his contact in her office in the maintenance department—right where she'd said she would be.

"Long time no see." She looked up from the maintenance logs she'd been working on. A smile spread across her round face as she pushed the escaped hair from her bun out of her eyes. "I got your message."

"Can you manage it?" he asked, hating that he was asking his late wife's best friend for such a huge favour. But then, when Swa was trying to stop alcohol being smuggled onto the Rock, he'd hidden Rosie's involvement.

"You could've swung by from time to time," she said as she stood. Her curly hair bounced with each movement. "You know I don't have the security access to visit you."

"Things have been...." His words trailed off.

She put a hand on his arm. "I know."

He nodded.

"Come with me," she said. "I've got something that should work if you are okay getting your hands dirty."

Rosie took him into the main maintenance shop. The cavernous space hummed with activity. At least a half-dozen ships were parked on the floor in various stages of repair—and these were only the small ones. Anything too big for the hangar remained docked in space during repairs.

Skirting the edge of the facility, Rosie led the way. All the technicians they passed smiled and said hello to their boss. She gracefully greeted everyone by name. Her warmth was just one reason her staff remained so loyal to her despite the frantic maintenance schedule.

She took him into a corridor that led off the back of the shop. The walls looked older here, less used.

"It's a bit of a junkyard back here." She gestured into the rooms as they passed their windows. "The army likes to hoard its old crap."

Instead of replying, Orin stared through the windows lining the corridor at the array of equipment haphazardly strewn about. There were small flying machines of all sorts, from the kind meant to stay in atmosphere to battle birds with guns big enough to blast through any dome.

"I need to be inconspicuous," he said, eyeing up a troop carrier with a huge hole in its side.

"You're always inconspicuous." Rosie opened the door to the last bay on the right. She went inside, and Orin followed. "That's your superpower."

Behind a battle-damaged ambulance sat an old survey ship. A jolly shade of yellow paint coated the hull as though the little ship was begging to be seen.

Its bulbous nose and stubby wings barely made it aerodynamic, but it would fly in atmosphere. Probably sluggishly. Orin cracked his knuckles, reminding himself it had been years since he'd flown anything.

It was a long-range ship, designed to be out for months or years. He walked up to the hull and put a hand on the metal surface. It felt rough beneath his palm, well-worn and past its surveying heyday, but it seemed solid.

"Where did you find a gem like this?" He turned to Rosie, but she was already opening the side door.

"Come on." She gestured with her head. "Check out the interior."

Orin nodded and followed her inside.

The interior was only marginally less worn. Aft, a workbench lined one side with cupboards on the other. At the very back was a narrow door currently closed, most likely leading to the engine room. Another door on the starboard side sat open, exposing the toilet inside. He closed the door to the bathroom and headed toward the front of the ship.

Forward of the next bulkhead, a small kitchen nestled into an alcove against the starboard side. At the end of the counter was a table that would barely accommodate two people eating a meal. Through an open door on the port side, he found a small cabin with four bunks—two on each wall.

Forward again sat the cockpit with a proper pilot and co-pilot seat and two pull down jump seats behind them.

"This is...." His word trailed off as he noticed staining on the deck plating—liquid splatter of various shades of brown. He hoped it was all just spilled coffee.

"It's something, isn't it?" Rosie grinned. "Got it at auction for way less than it was worth. This vintage beauty has so much potential."

Orin turned to his wife's old friend. "Does it fly?"

"Hell yeah. I've put my off hours into upgrading the engines —it's even passed inspection to earn a long-range license."

Orin nodded. He put his hands on his hips and slowly rotated, taking in all the details of the small ship. He took a deep breath in. The air smelled fresh with only a hint of lemon cleaner. Inside, the walls were just as yellow as the outside. Despite being worn and decades out of date, the ship felt right.

"Can I borrow your ship, Rosie?"

"No, you can't borrow it." Rosie looked him in the eye. "I don't know why you've asked for my help"—he put a hand up as Orin was about to speak—"and I don't need to know why."

"What are you saying?" A fluttering sensation formed in his gut. This ship was the best option he had for helping Veena. If Rosie said no...

"You've been above board in everything you've done since I met you. What, ten years ago now?"

"Something like that."

"Well, you're acting cagey now. Whatever is going on must

be important. Consider this ship my contribution to your effort."

Orin's jaw dropped. He swallowed. "Thank you," was all he managed to say.

"I'll set you up with tools and spare parts. This is a solid ship, but she needs a lot of work." Rosie smiled. "But first, this darling needs a name."

Orin surveyed the cramped interior a second time. It wasn't pretty, but it would take him where he needed to go.

"Buttercup," he said.

"You're naming a ship Buttercup?" Rosie cocked her head to stare at him.

"They were Mary's favourite flower."

After four hours of Rosie explaining the workings of everything on the ship down to the toilets, Orin was ready to go. *Buttercup* hummed to life as he started the main engines. A subtle vibration ran through the ship—the sign of a well-tuned engine.

He pulled back on the controls, and the ship lifted off the deck. The port wing drooped slightly, and the entire ship remained slightly tilted—issues to work on. After being granted permission to depart, he inched the ship forward and into the airlock.

His hand trembled a bit as he monitored the walls; he didn't want to scratch the ship within Rosie's view. As the airlock cycled, he pulled himself together. He checked the hull's integrity. *Buttercup* held its atmosphere just fine.

The outside door slid open, exposing the ring of asteroids circling Alpha system's twin suns. Accelerating as smoothly as the old controls would let him, Orin pulled out of the station.

New Haven, the only planet in the system with a breathable atmosphere, was out of view. Further out, a few other rocky worlds orbited, good for mining and little else.

A freighter pulled out of the spaceport from another berth. He angled onto a course that wouldn't intersect the lumbering beast of a ship.

Setting the autopilot, he programmed a course for Jupiter Station, Veena's last known destination. He'd find her, explain everything to her, then help her find Molly.

Chapter Twenty

Late in the morning, *Freighter 51* docked at Jupiter Station. After he snuck her off the ship, Veena thanked Sam for his help and ventured off on her own.

She'd been on Jupiter Station before, but this time, her world felt different, paler somehow. Like looking through the lens of her own anxiety desaturated her surroundings. But she couldn't afford to wallow—she needed to find a ship to take her on the next leg of her trip.

She marched along the docking arm, counting windows as she went. When she reached forty-seven, the corridor merged with the station's main concourse. With a similar purpose as the main street in a ground-based town, the station's main concourse looped several kilometres in circumference and was lined with businesses like shops and restaurants.

Topped with a clear glass ceiling several stories up, the wide concourse was designed to be spacious and easy to traverse. Now, refugees crammed together in the space. To make matters worse, the crowd exceeded the station's air purification system's capacity, leaving an unmistakable human stench in the air. Net access to the ticket agents was down due to the volume, meaning that to find a berth on a ship leaving the station, she had to visit the ticket agents in person—leg work made more difficult by such a crowd.

Veena realized she was counting all the people that passed—and the number was getting huge. She stopped next to a wall and took a deep breath. As the river of humanity passed by, she looked for familiar faces. Many of the people here were from New Haven. Most wore a blank expression and moved with hunched shoulders. This could have been her and Molly's fate, stuck here in limbo, waiting for somewhere to go rebuild their lives. After tightening the straps of Molly's pink backpack, she pushed forward. The crowd jostled against her with every step, dragging her along when she slowed to read signs. Any ship heading towards the Delta System would do.

It took Veena four hours to check every ticket agent, leaving her with aching feet, a throbbing right temple, and no ticket. New Haven refugees willing to go anywhere that might provide a less crowded life had already snapped up every spot leaving the station for the next week.

After being turned away from the last ticket kiosk, she let out a long sigh and pushed through the crowd to the side of the concourse. Tucking herself in next to the support beam, she ran her hands over her face.

"Think," she said. Counting the passing people tempted her. It would calm her down, but she needed to focus on the problem at hand.

What if she couldn't find a way off Jupiter Station? Leaving the station was only the first step of many—ultimately, she needed to find a secret base on an off-loop link. She swallowed and closed her eyes. Her task seemed impossible. With Hwicce out of touch, Molly needed her more than ever. Hell, Veena needed him more than ever—he'd know what to do.

"Get a grip." It was all up to her. She needed to keep going forward until she got Molly back. She opened her eyes.

A pink and powder blue sign across the concourse caught her attention. In bold neon letters, 'Molly's Diner' called to her.

In response, her stomach rumbled, reminding her she hadn't eaten since breakfast—and it was now mid-afternoon.

"Everything will make more sense once I've had something to eat," she said, her eyes fixed on the sign. Fortifying herself with a deep breath, Veena plunged into the crowd, leading with her elbows to force her way through.

Inside the diner, the cacophony of human noise subsided to a more reasonable level. The hum of hushed conversation overlaid with soft music soothed her. She'd found somewhere to figure out her next steps. A weight lifted from her shoulders, and she took a moment to study her surroundings.

A black-and-white checkered floor extended under the twenty-six tables—but patrons occupied only half, and no one paid her any attention. To her right, stairs lead to a second level, which she took. An unoccupied booth overlooking the concourse beckoned her. She sank down, keeping Molly's backpack at her feet. Her stomach grumbled loudly.

"First things first," she said as she brought up the holographic menu.

She ordered a big bowl of miso soup, then stared down at the crowd outside, giving in to her urge to count the people. A calmness washed over her, soothing her frayed nerves. A few minutes later, a robotic server brought her soup, and she began absentmindedly sipping spoonfuls while keeping her gaze fixed on the crowd.

A buzzing from Molly's bag drew her attention, and she lost count. She pulled the bag onto her lap and fished out the comms device from Gloria. A message was waiting for her—Gloria was on Jupiter Station and looking for her. Veena put a hand on her heart and let out a long breath. Her friend had come through for her; she wasn't alone anymore. She smiled as she sent Gloria her location. The umami flavours of her soup suddenly tasted more vibrant.

Ten minutes later, Gloria burst into the diner. Her pink dress and styled hair were a perfect match to the diner's decor. With a big grin, she slid into the booth across from Veena.

"Did ya really think I'd send you off on this adventure all alone?"

"Thank you." Veena grinned. "I didn't expect you to come." With Gloria's help, finding Molly no longer seemed so daunting.

"Just had to tie up some loose ends at the office and book some time off. And voila...." She turned over her hands and exposed her palms. "Here I am." She leaned forward, her face taking on a more serious tone. "How have things been going?"

"I haven't been able to find a ship with space even heading through the first gate." Veena ran a hand over her hair, grabbing her messy ponytail.

Gloria nodded and pulled out her datapad. "Well, I have some contacts. Let me check in with them."

Veena finished her soup as she watched Gloria type multiple messages. By the time Veena had finished the last of her tea, Gloria looked up.

"Find anything?" Veena asked as the shiny metallic server came and refilled her mug. It took her empty bowl away.

"We just need to wait." Gloria sounded confident as always. "Why don't we work on some decryption together? I heard your last assignment was a fun one."

Veena furrowed her brows. "That one was supposed to be classified."

Gloria paused for a moment as she scrolled through the menu. She ordered veggie tempura and tea before turning back to Veena. "I should've mentioned—your assignment got turned over to me once you left."

"So, Orin finally put his bottle down long enough to be efficient."

Gloria shrugged. "Or someone higher up is putting pressure on him."

"I didn't realize it was time sensitive." Veena smiled.

Helping Gloria with her work was the least she could do for her friend—but she was hesitant to divulge that she'd seen the code before it was assigned. "I barely got started before I left, but I'll help you where I can."

As Veena finished the last sip of her tea, a thud reverberated through the diner, so intense her ears rang. The teacup slipped from her fingers, bounced off the table, and dropped to the floor.

A man at the table behind them started to scream as the crowd on the concourse below merged into a stampede. Veena leaned towards the window, putting both hands on the smooth surface as she tried to see what happened. From around the curve of the concourse, smoke billowed out.

"What's going on?" Gloria followed Veena's gaze.

"I don't know."

More smoke obscured her view. She couldn't see anything other than a few dark shapes moving below. Decompression? Ventilation failure? The other diner patrons were already heading towards the exit.

"We gotta get out of here." Gloria dragged Veena to her feet and barely gave her enough time to grab Molly's backpack.

"Wait, our bill." Veena reached out to swipe her credit chip.

Gloria pulled her along. "No time for that."

As they descended the stairs, the station alarms sounded, sending a reverberation to Veena's core. Something was seriously wrong. She followed Gloria as she pushed her way into the crowd outside the diner. The two of them joined the throng of people moving away from the disturbance towards cleaner air.

Chapter Twenty-One

Orin set the toolbox down on the counter in *Buttercup's* tiny galley and pulled out the screwdriver. Holding up the tool, he stared at the coffeemaker. The damn thing had already spewed scalding coffee twice. His pride prevented him from calling Rosie over a crappy kitchen appliance, but a screwdriver would not help him.

He continued to dig through the toolbox until he found an assortment of gaskets. The range of sizes was astounding, yet not one fit the coffee maker. With a sigh, he went aft and hunted for sealant.

Rosie had outdone herself with organizing supplies in what would have been the survey ship's lab. She'd even labelled each cupboard. With the spares she'd given him, he could keep *Buttercup* flying for years. A new life was opening up before him. Once he helped Veena get Molly back, he could keep flying, going wherever he wanted.

He closed his eyes. Mary had always wanted them to go to New Venus. She'd claimed the floating islands there would be so romantic with their endless sunsets. He let the memories wash over him.

"Just look at these statues!" Mary grinned as she moved the holographic projection of the courtyard around them.

He studied the mock-Greek architecture and the white stone statues that circled the square. Everything on Seven Soaring Swans—the public floating islands—was ostentatious. *"It's a bit over the top, isn't it?"*

"The islanders are rich," she said with a shrug. She met his gaze and smiled. *"I'd love to get a commission. I've always dreamed of having a statue there."*

Orin let out a sigh. They'd argued that night, and he'd left the next day. Within the week, bombs had levelled New Haven. A wave of grief surged through him. He couldn't even remember what they'd argued about, but it ate at him that he never got a chance to apologize.

This time, he didn't pull out a bottle to numb himself. Instead, he found a tube labelled 'food-grade sealant.' Flipping the tube over in his hand, he let his thoughts go back to Mary's wish for one of her statues to grace the public square on one of the Seven Soaring Swan islands.

All of Mary's statues were gone, reduced to ash and dust by bombs—but he could still go to that square on Seven Soaring Swans and project a hologram of one of her statues there. He smiled. It would honour her memory.

Returning to the galley, he sealed the coffee pot's leak and set it to brew. As he waited, he leaned against the counter and took a long look at *Buttercup's* interior. Even though paint chips marred the jaunty yellow, the colour made him happy—Mary would've loved it. For the first time since New Haven was bombed, he didn't want a drink more potent than coffee.

Rummaging through the galley cupboards, he found a silver coffee mug emblazoned with a ship logo he didn't recognize. He filled it and returned to the cockpit. Just as he sat down in the pilot's chair, a ping alerted him to an incoming message. The docking master had approved his visit and assigned a berth. He acknowledged the message, and a few moments later, traffic control sent him *Buttercup's* assigned approach trajectory. He programmed the autopilot to take him in.

In only a few hours, Orin felt he'd mastered flying *Buttercup*. He'd even mastered the coffee machine in the galley. And now, he had a plan to honour his late wife's memory. With a smile, he took a sip of his brew. The bitter liquid tasted perfect.

Outside, the wheel of Jupiter Station hung in the vacuum of space dead ahead. As he flew closer, Orin could make out the ships parked at the station's docks. He adjusted *Buttercup's* trajectory to match Jupiter Station's rotation before angling in closer.

As *Buttercup* made its final approach, one of the huge luxury liners came into view. Its green and gold hull gleamed against the backdrop of the station's grey.

He couldn't help but stare as he passed the shining hull dotted with brass-lined portholes. Even from the outside, it looked ridiculously decadent. Oversized golden letters running the length of the ship announced its name as the *Garden Princess*. In contrast to the rest of the ship's clean lines, a clear bubble covered the top at the front—an observation deck so the privileged could experience passing through the gates up close.

Emitting a grunt, Orin looked away. The fact that a war had been going on while that ship took vacationing wealthy where they wanted to go grated on him. Surely a ship like that would be better put to use by the military to move casualties or bring in supplies.

On autopilot, *Buttercup* flew into its assigned docking bay and executed a perfect landing. He didn't spill a drop from his mug. He watched as the umbilical gangway approached his ship like a tentacle and secured itself to the airlock. An automatic message notified him when the gangway sealed. He was now free to enter the space station.

After finishing his coffee, Orin went through his post-flight checks before making the call he dreaded. Jan, his late wife's twin sister, lived on the station, and he needed her help. After powering down, Orin set the now-empty mug in the sink and left the ship. The station police had issued an alert around a recent riot but claimed to have it under control, so he continued on into the heart of the station.

Human chaos filled the main concourse. People were every-where as though the entire station's population decided to use the concourse at once. And the stench...a weird combination of burnt plastic and body odour with a hint of something floral.

Orin tried not to breathe too deeply as he headed towards his sister-in-law's apartment on Deck C. He passed through a sector of fancy shops before cutting down a lane to the accom-modation block.

Chapter Twenty-Two

"What happened?" Veena asked no one in particular as she moved with the crowd.

"Riot," a man moving beside her said. "Some New Haven refugees have had enough of being stuck here."

Veena stopped and looked at him. His dark eyes bored into her. "But they're alive and safe."

"That's just not enough," the man said before he was jostled away.

Veena spun around and realized she'd lost sight of Gloria. Her friend's pink dress should have stood out, but it was nowhere to be seen.

"Shit!" No one even looked at her as she spoke.

Like a twig caught in a river's current, the crowd pushed and pulled Veena forward and out of the smoke. With considerable effort, she made her way diagonally across the flow of people until she reached a wall. From there, she scanned the crowd for any sign of a pink dress, hoping Gloria wasn't ahead of her.

After a few moments, the crowd became angrier, more like a mob. People began marching in step and shouting angry words. Now concerned for her safety, she ducked into a nearby store.

Once the door slid closed behind her, she sent a message to Gloria.

"I was thinking of closing up." The perfectly coiffed shopkeeper frowned at her from behind a counter at the back of the shop.

"Um..."

Running her hands down her generic printed shirt and pants, Veena surveyed her surroundings. Indigo dyed dresses and hand-embroidered jackets filled the racks of this high-end clothing shop. Even the shopkeeper's clothing appeared hand-made. This kind of fashion was well above her pay grade.

She wished Gloria was with her—they'd only just linked up. Veena swallowed and reminded herself they'd find each other again.

"Station security sent out an alert about the riot," the shopkeeper said. "They recommend everyone shelter in place until the instigators are dealt with."

Veena nodded. "I was hoping I could browse. I leave on the *Garden Princess* in a few hours."

The woman nodded as though it was perfectly normal to browse while a mob raged outside. "Let me know if you need assistance." She returned her attention to her datapad.

"Leaving on the *Garden Princess*?" she whispered to herself as she began moving through the shop. "Why did I suddenly come up with that?"

On the wall, an old-fashioned poster made of pulp caught her attention—it must have cost a fortune. A stylized passenger space liner covered most of the paper, its hull covered in gold letters that declared it the *Garden Princess*. She let out a low whistle. Everything about the ship screamed luxury, and she had a ticket to board it.

She pulled out the ticket and studied it. It presented a way off Jupiter Station. Maybe she'd have better luck finding passage to the Delta System from Indigo Station. But Gloria was here, so maybe she had other options. As she gazed at the crowd outside the shop window, a lump formed in her throat. She hadn't heard from Gloria, but she needed to give her friend time. Drumming her fingers against the side of her thigh, she began counting the beats. Gloria would message her—she wouldn't just vanish. Would she?

Veena stared down at her feet for a count of fifteen before staring back out into the crowd. Her heart leapt into her mouth as she spotted a face she recognized. Orin Atkin, her boss, should be back on the Rock, yet there he was, pushing his way through the crowd on a path parallel to the shop window. Her mouth went dry as she took a step back from the window.

"Is he coming for me?" she whispered under her breath.

"What was that?" The shopkeeper looked up from her datapad.

Veena spun around and grabbed the nearest item of clothing. "Can I try this on?" She tried to keep her tone light.

The shopkeeper frowned as she studied the garment. "It's last year's fashion." She cupped her chin with one hand. "But it would be acceptable on the *Garden Princess*, and it would be versatile." She waved Veena to the change room in the back.

Once the change room door closed behind her, Veena sank down on the stool inside. With the garment pooled in her lap, she opened her comms device. Gloria hadn't responded to her message. Veena messaged her again.

"Respond, respond, respond," she chanted under her breath. But nothing came from Gloria. Where did she vanish to?

Veena realized she still held the cruise ticket in her other hand. It presented, perhaps, her best way off Jupiter Station. She re-read the writing on the back. She'd been in touch with Theo65 for years, and they'd never asked to meet in person. What could they possibly have for her? It was statistically unlikely that Theo65 would contact her within hours of the military assigning her to break the old alien code. And now

Gloria had been assigned to work on the same code. Why was the code so important now?

Biting her lip, she tucked the ticket into a side pocket of the backpack. She stood and lifted the garment she'd brought into the change room with her. Although she'd randomly selected it off the rack, it was stunning. Its emerald hue shone in the bright change room light. It was a full-length piece, somewhere between a dress and a coat—fancy at a level she hadn't seen since the bombing.

After slipping off her jacket and shoving it into the now overstuffed backpack, she picked up the garment.

"Nanotech," she whispered. By touch, it felt like silk. Nanotech had been all the rage last cycle, only recently replaced by a preference for handmade goods.

The garment could be reconfigured to either a dress or coat. She changed it to a long coat and put it on over her clothes. This configuration buttoned up the front and had a tie at the waist. She twisted her hair into a bun and studied her reflection in the full-length mirror.

She no longer looked like herself. The garment made her appear more elegant, like she might even be stylish. She brushed a stray lock of hair behind her ear. Orin might not recognize her out of the crappy 3D printed cargo pants she normally wore.

Plus, if she couldn't find Gloria, her ticket for the liner was her only way off the station. As much as she wanted Gloria's help, she needed to keep moving if she was going to get Molly back. She hoped she looked fancy enough to get on the *Garden Princess*. Decision made, she pulled herself up tall and left the change room.

"I've decided to take it." She forced a smile. "It's perfect."

"The dress highlights the gold flecks in your eyes," the shopkeeper said with a matching smile. "This scarf around your hair will finish the look perfectly." The shopkeeper out a green and gold silk scarf. Veena nodded, and the clerk tied it on her.

In the mirror behind the counter, Veena saw how ridiculous she looked. But Orin defiantly wouldn't recognize her now.

"How about we find you a new bag?" The clerk pointed to the pink backpack Veena held.

Veena shifted the backpack behind her legs and out of sight. "I'll just pay."

"Of course," said the shopkeeper.

Veena tried not to choke as she transferred the credits. The garment had cost her a month's pay. After checking one last time for a message from Gloria, Veena returned to the concourse. She carefully checked the crowd; Orin was nowhere to be seen. Continuing to hold herself as tall as she could, she headed towards the dock containing the *Garden Princess*.

Gloria would understand if she had to go on alone.

Chapter Twenty-Three

Wearing her new green garment as a trench coat and holding the pink backpack tight against her chest with her left hand, Veena pushed through the crowd, heading towards where the *Garden Princess'* berth. The air remained too warm with a lingering scent of smoke as the station's air handling system struggled. Getting on the ship was her best step towards getting Molly back.

Even though her mind churned through what had happened to Gloria, Veena was certain her friend was fine. And Theo65 had always been a solid contact—maybe they could help her find passage to the Delta System from Indigo Station. At the very least, once free of the chaos on Jupiter Station, she could take the time to figure out her next move. Against the back wall of the cavernous space, the green and gold poster of the *Garden Princess* hung above the far ticket booth like a beacon. Against the dingy walls, its crispness looked unnatural, similar to a holographic projection, but she suspected the poster was real.

Behind the ticket counter, a silver-faced android came to life as she approached. After only a glance at her ticket, they opened a door in the wall and waved her inside, where a different world embraced her. A glorious green carpet covered the floor while a pristine warm white blanketed the walls. The air smelled fresh as though recently purified by a forest, leaving a slight hint of pine. Best of all, she was the only person in the room.

Her lips parted, and she let out a long exhale. Tension melted away. This was an environment she could think in. Coming here was the right move. A brightly lit corridor connected the station to the ship. Her footfalls made no sound as she walked along the plush carpet. As she passed, she began counting the green and gold leaf-patterned wall panels. It felt as though she were walking back in time to an era pre-dating her ancestors' departure from Earth.

After passing through a gilded airlock, she stepped onto the *Garden Princess.*

"Dr. Oswiu, welcome aboard."

She turned and came face-to-face with the most realistic holographic person she'd ever seen. This image was of a caucasian man, slightly taller than her, with light brown hair the same shade as Hwicce's.

Where her husband resembled his nickname of Bear, this hologram was refined. He wore period clothing from old Earth, including a slate-grey pinstripe suit tailored to perfection. A green cravat, the same colour used as an accent for the *Garden Princess,* around his neck finished his look. She had to resist the urge to reach forward and touch his cleanly shaven cheek.

"Um..." She gripped the handle of Molly's pink backpack tighter as she stared at the perfect rendition of a prim and proper human. "Thanks."

He cocked his head slightly and smiled. "Are you ready for me to show you to your cabin?"

Veena looked around. No one else was in sight.

"Are all the crew on this ship holograms?" she asked. Technically, a sentient AI could run a ship of this size. She'd just never heard of it being done.

"Of course not. Let me introduce myself. I am Nigel 378, your personal steward for the duration of your voyage. If you would prefer a different avatar, there is a wide selection available."

"Hi, Nigel," she said. "You'll do fine. Please show me to my cabin."

Nigel executed a slight bow. "Right-o. Please follow me, madam." He turned and started walking deeper into the ship. Veena slung Molly's backpack over one shoulder and followed.

Her jaw dropped when they emerged from the passage into the massive and open central atrium of the ship. At one end, a waterfall cascaded from the ceiling several decks above into a pond another deck down. The falling water created just enough background noise to dampen the sounds of people milling about. Strategically positioned lights created dancing rainbows in the mist.

She couldn't find the words to describe what she saw as she stepped up to the edge of the nearest scalloped balcony to get a better view. Actual trees rose from the bottom level, reaching towards the glowing ceiling and filling the air with the complex scents of a forest.

More scalloped balconies lined the sides of the atrium. Tendrils from an assortment of vines wound around the metal railings, adding another layer of foliage to her view. Some had leaves bigger than Veena's head and others blooms so brilliant, she doubted they could be real but knew they were.

"Wow," she whispered, and an overdressed couple passing by gave her a sharp look. She nodded at them before chasing after Nigel.

"This way," Nigel said. "It's not far now. Your cabin is on the Peony deck."

They passed what Nigel described as the breakfast nook—a space bigger than the mess hall on Rock 13-A5. Next was a spa, a games room, and a gym. As they walked, Nigel told her about a complete list of other amenities Veena didn't need.

At the theatre, Nigel turned to port and showed her into a waiting elevator, likely timed to be there exactly when she needed it. Darkly polished wood, smoky mirrors, and gold fittings made up the interior of the car. A flower pattern of inlaid ivory wove around the walls like a vine. The elevator's gravity plating was so smooth, she couldn't even feel the extra pull from the elevator's acceleration.

Without a sound, the doors opened to a carpeted hallway the same colour as Nigel's cravat. More dark panels lined the walls, and crystal prisms hung from each light fixture. She resisted an urge to count them.

"How long will the trip to Indigo Station take?" Veena asked, wishing she could share this trip with Molly and Hwicce. Her ongoing sense of panic about losing Molly returned.

"It's a day to the gate from here," he said. "Then a day to pass through the two gates. When we exit the final gate, it'll be another day until we dock at Indigo Station."

"So three days total." Veena bit her lip and shifted the backpack.

"If you are worried about entertainment—"

"No, not that," she cut him off. "I just want to plan my time."

"Very good. Here we are at last." Nigel strode ahead, and a door slid open. He waved for her to follow him inside.

With a frown, Veena glanced both ways down the hall. The knot in her gut tightened. There was still time to leave and try to link up with Gloria. Glancing back the way they'd come, she took a deep breath. No, this was the best way off of Jupiter Station. Molly needed her, and she wasn't about to let her little girl down.

Pulling herself up tall, she followed the hologram into her cabin. For a second time, her chin dropped.

A large seating area filled with twin cream-coloured couches sat dead ahead. Behind them, floor-to-ceiling windows exposed a panoramic view of the vacuum beyond. Ornately patterned carpet added rich jewel tones of indigo, jade, and amethyst. Tone-on-tone cream wallpaper patterned with leaves covered the walls. It was serene and opulent at the same time.

A set of sliding doors, currently open, separated the sitting area from the bedroom. A web of dark blue covered the cream bedspread—no doubt hand-dyed indigo from Indigo Station. A pile of similarly patterned pillows rested against a wooden headboard. The windows extended into the bedroom—lying in bed, Veena would see the stars.

"And through here is your bathroom," Nigel said, pulling her attention away from her stateroom. She followed him down a short hall and into another luxurious space, including a marble bathtub also with a view of the stars. The bathroom was at least double the size of her and Molly's room back on the Rock.

"The *Garden Princess* will pull out of dock in seven minutes. You shouldn't feel a thing as the gravity plating is functioning at 99.8% efficiency. And you have dinner reservations at 7pm ship time."

Veena went back to the main room and put Molly's backpack down on a cream sofa. She bit her lip as she looked around.

"I'm sorry, but there is one more thing I need to tell you about before I go," Nigel said, following her and rubbing his hands together. "It's the standard safety briefing required by transport safety."

Veena sat beside the bag and looked up at him. "Go ahead."

He gave a curt nod. "In the event of an emergency, the first thing you need to do is put on your emergency spacesuit. In your cabin, they are located here." He pointed to a wall panel that slid open, displaying several spacesuits inside. Even the emergency spacesuits were the ship's signature green. The only exception was the bubble of clear metal that would form her helmet.

"There are suits located throughout the ship. In the event of an emergency, the doors to their storage compartments will open automatically."

"Good to know."

"The suits contain similar nanotech as your dress," he continued. "Pull it on, and the suit will take care of sealing you in." He pointed to an airpack hanging at the side. "There is at least four days' worth of air, so there will be plenty of time to rescue you."

"Are there escape pods on board?"

"Of course. My systems can access remote back-up power. Even if the ship loses power, I will guide you to the nearest one."

"So I put on the suit and wait for you?"

"That is correct. If there is nothing else, I will leave you be."

"I'm good," Veena said.

"Right-o. I will return at 7pm to escort you to dinner. Please note that the dress code in the dining room is formal. If you need anything, just call my name." Nigel blinked away, leaving Veena alone in the cabin.

She felt her energy drain away as she slumped down onto the sofa.

"Gloria," she whispered, remembering that she'd abandoned her friend and ally on Jupiter Station.

She put down the box and rooted through Molly's backpack until she found the comms device Gloria had given her. She activated a link.

Gloria answered immediately. "Hello?"

"I'm sorry I lost you on the concourse," Veena said, words tumbling out of her. "I'm on a ship headed to Indigo Station."

"Slow down," Gloria said. "You're on your way to Indigo Station?"

"I couldn't find you and didn't dare to wait." Tears welled up in Veena's eyes—she'd abandoned the only person who'd seemed willing to help her. "It's because I saw Orin."

"Orin?"

"Yeah! Why would he even be on Jupiter Station?" Veena asked. "I mean, shouldn't he be back at the office?"

"It seems strange."

"I'm feeling paranoid. Everywhere I look now, I see people following me." She closed her eyes and rubbed the back of her neck.

"What ship are you on?"

Veena fell silent for a moment and bit her lip. "The *Garden Princess*. It's a luxury liner."

"I saw it on my way in. How in the hell did you afford a ticket? You didn't stow away, did you?"

"No, of course not. I..." Veena paused. She didn't really want to tell Gloria about Theo65 and accepting a ticket from someone she'd never met. "I used up my savings."

"Okay. Sounds like you'll have a comfortable ride. Just keep to yourself until you get to Indigo Station. Finding transport to the Delta System will be easier there."

Veena stood and paced over to the windows. She hadn't even noticed the ship leaving port. Jupiter Station was already out of reach—she couldn't get off now. "It's going to take three days to get there. I don't know what to do with myself."

"You could work on those codes," Gloria said.

Veena almost groaned—the last thing she wanted to do was decode anything.

"Maybe if you crack them, you can use them to barter for Molly's return."

"I won't work for the army again," she said.

"Okay, but working on those codes will give you an escape from your worries. I know how that stuff pulls you in."

Veena scratched the side of her neck as she stared out at the receding space station. "Yeah, you're right."

"Keep in touch, okay?" Gloria said. "I'll ask around and see if I can dig up any info that'll help you find Molly."

"Thanks." Veena glanced down at her datapad where she'd

tossed it on the sofa. "I'll call you tomorrow." She disconnected the line.

Chapter Twenty-Four

Outside his sister-in-law's door, Orin stopped and wiped his sweaty palm on his pants. Even though Jan kept inviting him to visit, he'd avoided coming. Since the bombing, he hadn't been willing to face Mary's side of the family, Jan least of all. Steeling himself, he rang the buzzer.

A moment later, the door slid open. Jan smiled at him from the doorway, and a lump formed in Orin's throat. Jan was a splitting image of her twin. His heart cracked a bit more. Mary was gone, and nothing would bring her back. But Jan was still here.

She waved him in. "Long time, no see."

Inside, the flotsam that came with several small children coated every surface. He racked his brain to remember their names. Jan had three boys: Simon, Jake, and—he scratched his head—Pete. Pete was the youngest one.

"Uncle Orin!" Simon, the oldest, shouted as soon as he spotted Orin. "Check out what I made with the bucket-o-stuff you sent."

Orin smiled as the boy brought out a parade of mythical beasts, including an elephant, a giraffe, an alligator, and several lions.

"That's great." Orin picked up each nano-constructed beast and studied them as Simon watched. The bucket had been an expensive gift but clearly appreciated.

"You still drinking?" Jan asked as she cleared a spot on the sofa and sat.

Orin glanced her way. "More than I should." He handed the animals back to Simon before clearing space on a chair. He sat facing his sister-in-law.

"She's only been gone a few months," Jan said. "Be kind to yourself."

"I should have been on New Haven." Like every time he was reminded, the memory of sitting at his desk on the Rock while the bombs fell surfaced. As the intelligence reports poured in, there had been nothing he could do but sit helplessly and hope.

"Bullshit," Jan said before glancing around to see if the kids heard.

Orin sighed. "I should have been with her."

"They needed you for the war effort."

"Not that day." That day, he'd sat alone in his office. With the doors closed, he'd watched his hometown burn.

Jan put a hand on his arm, bringing him back to the present. "You need to stop beating yourself up."

"The war is over." He took a deep breath. "The Nader Alliance doesn't have enough soldiers or ships left to make a counterattack."

"I saw on the news that a peace treaty was signed."

Orin nodded. "Yes, it's official."

Pete grabbed one of the nano-constructed lions and ran screaming through the house with his brother hot on his heels. Orin smiled at the boys' fun.

"You should visit more often. You're always welcome here."

"Thanks." Orin took a deep breath.

Jan looked him in the eye. "From the look on your face, I can tell you didn't come here just to visit."

"I have a favour to ask."

Jan cocked her head but said nothing.

"I'm trying to help a friend, but I've lost track of her in the crowd." He hated lying but didn't want to explain everything—especially his compliance in letting a child be kidnapped.

Jan pursed her lips together. "And you want me to see if she's boarded a ship leaving the station."

"Yep."

"If I check, you need to promise to stay for dinner."

"Sure." Orin had suspected that would be her price.

———

Somehow, Veena had booked passage on *The Garden Princess*, which finished boarding while he debated the merits of green peas with Jan's youngest. The voyage was slated to be going to Indigo Station—two gates away. At least there weren't multiple stops.

He checked the ticket price, and it cost more than her yearly salary—money she didn't have in savings—which implied someone was backing her. But who? He'd seen her file, and other than occasionally dabbling in decoding on the DeepNet, nothing about her had seemed out of the ordinary. Yet, she was turning out not to be who he thought she was. Still, he doubted General Swa was right about Veena.

As he walked down the concourse back to his ship's berth, he considered his options. Maybe Veena had all the help she needed to get her daughter back. Maybe she wouldn't accept help from him. Did that make following her pointless?

"Maybe I should just go home," he whispered as the throngs of people pushed past him. He swallowed. The Rock was where he lived, but home was gone.

He turned off the main concourse down a passage that led to the docks. Just outside his ship, Gloria Norton stood waiting for him.

She waved as soon as she spotted him. "Orin!"

He froze. How did she find him? And why was she here? With a sigh, he continued towards her. The most important question was, how quickly could he get rid of her?

After taking a deep breath, he fortified himself for Gloria's nonsense. "I didn't expect to see you here."

"You signed my leave request, silly." She tilted her head as she spoke.

"Right." Orin didn't remember approving a leave request for her, but then he signed lots of things. Maybe he just forgot.

"Nice ship you've got." She gestured towards the *Buttercup* behind her with a coy smile. "And I brought you a gift." She held up a bottle of his favourite whiskey.

His eyes fixated on the bottle. The amber liquid spoke to him, filling his head with numbing promises. He made no move to accept the bottle. Numb was not what he needed to be.

"Why are you here?"

She lowered the bottle and bit her lip. "I was hoping you would give me a lift."

"Where are you trying to get to?" He frowned. Gloria didn't normally put on her cute act for him. Something was definitely up with her.

"Just back to the office." She smiled. "That's where you're going, right?"

"I just came down to do some repairs," he said. "Rosie's going to be online in a few minutes to walk me through them."

"Perhaps there's something I can help with? I used to tinker with old hovercraft back on New Haven before..." She trailed off.

Orin took a deep breath. He didn't want Gloria along for the ride—nor did he want to take a trip with her down memory lane.

"My sister-in-law is bringing down her boys to see the ship later. You know how crazy a group of boys in a small space will be. Now's not a good time for you to be here."

"Right." Gloria drew her eyebrows together, and a moment of silence fell between them. "I guess I should get going. When will you be back at the office?"

"I'm going to stay on Jupiter Station for a while. My sister-in-law needs my help."

"Okay." Gloria opened her mouth as if to say something, then she closed it again. "Are you sure I can't come with you? You wouldn't need to work on this ship if you were just planning on sitting around on the station. I don't think you're really staying to help your sister-in-law."

"I'm going to insist you mind your own business." Orin frowned.

Gloria seemed to deflate. "Right. I'll see you when I see you." She turned and walked away.

Orin sighed as he watched her go. He'd always struggled with Gloria's tendency to be nosy, but her behaviour this time seemed out of character for her—she'd seemed desperate to get on his ship. Fortunately, there were plenty of shuttles that could take her back to the Rock—if that was really where she wanted to go.

To follow *The Garden Princess*, he needed to get going.

Chapter Twenty-Five

Hwicce grimaced as yet another twinge shot up his back. With a sigh, he tossed his scrub brush into the bucket and pushed himself back onto his heels. After a morning spent scrubbing algae out of the floor grating, he'd barely progressed two metres. He stood, put his hands on his hips, and arched his back. His vertebra sounded off like popping popcorn.

"Hey, old man, we're on cargo duty today," Emiko said as she strode into the algae generator room.

"A change would be good." In fact, he'd be willing to do almost anything to get out of more scrubbing. "Have we arrived somewhere?"

"We're about to dock at Hamber's Hole. It's a Beta System mining outpost drilled into an asteroid."

Hwicce nodded, picturing the figure eight of the loop system. The Beta System was two gates away from the off-loop link Gloria told him about. "What are we picking up?" he asked even though he'd seen the logs. Boris was here to meet someone —someone Hwicce was interested in talking to.

Emiko shrugged. "Didn't think to ask. We'll arrive in an hour. Hamber's Hole is far from fancy, but it's still worth hitting the showers before we arrive."

"Right," Hwicce replied, but Emiko was already gone—probably looking for Baker.

Still damp from his shower, Hwicce leaned against the wall next to the Hamber's Hold dock master's office. Just getting away from the relentless stench of rotting algae was a relief. The asteroid's size and slow spin gave it about a third of standard gravity, but it felt natural—unlike the lumpy gravity field on the ship. *Shimmer's* bulky hull filled half the docking bay. Fortunately, it was the only ship around.

"Hey, sir." Snacking on something out of a silver bag, Baker leaned against the wall next to him. "There must be better access to the net here. You could try again to reach your wife."

He slowly nodded. Veena needed to hear from him. What was she thinking? How was she faring? He closed his eyes and tipped his head back against the rock wall. And Molly? His little girl must be terrified.

Licking her lips, Baker crumpled up the bag and stuffed it in her pocket. "Something up? Sir."

He opened his eyes to find Baker staring at him with her lips pursed.

"Sorry." He ran a hand through his hair. "I..." He'd held off telling Baker about Molly's kidnapping, but he could trust her—she'd always been a solid ally, and he needed to get the weight of his news off his chest. "Molly's been kidnapped."

"What the fuck? I thought they were on a secure military base?"

"Some army doctor took her." Hwicce took a deep breath, then looked Baker in the eye. "Veena and I have known for some time that Molly could do...things."

Baker just stared at him.

"She can make things move when she's angry." The knot in his gut tightened as he pictured that super soldier he'd encountered at Candy Cane Lane. His side would want soldiers that could do what she did. Was Mol the first step towards that?

"So what? I've known lots of kids who can throw an epic tantrum. It doesn't mean they get ripped from their family. That's bullshit."

"I think our side is starting a super-soldier program."

"Those assholes!" She slapped her hand against the wall. "They can't snatch kids. We'll get your girl back."

"We'll get who back?" Emiko walked up and leaned against the wall next to Baker.

"It's a family matter," Hwicce said, and Emiko was smart enough to leave it at that.

"Hey, sir, what do ya think's in those?" Baker pointed to the pile of crates off to one side of the bay. All were identical cubes about waist high and without marking of any kind. If any cargo could appear suspicious, those did.

"No idea." He turned back to Baker. "And you can stop with the 'sir'—I'm no longer your boss."

"Well, if you aren't my boss, I don't need to do what you say. Sir." She continued studying the crates.

Hwicce just shrugged in response.

A few moments later, Boris emerged from the office red-faced and twitchy. "Load 'em up." He waved at the pile of crates. "I want us out of here in an hour. Emiko, go get the ship's engines warmed up."

"But we just got here." Emiko put her hands on her hips.

Without answering, Boris left the docking bay and headed deeper into the mining outpost.

"Well...shit." Emiko turned to the others. "I guess we don't get time to wander around."

"I was hoping to add to my crystal animal collection." Baker stepped forward and looked down the hallway leading out of the docking bay. "Maybe a mythical creature or two."

"I hear there are shops and shops full of fine crystal at

Hamber's Hole." Emiko stood so close to Baker, their shoulders almost touched. "Too bad we can't check 'em out."

Baker laughed. "I guess I have to find my fancy shit elsewhere."

"Maybe at our next stop." With a grin, Emiko turned and headed back to the ship.

"Well..." Hwicce let out a long exhale as he regarded the crates. There were a lot of them. "Let's get this done."

"Roger that."

He and Baker walked over to the crates.

"Contraband?" Baker ran her hand over the closest one.

"That'd be my guess." Hwicce picked up one; it was surprisingly heavy for the low gravity. "I wonder what's inside."

Baker picked up her box as though it weighed nothing. "Boris isn't up to anything good." She passed him on her way up the *Shimmer's* cargo ramp.

Hwicce snorted but said nothing. The sooner they got this task done, the better.

When all the crates were stacked two high in the cargo hold, Hwicce turned to Baker. "Keep watch."

Baker raised an eyebrow and leaned against the doorframe to the cargo bay. As usual, she managed to look completely relaxed in a split second.

"You headed out to do something stupid? Sir."

"Probably," he said as he left the ship. Boris had said they'd been leaving soon, but his new boss hadn't returned yet—and Hwicce was curious what business he had beyond cargo on a mining outpost.

Trying to look like he belonged here, Hwicce sauntered towards the inside doors of the docking bay. No one came out to stop him, so he walked through and down a long corridor.

A metallic scent best described as 'sharp' hung in the air,

leaving Hwicce with a lingering need to sneeze. Something skittered out of sight just ahead of his boot, but he didn't look closely. Insect infestations were common on the remote communities. Fifty metres on, he emerged into the main habitation area.

Emiko had been right—Hamber's Hole was far from fancy. Dust hung in the air, slightly obscuring everything. A few shops circled a crudely hollowed out space while nets across open areas prevented anyone from accidentally drifting away. Off to one side, a dilapidated residential wing rose up several stories. He wouldn't have been comfortable letting his soldiers stay in it, yet from the laundry hanging on the balconies, he assumed it contained families.

The majority of adults must have been on shift, as it was mostly children in the area. The dingy surroundings didn't stop them from playing, and their presence added a friendly feel to the place. They ran in packs, screeching with joy as they chased each other through the grubby environment. Their voices bounced off the walls, creating a cacophony of half-echoes.

In a tea shop across the way, Boris sat with an elderly woman at a table next to an open window. Keeping out of their line of sight, Hwicce made his way closer. Was this the Long Enterprises representative? Next to the window, he leaned against the wall and tried to look casual.

"Grandma," Boris said. "Had I known you'd be here, I would've taken more precautions."

The woman grunted. "Like what? Strategy has never been your strength."

"But...but...I didn't expect you'd make the delivery in person." Boris sounded like a whiney child who'd just been denied a toy.

"Boris, my sweet Boris," the woman said. "Trust me. As soon I'll be trusting you to do your part."

"I'm ready. I've even brought on more crew to help move that scientist's work to our lab."

"My sweet Boris, I'm so proud of you. Unfortunately, our plans have changed."

"What? Why wasn't I informed?" Boris still sounded like a child.

"There's a new cargo ready for you to take on—"

A group of screaming children ran by, making it impossible for Hwicce to hear the conversation. He leaned in as close to the window that he dared.

"But is it really necessary? There are so many people on that ship."

"My dear, we're playing the long game here. Don't lose sight of that."

A silence stretched between the pair, and Hwicce assumed they were sipping their tea. He leaned his head back against the wall and watched the playing kids.

"But—" Boris started again.

"Don't let your conscience weigh you down," Boris' grand-mother cut him off. A gentle sound of flesh on flesh suggested she'd patted Boris' hand. "The army needs to pay after cancelling my contract like that—and it'll cost them dearly."

"But—"

"We can't let them push us around."

Hwicce heard the clink of mugs settling back on the table.

"After all this, I've got a nice safe job for you back on Indigo Station. All you need to do is follow my instructions," she said. "And soon you'll be back where you want to be."

"Do they still sell those spicy cricket tacos on D-concourse?" Boris now sounded like a whiny child.

"Of course, dear. I bought up the shop years ago just to make sure it'd be around for the long haul—just like our family."

"I love those tacos."

"Maybe when you get to the station, I'll set you up with a nice girl. I think it's time for you to settle down and start a family."

"Yes, Grandma."

"Now, promise me you'll do your part." Her voice took on a harder edge.

"I promise."

The squeak of his metal chair moving signalled the end of Boris's visit with his grandmother.

Hwicce turned away as Boris exited the teahouse. He kept his eyes focused on the ground just in front of his feet, oblivious to his surroundings.

A moment later, Boris' grandma emerged out into the common space. Standing up tall, her head would barely reach Hwicce's chest. Her silver hair was pulled back from her wizened face.

He would have discounted the woman, except her eyes were bright, taking everything in. She stared him up and down before turning in the opposite direction. As tempted as Hwicce was to follow her, he knew he had to get back to the ship.

Chapter Twenty-Six

Back on the *Shimmer,* Hwicce found Baker lounging near the crates in the cargo hold. She flashed him a wide grin as he approached.

"How'd your recon go?" She raised an eyebrow as she met his gaze. "Do anything stupid?"

"Sorry to disappoint you," he said.

A few paces away, Emiko sat on a crate studying her data-pad. On the surface, she appeared to be ignoring them, but every now and then, she glanced Baker's way. In the few days they'd been on the *Shimmer*, Emiko Green had done wonders for Baker's mood.

Hwicce pressed his lips together to keep from smiling at the pair. If they wanted to pretend to be disinterested in each other, he wasn't going to get in their way.

"What's next? Sir."

"Just hang tight for now." As he leaned against the crate next to Baker, he began dissecting the conversation he'd overheard.

"Tight's my middle name." After a few moments of silence, Baker leaned forward. "Hey, slime girl, we waiting for passengers or what?"

Emiko glared at Baker, who grinned in return.

"Careful, or I'll find more slime for the two of you to scrub away."

Baker slapped her leg and laughed as though Emiko had told a joke. With a snort, Emiko returned her attention to her computer, but now her expression was softer.

Heavy footfalls ringing out on the metal deck announced Boris' approach. He strode onto the cargo bay deck and towards the pile of crates.

"Good, you're all here." Boris' earlier childish tone was now gone. "There's been a change of plans."

Baker stood up tall and stared the captain in the eye. She was much taller than Boris and did intimidating well—many had crumbled under her gaze.

But Boris refused to look her way. Instead, he made a sweeping gesture that encompassed the three of them. "Take the rest of the day off. Go enjoy what this outpost has to offer."

"Don't we have a schedule to maintain?" Emiko cocked her head slightly as she put her datapad away. "I thought we had a tight deadline to deliver all of this?" She waved at the unmarked crates. "Where did you say we're taking this stuff?"

"I'm waiting on the client to let me know," Boris said without making eye contact with her either.

The three of them continued staring at their captain.

"I gave you all an advance on your pay. The credits should be in your accounts." Boris pulled himself up tall. "Get off my ship and blow off some steam."

Emiko narrowed her eyes as she stared at Boris. "You sure?"

"Yes. Now get the hell out of here." Boris turned and strode off towards his cabin.

Frowning, Emiko led the way back to the outpost. Without a word, Hwicce and Baker followed.

Once they reached the open area, Emiko turned to the others. "Well, that was fishy. I've been working for Boris for the last year, and I've had to fight to have him pay me what I'm owed. He has never offered to advance me anything."

A group of shrieking kids ran by, nearly bowling them over.

"Let's grab a bite." Baker stared at Emiko with an expression Hwicce didn't recognize—it was almost a shy smile, as though his normally tough companion had suddenly been overtaken with self-doubt.

"There's a tea house back here." Hwicce pointed to the teahouse where he'd eavesdropped on Boris and his grandmother.

Emiko nodded. "That'll do."

Inside the teahouse, the rattling of ongoing generations dice games competed with the sound of playing kids outside. Dingy white walls and well-worn metal furniture greeted them. About half the tables were filled with patrons sipping from steaming mugs—the dice games were happening somewhere out of sight, suggesting gambling was going on.

Emiko selected the same table Boris and his grandma had used near the window. Hwicce sank into the metal chair and gazed out into the common space beyond. It actually wasn't that bad in Hamber's Hole. As a gang of shrieking kids ran by, he could almost picture Molly in there with them. Maybe when the three of them were back together, they should find some out-of-the-way corner to live a simple life...

"Sir?"

Baker brought him back to the present. Hwicce sighed. He needed to put his family back together before planning their future.

After ordering a pot of green tea and a pile of dumplings, he leaned back in his chair and stared at the two women. Sitting side-by-side, they made an odd couple. Even though Baker's dark hair was starting to grow in as fuzz that covered her normally clean-shaven scalp, it did nothing to soften the tough angles of her face. In contrast, Emiko's delicate features would have fit on an antique high-end china doll.

He stared at Emiko. "What kind of stuff does the *Shimmer* normally transport?"

She glanced briefly at Baker before leaning back in her chair. "Low end goods mostly. Unprocessed ore, bales of food, raw printer fodder." She shrugged. "Nothing out of the ordinary."

"How do the crates we just loaded fit in?"

"I have no idea what's inside," she said. "I had assumed you two were going to take a peek."

Hwicce ran a hand over his face as he wondered how much he could trust Emiko.

"You've got solid mechanical skills. Why work for Boris at all?" Baker asked. "He doesn't appreciate you in the least."

"He needs me," Emiko said. "And he doesn't hit on me. He just leaves me alone to do my work." She glanced down at her hands. "It wasn't like that on the other ships I worked on."

"Where are you from?" Hwicce asked.

Emiko shrugged as a battered serving robot clanked a tray onto their table. Tea sloshed out of the printed mugs, but the dumplings remained piled in their pyramid. The robot released the tray and wobbled as it turned.

Emiko stared at the robot as it rolled away. "I could fix that."

"And build a rescued robot army?" Baker grinned.

"Hell yeah."

As the two women continued to natter on about robots, Hwicce picked up a dumpling with his bare fingers and popped it in his mouth. He resumed staring out the window as he chewed. The homemade savoury tastes made for a refreshing change to the packaged fare he'd been subsisting on. He sipped his tea and took another dumpling, allowing his thoughts to wander back to his family.

As he finished his third dumpling, a shift change occurred,

and more adults began moving through the space. In the crowd, he spotted the woman Boris had been speaking to—his grandmother.

Across from him, Emiko choked on her tea. "I know her," she said, clearly looking where Hwicce was.

"Who is she?" Emiko set her mug down. "Mrs. Long, the head of Long Enterprises. Why in the hell would she be here?"

Baker shoved another dumpling in her mouth before following their gaze. "Don't recognize her. But she's got the same last name as Boris."

Hwicce decided he needed to trust Emiko. "I eavesdropped on Boris and Mrs. Long earlier. Boris called her Grandma."

"What were they talking about?"

"They had a cryptic conversation about a job after which Boris is going to retire on Indigo Station."

"Huh." Emiko leaned back and crossed her arms over her chest.

"She's got security." Baker talked with her mouth full dumpling.

Hwicce studied the crowd. At least two guards trailed Mrs. Long, keeping a few paces between them.

He frowned, then paid the teahouse bill. He needed to have a conversation with Mrs. Long—she just might know where the lab Molly had been taken to was. "I'm going to follow her."

Outside, Mrs. Long continued to converse with a woman dressed as a miner but cleaner, suggesting she was part of the mine's administration.

"Don't be fooled by how she looks. Mrs. Long is the head of organized crime on Indigo Station," Emiko warned.

Baker tossed another dumpling in her mouth, then stood. "I'm coming with you, sir."

"Um...." Emiko stood. "I'll come too."

Chapter Twenty-Seven

"Supplies, I need supplies," Orin muttered as he went through the *Buttercup's* kitchen cupboards. Rosie had loaded on a few days worth of fresh food before he left the Rock, and there was the obligatory six months worth of hard rations that would taste like chalk. In the supply closet off the airlock, he found four cans of peaches and a dozen cans of extra-hot spicy crickets that would leave him with heartburn.

Letting out a long exhale, he leaned against the wall. He could end up following the *Garden Princess* for a week or more. Beyond that, he had no idea where he might need to go. *Buttercup* had enough fuel to keep him in motion for three years with air to match. Would he need to keep going that long? He had no idea where his voyage would take him.

Orin headed up to the bridge and sat down. The *Garden Princess* had already slipped its berth, but the liner was slow—he had plenty of time to catch up.

"*Buttercup*, where is the nearest shop with food supplies?"

"Interfacing with Jupiter Station directory," the genderless voice replied.

Orin got up and paced back and forth between the bridge

and common room until the ship gave its 'job complete' ping. He slid back down into his seat.

"Long Haul Supplies will have what you need, and it is currently open," the ship said. A map flashed up on the nearest screen with the route to the shop highlighted in green. It was just at the mouth of the docking bay he was using.

Orin pulled out a wagon-like cart from the supply cupboard and left the ship. Long Haul Supplies was, in fact, open when he arrived. But most of the shelves were bare.

"What happened?" Orin asked the mountain of a shopkeeper.

The man snorted and ran a hand over his bushy beard. "Looting."

"Looting?" Orin added a flat of canned peaches to his cart, then a 25kg bag of split peas.

"Yeah, them rioters broke in last night. Cleaned me out of a lot of stuff."

"That's unfortunate." Orin added a flat of canned baked beans and another of Click-shaped pasta in tomato sauce. "Do you have any rice left?"

"Nope. Those assholes took all I had, along with all my snack food, candy, and coffee."

"You have no coffee?"

"None."

Orin stopped and scratched his head. He'd run out of coffee within a day—a thought that almost made him reconsider setting out. Since he'd given up alcohol, coffee had become his crutch. It was going to be a long trip without coffee; he'd have to make a pit stop somewhere along the way.

The shopkeeper held up a green package. "But we have plenty of fucking tea." Orin took the package and turned it over in his hand. It was mint, dried and harvested from the floating islands of New Venus. "I guess it'll have to do." He sighed and added it to his pile of supplies. After pausing for a moment, he added three more boxes of the herbal brew—fucking tea was slightly better than nothing.

Resigned to taking what was available, he went up and down the aisles and added a few more flats of canned food. He paid and headed back to *Buttercup*. Inside, he left the wagon in the middle of the kitchen. Then he went forward, powered up the ship, and requested permission to depart.

A few moments later, his departure authorization came in, and he lifted off. Once he cleared the docking bay, the green hull of the *Garden Princess* shimmered like a gem in the distance as it lumbered towards the gate.

It would be no problem to accelerate and be at the bigger ship's side as they passed through the gate—maybe even ahead of it. Orin programmed the ship's AI to take over piloting, wishing for the first time that it was a sentient model. At least then he'd have someone to talk to.

"You've made some interesting food choices here. I see we're not going to be doing any gourmet dining."

"What the..." Orin stood and spun around. Gloria stood at the table, going through the groceries he'd purchased. A breath caught in his throat as he stared at her. He rapidly blinked as though she might just disappear—but she didn't.

"Looks like there's enough for both of us on our trip to Indigo Station." She pushed a lock of her golden hair behind an ear before smiling at him.

Orin's heart sunk. Being alone was a better option to being with Gloria.

"What the hell?" With narrowed eyes, he paced into the galley. "Why are you on my ship?"

"I noticed your flight plan listed Indigo Station as your destination. I thought I'd go visit my aunt there."

"I already told you I didn't want you on board." Orin could feel his face flushing. His flight plan hadn't been public; how in the hell did she know where he was going? He narrowed his eyes but didn't inquire.

Gloria shrugged as she started putting the groceries into the cupboards. "And yet, here I am."

He glanced back over his should and at the view outside. Did he have enough time to turn back and drop Gloria off? He'd given up his berth and would have to put his name in the queue to dock again, and he had no idea how long that would take.

He ran a hand over his scalp as he stared at his unwanted passenger. A headache threatened to emerge. The tiny interior of *Buttercup* couldn't contain Gloria's oversized personality. He let out a long exhale.

"You shouldn't have just stowed away!"

Ignoring his comment, Gloria continued putting groceries away. "Peaches, peas, mealworms, protein powder...extra-hot spicy crickets? It's going to be near impossible to make a proper meal out of these ingredients."

"I was in a rush, and the options weren't great." Orin frowned as he realized he was justifying himself to Gloria—she was the stowaway, not him. This was his ship!

"You know what?" She turned to him and smiled again. "I don't think we've ever taken the time to get to know each other."

Orin nearly groaned. Gloria was way more chatty than he could tolerate. No coffee and now Gloria's full attention...it was going to be a long trip.

"You're getting off at our first stop." He didn't wait for her answer before returning to the cockpit and sliding the door shut behind himself.

Chapter Twenty-Eight

After spending enough time in the large bathtub that her fingers ended up looking like prunes, Veena programmed her nanite garment to be a dress. Once she had it on, she felt like a different person. Her cheap, printed clothing sat in a pile on the floor beside the clunky combat boots she'd been wearing.

The closest thing she had to glamorous footwear were the black satin slippers Hwicce had given her. If no one looked too closely, they would pass. She sighed as she stared at her slippers. Hwicce didn't know where she was—and she had no idea of his location.

Veena almost opened her datapad to see if he'd messaged her, but she sighed again. What if Swa's assessment that he'd run off with another woman was true? A heat welled up in her, and she felt her cheeks flush. She refused to believe it was true.

"I'll send him a message after I have a full night's sleep," she said to herself. Maybe by then, he would have sent her a message explaining himself.

She glanced up at the ceiling as though direction mattered. "Well, Nigel, I think I'm ready to go."

The holographic steward materialized next to her and smiled. "Right-o, madam. Please follow me."

Out in the corridor, the lights had already begun dimming to nighttime levels. Under lower illumination, the gilded decorations glinted, adding to their opulence.

Veena pulled herself up as straight as she could as she fell into step beside Nigel. She started counting the light fixtures as they went.

"Are you finding your accommodations comfortable?"

"Huh?" Veena stopped at thirty-two, her concentration broken.

"Is your cabin satisfactory?" The hologram's expression mimicked genuine concern.

"My cabin?" She paused, thinking of the elegant space. Cabin was selling it short. "Yes, it's more than adequate."

"Excellent." Nigel put out a hand to guide her along. "Dinner awaits."

Nigel evaporated once he escorted her to the human maitre d', who glanced up from a screen as Veena approached. His eyes were the colour of pickles, as sour as his expression. As he glanced down at her shoes, a frown spread across his face.

Adjusting his jacket, he met her gaze. "Are you meeting someone?"

"No."

Pursing his lips together, he glanced down at his screen again. "Dr. Oswiu, your steward booked you a table with a forward view."

"Sounds good." Veena started wondering if she should just ask for room service instead. She didn't want to eat in such a fancy restaurant by herself. If only Hwicce... She cut her thought off, endlessly mulling over what he was up to wouldn't help her.

"This way." The maitre d' started walking down a plushly carpeted corridor. Veena followed.

Around a corner, the corridor opened up into a massive wedge-shaped space surrounded by windows on three sides. Tables full of patrons sat on multiple levels, their hushed conversations adding a conspiratorial air.

As she glanced up at the ceiling, her jaw dropped. Tentacle-like clear tubes wound around each other like a writhing kraken descended from above. Bioluminescent algae filled the tubes, emitting a soft green glow. The complex shapes mesmerized her. Each time she tried to count the tentacles, she lost track and had to start again.

"Madam?" The maitre d' had stopped and was staring at her.

"Sorry." Veena felt her face flush. She stayed on the maitre d's heels as he led her up winding steps until he reached a table against the forward windows. Beyond, stars twinkled back. In the centre of the view, the aqua surface of the gate shimmered. Her focus fixed on the gate.

Two years ago, before the war, she'd stood beside Molly as they went through the very same gate. The ship wasn't fancy like this one, just an ordinary ferry. Molly had been so excited, bouncing at the thought of going through a gate.

Swallowing, she looked away. This time, Molly was making this trip alone—and without the luxuries that now surrounded Veena. She focused on the plush carpets and fancy chandelier; this space was beyond any she'd been in before. Why did Theo65 splurge on such a ticket? What did they want to give her? There were too many things she needed to think through.

"This is your table," the maître d' said. She sat and took the old-fashioned menu he offered. "Your server will be with you shortly." He turned and left.

Veena sighed and studied the menu—21 options, a Fibonacci number. But the font was wrong, too rounded and not trustworthy. She scratched her head and told herself she needed to pick something. Rokan mushroom risotto, perhaps? The menu claimed the mushroom's bioluminescence would provide a lasting sensation of calm...

"What we need..." a man's voice startled her. She glanced up from the menu, but no one was at her table.

"No, James. There's no way the Protectorate will grant us more resources until we've shown them results," a woman said.

Veena swivelled her head around, hunting for the source of the voices.

"We'll have results soon." The man let out an audible exhale. "Being forced to work at that...facility—"

The woman cut him off. "The X-ray System is off-grid. It's probably the best place to do your research. Far away from the prying eyes of our superiors."

"My work should be celebrated," he said. "Not hidden away on some backwater moon."

Veena finally pinpointed the source of the conversation she was eavesdropping on. The hard surfaces of the windows focused the words said at a table a level lower than her on the other side of the restaurant. Trying to be subtle, she studied the man and woman.

The woman's back was to Veena. Beyond having impossibly glossy black hair, Veena couldn't tell much about her. Across the table, the man faced her. The familiarity to his face made her shift in her seat. Veena had seen him before—but where?

"Your work violates the GenEn protocols," the woman said before sipping her minty-green cocktail. "No one wants to celebrate that."

"Those are outdated laws."

"Yet, the Protectorate just went to war to defend them."

The man huffed. "I work for a backwards government who'll never fully appreciate my work."

"Madam."

Veena looked up to find a server standing over her.

"Are you ready to order?"

Lifting the menu to obscure her face, Veena glanced at the

man again. His brown hair was ordinary, and his tailored dinner jacket showed off his fit physique. Veena couldn't place where she'd seen him before, yet her heart now thumped in her chest. She licked her lips and looked up at the server.

"Can I have dinner delivered to my cabin?"

"Of course."

Veena ordered the risotto and left the restaurant, taking care not to be in full view of the man she recognized for fear he would recognize her too.

Back in her cabin, she slumped down onto the closest sofa. Her hands trembled. Seeing that man had unnerved her. If only she could figure out where she'd seen him before.

"I need to do something."

"May I suggest an evening at the theatre?" Nigel appeared in front of her. He smiled. "The ship's production of *Much Ado About Nothing* will begin in a half-hour."

Veena blinked as she stared at the intrusive hologram. She started counting the petals on the rose he wore pinned to his jacket. Stopping herself, she took a deep breath.

"I'm sure the play is fantastic, but I was thinking more solo." She pulled Molly's backpack onto her lap and pulled out her scroll. "A puzzle is what I need."

"Right-o," Nigel said with a smile. "May I be of assistance?"

Veena brought up the alien code and studied the text. 101 distinct symbols arranged over thousands of lines. She took a deep breath. "Do you have access to any advanced processing?"

Nigel shook his head as he sat on the couch across from her. "My apologies, my base algorithm is incapable of that. I can query the bridge to see if they can arrange access for you."

"No need to bother them." Veena scratched her head and started one of her own routines to go through the symbols.

"Does your archive include anything about the alien civilization that pre-dated human arrival?"

Nigel pulled himself up tall, then glitched. A moment later, he re-coalesced. "Yes. What do you want to know?"

"Is there any record of symbols they might have left behind?"

He shook his head. "Negative. The gates and a few ruins on the anchor worlds are all that remains. Alien writing is only a rumour."

Veena nodded. Alien writings were a fringe idea, never sanctioned by the official archives. When she'd worked on the codes before, Theo65 claimed the Protectorate was suppressing the knowledge. But now, the Protectorate wanted them de-coded. What changed?

She scrolled through the text again. Some of the symbols seemed similar. She isolated them and copied them to a separate file. Filtering out four of the symbols, she lined them up. They were identical. Their orientation was the only difference.

A slow smile spread across her face as she ran her finger along the symbol set. She'd made progress. Did orientation change meaning? Going back to the original text, she started another algorithm, not hearing the chime that announced her dinner's arrival.

Chapter Twenty-Nine

Hwicce kept his eyes fixed on the back of Mrs. Long's head as they moved through the shift-change crowd. The administrator stayed at Mrs. Fong's side, the two of them deep in conversation. The expression on the administrator's face suggested she wasn't happy about what was being said.

Baker brushed up beside him. "I count three."

Before he could reply, she fell back a few paces to walk beside Emiko. He picked out Mrs. Long's security detail easily—two men and a woman. The trio stayed in a loose triangle around their boss and her contact, keeping most of the crowd away.

Dodging the playing children, Hwicce followed Mrs. Long's group as they descended to the bottom level, a wide corridor with arched walls created when a giant drill bit ripped a hole through the rock led away from the habitat cavern. At least three times his height, the very top hosted a single strip of illumination so bright, he couldn't stare directly at it.

Down the corridor, a cloud of dust rose behind every person on the move. He could taste the fine particulate in the dry air—it reminded him of the air in the armour workshop after they'd been grinding out battle damage. He licked his lips as he wondered if he was breathing in something dangerous; he had no idea what they mined here.

Baker and Emiko pulled up beside him.

"This seems very fishy," Emiko said as she kept her eyes on Mrs. Long up ahead. "Are you sure we should follow her?"

"Yes. At the very least, I'd like to talk to her. Besides, I'm curious about the facility here," Hwicce said, hoping the old woman would give him some answers—assuming he could bypass her security somehow. "We stay well back; hopefully, we won't be seen."

"That's not much of a plan. Sir."

He looked Baker in the eye. "We don't know what we could be walking into. We follow at a distance."

"Yes, sir."

Once in the corridor, the crowd thinned, but enough people remained on the move that the three of them didn't stand out. Hwicce made sure a few miners walked between him and Mrs. Long's rear guard. He wished he was close enough to hear their conversation as the administrator kept shaking her head.

A hundred metres on, the corridor ended at a bank of three elevators descending into the asteroid's interior. A metal fence separated the crowd from a shaft heading down.

Hwicce raised his hand to stop Baker and Emiko as they entered the cavern behind a group of miners talking loudly about their upcoming shift. He turned his back to Mrs. Long as the three of them huddled together.

Baker casually glanced over his shoulder. "They're just waiting for an elevator car to arrive."

"We need to figure out where they go," he said in a whisper. "There are probably multiple levels below, and we won't be able to take the same car as them."

With her right hand, Baker slapped him on the shoulder. "Sir, we've got this." She grabbed Emiko's hand.

The pair continued forward into the crowd waiting for the elevator. Baker plowed her way towards where Mrs. Long stood still, deep in conversation. Just as one of Mrs. Long's guards moved to block her way, Baker turned, pulled Emiko into an embrace, and kissed her. The entire crowd turned to watch Baker's romantic gesture.

As Emiko wrapped her arms around Baker, the waiting crowd broke into grins. The guard shook his head and retreated, leaving Baker with an unobstructed view of the buttons.

The elevator car arrived, and Mrs. Long led her people inside. Behind them, the last guard prevented anyone else from cramming in. With a clang, the wire mesh doors slammed shut, and the elevator descended out of view.

Baker released Emiko. Keeping her eyes averted from the others, Baker stepped forward to see over the railing. Emiko's face flushed red, then she wiped her mouth with the back of her jacket sleeve. Uncertain if he was stepping into a hornet's nest, Hwicce joined them.

"I heard them mention level seven." Emiko didn't look at him as she spoke.

Hwicce nodded, then stopped a passing miner. "Excuse me, we're trying to catch up with some friends. What's on level seven?"

The haggard-faced miner stared at him for a moment before grimacing. "Why the hell would you want to go there?" Her voice was rough. "Ain't nothing on that level, just some abandoned corridors that produced nothin'."

"Okay, thanks," Hwicce said.

With a grunt, the miner walked into the open car of the next elevator. Behind her, the remaining miners crammed in. The doors closed, and the car descended out of sight. The three of them were now alone on the platform.

Baker pressed the elevator call button. After a few minutes wait, a car arrived, and the three of them stepped inside. Baker hit the button for level seven.

"You're all about pushing buttons today." Emiko's tone was

flat. She stood on the far side of the car from Baker and leaned against the metal mesh wall.

Hwicce realized he was now between the two women. He swallowed and said nothing.

"I can push buttons all day." Baker grinned, and Emiko snorted.

The door rattled as Baker slid it shut. With a lurch, the elevator descended. The motion was faster than Hwicce expected, forcing him to grab onto a handhold to keep his balance. The car stopped just as fast.

Baker took the lead as she opened the door to level seven. She darted out and ducked behind a nearby wall.

"Clear," she said, and her voice echoed off the surrounding rock.

Hwicce exited. Other than a few piles of rock and the overhead lights, the cavern was empty.

"Crap, we lost the car," Emiko said. The elevator car ascended as soon as she stepped off.

With a frown, Hwicce gazed up. He couldn't even see the top of the elevator shaft from his vantage point. Then he glanced down; he didn't see the bottom either.

"We can call it back when we need it," he said, hoping that would be true.

A single passageway led off from the platform, its dimensions identical to the corridor above, suggesting the same equipment bore it out. Staying close to the wall, he moved enough of his head around the corner to see down the corridor with one eye. It was empty except for a hint of dust in the air.

"Okay." He turned to face the other two. "I don't see anyone, but there's no cover."

"Shit, I should've brought a pistol." Baker ran a hand over her hip where she used to keep a holster.

"You turned your weapons in," Hwicce said.

Emiko shrugged. "I would've loaned you mine if I'd known you'd want it."

Baker turned back towards the elevator. "Maybe we can go back and get it."

"We don't want to risk losing Mrs. Long," Hwicce said. "Besides, if we get caught, we can just say we got lost—an excuse that won't work if we're armed to the gills."

"I still fucking hate it." Baker crossed her arms over her chest, but she made no move to leave.

"Okay, we move quickly and quietly to the first junction." He looked both women in the eye. "Once there, we reassess."

Without waiting for their response, he started at a brisk pace down the corridor. The women followed.

Two hundred metres on, the corridor made a right-angle turn. After gesturing for everyone to stop, Hwicce crouched down to peek around the corner. Roughly ten metres on, the corridor opened up into a cavern as big as the *Shimmer's* cargo hold.

A massive metal wall ran down the middle, bisecting the space. A door in the wall stood open. Bright lights cascaded through the door, making it impossible to see what was on the other side. He thought he saw multiple shiny surfaces, but he couldn't make out more details than that. Mrs. Long and her entourage stood talking between them and the wall.

"You can't keep this facility here," the mine administrator said, shaking her head.

"Hmmm." Mrs. Long pursed her lips together. "Indium ore isn't worth what it used to be."

The administrator bit her lip and glanced at the security guard. "Once your lab is fully staffed, the miners are going to notice. People will start asking questions."

"My funds are meant to smooth away those questions."

"It's too risky." The administrator rubbed her hands down her pants. "Besides, there are laws against human experimentation. Hell, for all I know, you plan on violating the GenEn laws."

"So you've suddenly developed morals—after accepting my

money." Mrs. Long used the same tone one would use on a misbehaving child.

"We need—" The miner was cut off.

"Then I'll find someone else to run this place." Mrs. Long gestured to one of her guards. He raised his blaster and pointed it at the administrator.

Hwicce couldn't believe what he was seeing, and he couldn't let it happen. He picked up a rock and threw it at the wall. It hit the metal with a loud clunk before tumbling down to the ground. Everyone twisted to look, turning their backs on Hwicce's group.

A blur of speed, Baker charged, tackling the nearest guard. At the same time, Emiko bolted forward and threw another rock —this one contacting the forehead of the guard with his blaster out. The blaster fell out of his hand and bounced once on the rock ground. So much for taking their time to reassess.

Now alone in his hiding spot, Hwicce took a moment to study his adversaries. Two guards focused on Baker—and he had confidence she could handle herself. The one Emiko hit with her rock was now on his feet and reaching for his weapon. Before he could pick it up again, Hwicce darted forward and kicked him in the gut. With an 'oof,' the guard doubled over.

Hwicce punched him in the face, hitting his nose and releasing a torrent of blood. Putting both hands on the guard's shoulders, Hwicce shoved him backwards. The guard landed on his back on the stone floor, his head smacked off the rock, and he went limp.

"What the hell?" the administrator said as Mrs. Long turned and ran the other way towards the metal wall.

"Stop her!" Hwicce sprinted forward past the administrator.

Despite her apparent advanced age, Mrs. Long moved fast. She made it through the open door and closed it behind herself before Hwicce could reach her.

"Crap!" Hwicce pounded on the door, the dull thuds of his

fists reverberating through the cavern. Then he turned and surveyed what was left of the others.

Baker had dropped the two other guards, and she hadn't broken a sweat. Emiko stood next to the confused-looking administrator.

"Who the hell?" the administrator repeated, staring at the fallen guards with wide eyes.

"What kind of experiments were they planning on conducting here?" Hwicce used his most authoritative tone.

"She..." The administrator gestured towards the now closed door that separated them from Mrs. Long. "She was never specific. My people pieced it together based on the equipment delivered."

"So, human experimentation of some kind." Emiko stood next to Hwicce, barely coming up to his shoulder.

The administrator shrugged. "We have extra space and a cash flow problem. Mrs. Long offered us a solution."

"We need more than that." Hwicce took a pace closer to the administrator.

She scratched her head. "They wanted me to clear the dock and common areas above to bring in their first subject. Someone from Rock 13-5A. I don't know more than that."

Hwicce kept his face neutral while he stared at the miner. Rock 13-5A was where Veena and Molly had been. Was this where Molly was being taken—to be a lab rat for criminals? For what purpose? It seemed a bit of a stretch, but then, the army he used to believe in had kidnapped his child.

"Look, I don't know anymore," the administrator said. "I'm calling the authorities. Long Enterprises won't be conducting those experiments here."

"Is there another exit?" Baker pointed to the closed door.

The administrator sighed and nodded. "The cavern extends to the surface where they keep a shuttle waiting. I suspect Mrs. Long is already gone."

"We'll be on our way then," Hwicce said, and Baker gave a curt nod in agreement.

The three of them strode out of the cavern and back to the elevators. All the while, Hwicce worried about where Molly had been taken and for what purpose. The only thing he now knew for sure was that his girl wasn't being brought to Hamber's Hole anymore—if that had ever been her destination.

It wasn't until they were in the elevator car heading up that Baker turned to him. "I don't think we learned a single thing of use."

"Just that Long Enterprises is up to something—but I could have told you that without a fistfight," Emiko said.

Hwicce closed his eyes. He felt like he was staring at half a puzzle without any clue what it was supposed to be.

"We know Mrs. Long is driving Boris to complete some sort of task he's not keen on doing and that there were supposed to be experiments done on humans in a private lab on this station, but not anymore," Hwicce said.

"That's about it, sir." Baker turned as the elevator reached the top floor and the door opened. "But the fighting was fun. I've worked some kinks out."

"I didn't know you had kinks that needed working out." Emiko brushed a lock of hair behind her ear.

Hwicce suppressed a groan and walked ahead.

Boris was pacing the cargo hold as the three of them walked through the cargo bay doors of the *Shimmer*. He seemed to be muttering to himself, but as soon as he spotted them, he stopped.

"Emiko, rev this ship up. I want to be out of here in ten minutes."

"Aye, aye, Captain," she said without even a hint of sarcasm. She headed towards the engine room.

"Boris," Hwicce said, just as the captain half turned to leave. "Where's our next port?"

Boris stared blankly at him for a moment, then licked his lips. "We're on our way to Jupiter Station." He spun around and strode off towards the bridge.

"We'll get off this rust bucket there," Hwicce said once Boris was gone. "You should invite Emiko to join us."

"Uh, sir." Baker made a sweeping gesture around the empty cargo hold. "Notice anything different about the place?"

Hwicce slowly rotated, staring at the cargo hold—the crates were gone.

"Well, that's weird."

Chapter Thirty

A reverberating thunk dragged Orin out of his slumber. His thoughts stalled as he listened to the unfamiliar sounds around him. For a moment, he had no idea where he was. Then he smelled smoke.

His heart and mind raced as his adrenalin started to spike. He rolled out of his bottom bunk and landed on the metal decking on all fours. Dazed, he coughed. His bare hands and knees throbbed from the short fall.

Gloria jumped down from the top bunk. "Something's on fire!" She charged out of the tiny sleeping cabin.

Orin pushed himself up and followed her. In the main compartment, a haze of smoke blurred the lines of the common room. His eyes burned as tastes of burning metal and charred electronics flooded his mouth.

"Why didn't the alarms go off?" Ignoring the tears streaming down his face, he grabbed the fire extinguisher from its mount on the kitchen wall and pulled its pin. "The alarms should have gone off."

"This bloody rust-bucket is antique." Gloria enunciated every word. "Hell, it should be in a museum!"

Orin swung around, trying to pinpoint the smoke's origin.

All the lights were on full, suggesting the power system hadn't automatically shut down like it should.

Smoke billowed out of an air vent just aft of the kitchen. It moved like a living thing, undulating as it spread out across the ceiling. Its acrid scent suggested circuit boards and rubber smouldered somewhere out of sight.

Grabbing a towel from the kitchen, he wrapped his hand before shutting the vent. Smoke still creeped out between the metal slats, but it was less. He racked his brain, trying to remember where that vent originated.

The ship alarms sounded. The high-pitched sound drilled into his head, amping his stress levels even more.

"Automatic fire suppression system has failed," the ship's computer announced between alarms.

"Shit!" Orin gripped his fire extinguisher tighter. His only option was to fight the fire.

At his side, Gloria doubled over, coughing. She tugged on his pyjama sleeve as she pointed at a door. "Bathroom."

Blinking rapidly, Orin advanced towards the closed door. He held the fire extinguisher nozzle in one hand and the trigger in the other. The smoke thickened with each passing second, dulling the yellow hues of the walls.

"Orin!"

He turned. Behind him, Gloria pulled an emergency air mask over her head. She held a second one out towards him.

For a millisecond, Orin froze. Air...he needed fresh air. Letting the nozzle drop, he reached out a hand. His world began to spin, and blackness started forming at the edges of his vision.

"Shit," he muttered through parched lips. He had waited too long.

Everything went black.

A body-racking series of coughs brought Orin back to consciousness. He smacked his lips, surprised at how parched he felt. His eyes burned as he opened them to a hazy view of yellow. Blinking rapidly, he tried to clear his vision. Over what may have been seconds or hours, he finally realized he lay on his back looking up at the yellow paint on the cciling.

"It's the colour of buttercups." His voice sounded rough. For a moment, he was back in his and Mary's kitchen on New Haven. Then reality crashed in. "The fire!" He sat up and started frantically looking around.

"Welcome back." Gloria sat on the deck plating beside him, soot coating her from head to toe. "By the way, the fire's out."

"How'd you put the fire out?"

"I got rid of the air." She grinned. "I'm not just a pretty face."

A shaky laugh spilled out of him. They'd survived a fire followed by a fire system failure. More laughter came, then Gloria joined in.

He looked around. The two of them were in a tiny metal box—the airlock. She'd had the presence of mind to get the two of them into the airlock and vent *Buttercup's* atmosphere. Her actions saved his life. Maybe having her with him was a good idea after all.

He met her gaze. "You saved me. Thank you."

"I sure did." She pushed herself onto her feet and went to the console next to the inside door. "Aren't you glad I'm here now?"

Orin stood and leaned against the wall. He still felt woozy from lack of oxygen. Was he happy that she was there? He took a deep breath.

"It's been a long time since I took a spaceship out," he said. "A long time."

"I gathered, considering you forgot to sort out breathing before charging into a fire." She consulted the panel again. "Air inside is good to go." She opened the door and waved him through.

Orin hesitated for a moment, then said, "I'm glad you stowed away."

"I knew you'd come around." Gloria grinned. "You better have plenty of water, so I can take a hot shower."

"Tell you what: you can go first and use it all up."

Orin stepped back into the main part of his ship. Even though all the air had been cycled, he still caught a whiff of burnt conduit—it would probably take days until the air smelled truly fresh again.

"Your ship sure as hell isn't so pretty anymore," Gloria said as she stared up at the once yellow ceiling that was now covered in soot.

"*Buttercup* will scrub up." Orin smiled. "But that's a task for later."

"At least we shut the door to the cabin. I'm going to change." Gloria vanished into the small sleeping cabin and closed the door behind herself.

Orin stared at the door. He didn't recall any ship-based training on Gloria's file. Before he seconded her to the Rock, Gloria had been a research associate at New Haven University —a post she'd had since finishing her graduate studies. She had never lived off-world, never served on any ship. He frowned. His stowaway was demonstrating unexpected skills.

"I'm alive because of her," he said to himself. Other than being annoying, Gloria could prove to be a valuable crew member—maybe he'd missed something in her file.

With a sigh, he continued forward to the cockpit and opened the door. No soot covered the controls. He slid into the pilot's seat and ran a full diagnostic on the system.

Gloria had helped Veena get off the Rock; maybe he could trust her with his real mission. He leaned back into his chair and stared at the gate shimmering far in the distance. Gloria might make a powerful ally.

A thought hit him, and he froze for a moment working through the ramifications. What if Gloria had been sent by Swa to keep an eye on him? But why would Swa go to such lengths? He scratched his bald head.

"Maybe Swa knows I'm heading to help Veena." He glanced back into the main cabin, half expecting to find Gloria watching him. Either way, he was stuck with Gloria for the time being.

The ship pinged, indicating its analysis was done. He leaned forward to read the report. A power line behind the bathroom wall had shorted, lighting the nearby insulation on fire. As for why the fire suppression system failed, he had no idea. He sent the diagnostic file back to Rosie before heading to the bathroom to start on repairs.

Chapter Thirty-One

A musical chime brought Veena out of her slumber. She lingered with her eyes closed, savouring the smooth sheets and soft bed.

"We will pass through the first gate to the Beta System at 10 am ship time," Nigel said from her bedside.

She opened her eyes and blinked a few times. The low lights in her stateroom meant it had to be early. With a sigh, she rolled over and stared at the hologram.

"What time is it now?" She stretched her arms out and yawned.

"It is 6 am."

Veena snorted. "Is there a reason why I needed to be woken at 6 am?" As she sat up in bed, the lights in her cabin cycled to a brighter setting.

"No. I just thought..." Nigel made a very human gesture of pursing his lips. "You seem like the type of person who would seize the day. Since you became so engrossed in work last night, I assumed you would want to continue first thing."

Another chime sounded.

"Ah, I took the liberty of ordering your breakfast. And here it is."

The cabin's door slid open and a server-bot rolled through, bringing the scents of toast and coffee with it. Veena's stomach grumbled as the robot slid a tray onto the table before retreating out the door.

She pushed back her covers and went over to the tray. A shiny carafe stood beside a blatantly handmade mug. Next to it were two slices of toast—no doubt hand-cultured sourdough or something equally labour intensive. Even the plate holding the toast appeared to be handmade stoneware. She poured herself some coffee and returned to bed, holding the mug and plate of toast.

Nigel remained next to her bed, staring at the bedspread as though contemplating the indigo design. All the while, he rubbed his hands together. His holographic form failed to fully mimic the human movement; instead, his fingers regularly passed through each other—a motion disturbing to watch. Certainly he hadn't been programmed that way.

"Hey, Nigel, can you tell me about your mandate?" she asked after taking a bite of toast and letting the crumbs land on the fancy linens. She opened her datapad.

His impossible hand motions stopped, and he focused on her. "I am here to assist guests assigned to cabin 378."

Veena took another bite of toast. "I suspect you might be a little glitchy."

There were no new messages for her, either from Theo65 or from Hwicce. Forcing herself not to dwell on her husband or what he may be doing, she brought up the potentially alien code and stared at it while sipping her brew.

"I..." Nigel started, then stopped. He cocked his head to the side and fiddled with his cravat. "They missed my code during the last steward upgrade. I can report myself right away."

"Please don't. I prefer you as you are," she said, setting her half-eaten piece of toast back on the plate. It was foolish on her part, but Nigel's glitches made him seem more honest somehow, more real.

"Right-o," he said with a smile.

She stared at the code for a while more. There had to be more to the pattern hidden in the symbols. She scratched her head and took a sip of coffee.

"Nigel, do you think the aliens that made the gates are still around?"

"I have overheard many conversations around that very topic," he said. "And whoever created the gate system had to be much more advanced than us—but no one has found official evidence to prove they are still here."

"Hmmm." She ran a finger across her screen. "There are the anchor worlds."

"Yes, every gate has one." Nigel projected an image of the local system above the foot of Veena's bed.

New Haven, Jupiter Station, and Rock 13-A5 were all clearly visible, along with Alpha System's shimmering gate. Beside the gate was the rocky orb that anchored it through technology no one understood.

Nigel pointed to the anchor. "An atmosphereless, iron-cored rock world—each one heavier than they should be for their size. Multiple expeditions to these worlds have found nothing to help us understand how the gates use them."

Mug in hand, Veena leaned back against the padded headboard. "That's not true. We have found artifacts—including text."

"Really?" Nigel came over and sat next to her. His incorporeal form made no impression on the bed. "What do the texts say?"

"No one has deciphered them." She took another sip of coffee while staring at the system map. "Can you bring up the gate map?"

The three-dimensional map morphed into the familiar figure eight that connected the gates. Most were in the Protectorate's territory, but the Nader Alliance held a few, and fewer still remained independent. The Golf System, containing

Candy Cane Lane, sat where the two loops crossed, making it a strategic location. As her eyes followed the loop, she examined the offshoots leading to Indigo Station, Rokan, and Vortex View.

She paused, remembering the off-loop link between Candy Cane Lane and the Beta System—a well-documented shortcut. Gloria implied there was another secret, off-loop link from the Delta System to where Molly was being taken. No doubt the gates held other secrets as well. There was so much about them that humans didn't understand.

"Do you think there're more arms off the main loop?" she asked, holding a faint hope her glitchy Nigel might know something.

"That information is not in the ship's database."

Her shoulders dropped. It had been a long shot. "Right."

She spied a shiny pink corner of a comic cover peeking out of Molly's backpack. After setting her coffee down on the bedside table, she got up and retrieved it along with Molly's Click stuffy.

On the cover, Bubble and Click both wore expressions of glee as they slid down a pink mountain on an alien world. Holding the Click stuffy, Veena ran a finger over Bubble's face. Then she counted the pink polka dots on Bubble's spacesuit.

After finishing both the comic and the rest of the coffee, Veena got out of bed. It was still early, but her mind wouldn't stop racing. She needed to move.

The man she'd seen at dinner the night before re-surfaced in her thoughts. He'd seemed so familiar, yet she couldn't place him. Was he a friend of Hwicce's? No, he'd seemed much too fancy for that. Was he someone she'd met at the university on New Haven?

She reformatted her nanite clothing into a shirt dress complete with spacious pockets before pulling in on. After putting on her slippers and stashing her rolled-up datapad in a pocket, she stepped out into the hall. She started walking, her footfalls silent on the plush carpet.

Three corridors and an emergency stairwell later, Nigel appeared beside her.

"Do you require assistance?"

Although she now stood on a different deck, the hallway appeared similar to hers. Golden numbers graced the centre of each stateroom door while gilded signs pointed the way to the centre courtyard. It seemed impossible to get lost on the *Garden Princess*.

"No. I'm sure I can find my way back to my cabin." Veena resumed walking.

"If you are looking for some exercise, may I suggest the ship's fitness centre?" Maintaining a realistic walking motion, Nigel kept pace with her. "A dance class starts in twenty minutes. I could reserve a space for you."

"No, thank you." The corridor branched. She stopped and glanced both ways. "I'm just looking around."

Nigel stopped beside her and began clasping his hands together in his glitchy way. "Do you require my continued assistance?"

"Not really, but I don't mind your company." She took the hall to the right.

"Oh." Nigel fell silent but stayed by her side.

She continued on, walking around three decks on her hunt for the man from dinner the night before. As she went, she added together the digits of each door number in her head before starting again with the next set. The corridor turned again, and fifty-one paces on, it opened into the main courtyard.

The daytime lighting glowed warm and inviting. A subtle wind-instrument melody augmented the sound of cascading water, creating a melancholy mood. Veena sighed.

Avoiding groups of wandering passengers, she stopped at the railing and took in the constructed view. Three more decks extended below her, their railings nearly obscured by all the vines. In the pool on the bottom, people frolicked in the water while others lounged in chairs on the deck.

Scanning all the faces in view, she continued her hunt for the man from the dining hall.

"I don't see him," she whispered.

Nigel leaned beside her, his elbow extending about a millimetre into the railing. "May I ask, whom are you looking for?"

She faced him. "I saw someone at dinner last night that I thought I recognized."

The elevator on the far wall opened, and out stepped the man in question. Veena's breathing quickened, and a fluttering sensation formed in her gut as she studied him.

His handcrafted suit fit him perfectly. Even amongst the elite of the ship, he stood out. As he passed a group of other passengers, he looked down his nose at them.

She turned back to the railing. "It's him; he just came out of the elevator. Who is he?"

"I'm not supposed to give out information on guests," Nigel said.

"You're glitchy, remember." She turned her head slightly to the side to see the man in her peripheral vision. He took no note of her. Instead, he turned the other way and started walking.

"Right-o, there's the glitch." Nigel leaned his back against the railing next to her. "That's Dr. James Greer. He came on board with a shocking amount of luggage."

"Like what?" Veena watched the man circle around to the glittery spiral staircase opposite the waterfall. He wasn't the sort to stop in at a mathematics department at a university.

"They looked like military crates and—"

Veena cut him off with a hand motion and let out a long, ragged exhale. "I remember where I saw him before." Her breath caught in her throat—he was there when they took Molly. Her heart pounded as she watched Dr. Greer take the stairs towards the pool level below.

If that bastard was here, where was Mol? She exhaled through her teeth, trying to maintain a dignified air.

"Shall I arrange an introduction?"

"Absolutely not." Veena turned and stared back at the elevator he'd emerged from. A bud of hope formed within her. What if Molly was here, on the *Garden Princess*? "Was there anyone else with him when he boarded?"

"No."

"How big were the crates?"

"There were a range of sizes, with the biggest being a 1.5 metre cube."

"So…big enough to fit a child inside?"

Nigel looked at her and cocked his head. "This is an adult-only cruise."

"I need to look at his crates. What cabin is he in?"

"Most of the crates went to our cargo hold on the bottom deck," Nigel said. "Including all the big ones."

"Can you show me to them?" Veena turned to the hologram, hoping his programming was compromised to the point he would help.

"It will be fastest if we take the service lift."

Chapter Thirty-Two

The elevator doors swished open into a different world. The opulence of the decks above was gone, replaced by a decor that could only be described as drab. The grey walls and deck reminded Veena of being on Rock 13-A5—without the same military-grade level of cleanliness.

"This way, Dr. Oswiu." Nigel gestured for her to follow as he took the corridor to the left. "Dr. Greer's belongings are stored in here."

A flickering ceiling light cast a sinister strobing effect. Veena paused and ran her hands down the smooth surface of her dress. A shiver passed through her. Then she pulled herself up tall, firmed her resolve, and strode after Nigel.

After one hundred and seventy-three paces, they turned a corner. The hallway expanded into a cavernous space where the air was dry with a slight scent of mould. Like a wave starting at the entrance, the overhead lights clicked on row by row. The clinical illumination exposed a variety of boxes and crates. Some were as gilded as the corridors above, while others were basic 3D printed storage units. The *Garden Princess'* passengers were not traveling light.

Nigel stopped mid-step and cocked his head to the side. For a moment, his image wavered, then winked out.

"Nigel?" Veena slowly turned around, looking for him.

He reappeared right beside her. "This way."

He set a course into the maze of luggage, and Veena followed. Grouped separately in the back corner were seven very ordinary crates with Greer stencilled on their sides. On each, an old-fashioned padlock secured them shut.

"Crap." Veena ran her hand over the first lock. It rattled as she touched it.

"I'm sorry, madam." Nigel hung his head. "My memory banks didn't record that the crates were locked."

"No worries," she said. "Forgetting happens to the best of us." Veena ran her hand down her dress, staring at the old-school locks on the crates—the kind only a physical key would open.

She glanced down at the fabric of her dress. It wasn't fabric at all; it was nanites. She pulled out her datapad and sat on a nearby suitcase decorated with glittering fleur-de-lis. Within a few moments, she'd hacked the dress' nanotechnology control system and directed a small piece to break off from the hem.

The sliver of nanites glistened in her hand, appearing more like a pool of coloured mercury than a scrap of fabric. After putting them on the suitcase beside her, she returned her attention to her code. Once she isolated the broken-off nanites, she told them to reorganize into a lock pick. Beside her, the green glistened as though wet before changing shape. She picked it up and turned it over in her hand.

"I hope this works," she said as she stood.

Nigel smiled. "I am optimistic."

At the nearest crate, she tried her lock pick—it didn't work. "Shit!" She continued on and tried it on the rest of the crates.

"I suspect in addition to a physical key, there's a ..." Nigel scratched his chin with jerky movements.

Bending down close, she studied the lock. Even though it

appeared old-fashioned, there was just enough space above the keyhole for a fingerprint scanner. She sighed.

"A biometric lock of some kind."

Nigel glitched from standing to crouching beside her. "Yes. That's it."

"Can you scan the crates?"

"Let me check." He went completely still for a moment. Then, in a blink, he was standing a few paces away. "All I can confirm is that there is nothing organic within the crates. I'm sorry. I cannot do more."

Veena bit her lip as she stood, keeping her eyes fixed on Dr. Greer's crates. Part of her was relieved none of them were in use as an inhumane prison for Molly—but that didn't mean she wasn't on the ship.

"Can you get me into Greer's cabin?"

Nigel's eyes widened. "If I'm caught, my existence would be compromised." He started wringing his hands together in his glitchy way. "The AI manager would delete my entire code."

Veena pursed her lips and nodded. His assessment was most likely correct. Even though she knew Nigel was just a piece of code, she felt bad for him. Her glitchy steward had grown on her.

"I'm prepared to download your program and take you with me," she said, hoping that would be possible.

He froze, and his pixels went transparent for a moment. As soon as he reformed, he stared at her. "I've never existed outside this ship. I cannot even fathom who I would be."

"I'll be challenging to find your place, but I'd be with you." Veena smiled. "I'm confident you'll figure out who you are and where you belong."

Nigel winked out, and Veena bit her lip. Did she push the AI too far? Just as she opened her mouth to call out for him, Nigel reformed. He seemed shinier and more solid.

"Right-o. Let's do it," he said with a curt nod.

After confirming that Dr. Greer was engaged elsewhere, Nigel led the way to the doctor's assigned cabin. As it was a ship's lock on the cabin's door, Nigel had no problem overriding it. The door slid open, and he slipped inside.

Veena paused at the threshold and forced herself to take a deep breath. Butterflies formed in her stomach at the prospect of breaking into Greer's cabin—even though it was her best option to find clues about Molly's abduction. She looked both ways down the hall. No one was in view. After swallowing, she stepped inside just enough to allow the door to slide closed behind her.

The space was a mirror of her cabin to the point she almost expected to see Molly's pink backpack on the sofa. Instead, Dr. Greer had scattered multiple datapads about the space. She counted five in total—each one identical. Veena picked up the first one to find it had a fingerprint lock.

"Oh, shit."

"May I suggest, madam..." Nigel adjusted his cravat as he looked at her. "That your nanotechnology reprogramming hack from earlier may work here." He pointed at a glass on the bed stand.

"Right." Veena reprogrammed the small piece of her dress to pick up Greer's fingerprint off the glass. It worked perfectly to unlock the datapad. Instead of taking time to look through what was on the computer, she transferred its contents to hers. After putting it back where she found it, she moved on to the next one and repeated the process, grateful for the custom holographic storage on her datapad.

Just as she finished downloading the last one, a loud thunk sounded from the bathroom. Veena's breath caught in her throat. What if Nigel had been wrong and Greer was here? Her heart started pounding as she turned to face the bathroom door.

"What was that?"

"I can confirm that Dr. Greer is still engaged in a dice tournament on the casino level." Nigel stood at her side.

Veena didn't feel the least bit reassured. She crept towards the bathroom. "Can you access a camera in there?"

"Madam!" Nigel sounded outraged. "The *Garden Princess* does not have cameras installed in the bathrooms."

"Good to know." Veena slid the door to the bathroom open just wide enough to see inside. A small crate sat in the middle of the floor. It matched the crates down in the cargo hold—except this one had 'Subject 33' stencilled on the side.

"What is it?" Nigel stood so close that part of his chest had vanished into her body.

She took a deep breath and opened the door fully. Nothing happened. She stepped forward to examine the crate. Another thunk sounded—and it clearly came from the crate. It was latched shut, but the lock hung open.

Veena paused and stared down at the crate. It was too small to fit a child, so what was in it? She swallowed. Did she really want to know? She took a deep breath in, then slowly exhaled. Whatever Greer was up to, she needed to know. She bent down and opened the crate.

In a whirl of shifting colour, something emerged from inside.

Veena gasped and stepped backwards until she contacted the bathroom vanity's sharp corner with her hip.

Still flashing colours, the organic being slopped over the crate's edge and down to the floor, landing in a pile of writhing tentacles. For a split second, it struggled to right itself. Then it darted out of the bathroom. The door in the other room swished open—whatever it was, it had just escaped the cabin.

"What was that?" Nigel asked.

"I have no idea." She leaned forward and examined the inside of the crate. Water filled the bottom third, and there was nothing else of note.

Veena turned and looked where that thing had passed—water splotches glistened, creating a track to follow.

She stowed her datapad in a pocket. "Let's follow it."

———

She and Nigel ran out of the cabin and easily spotted the damp marks on the hallway carpet. They followed the path until they reached the upper observation deck.

"This observation deck will be closed until tonight's gala." Nigel opened the door.

Veena stuck her head inside. No one was in the cavernous space.

Nigel appeared directly in front of her. "Shall I reserve you a ticket for the gala?"

"Fancy dos aren't really my thing." Veena moved forward, passing directly through Nigel. The path of small drops of water continued towards the dance floor. She followed them.

The upper observation deck jutted out in a clear bubble on top of the ship's bow. When she glanced up, Veena's jaw dropped, and she stopped. Through the massive window, the approaching gate loomed, its shimmering aqua surface reminiscent of a water's edge complete with small waves.

"Wow." She took a few steps forward before remembering she was here with a purpose. "Let's keep looking."

"I'll access the scanners." Nigel blinked away. A moment later, he rematerialized. "Whatever it was, it didn't register on the sensors."

Veena nodded and slowly turned. She didn't see any more drips on the floor, and no weird animal was in view. "I guess we lost it."

Nigel nodded. "I guess so."

"Let's go look at what Greer had on his datapads." She set off back towards her cabin.

Something nagged at her. As she walked, she tried to figure

out what. Statistically, ending up on the same ship as Greer was unlikely to be a coincidence. She pondered that for a few minutes, then shook her head and re-did her calculations. Factoring the lack of berths on ships leaving Jupiter Station, there was more than a 50% chance they'd be on the same ship.

She scratched the side of her head. Was it the crates then? Moving a child in a crate was beneath what any reasonable person would do. Besides, Molly wouldn't stand for it—and would shake the ship to show her displeasure. No, it would be better for them if they bribed Molly with candy and comics instead.

"Are you alright, madam?" The concern on Nigel's face seemed real.

"I'm trying to put all the pieces together," she said. "Did you get a good look at that animal?"

"Sadly, no. However, what I saw seemed very similar to the animal in your comics."

Veena stopped. That was it. The animal in Greer's bathroom reminded her of the octopus in Molly's comics, bright colours and all.

Chapter Thirty-Three

In the middle of his sleep cycle, Hwicce woke with a jerk. He thought he heard a noise. As he ran a hand through his hair, he tried to determine if the sound had been in his dream or real. He lay flat on his back, staring at the ceiling, waiting. After a few minutes of nothing, he decided to get up.

He slid open the privacy curtain and rolled out of his bunk. The privacy curtain in the bunk across from his was pulled closed, and he could hear Baker snoring on the other side.

"At least one of us is getting a good night's sleep," he muttered as he pulled his clothes on.

Out in the common room, the low nighttime light level created the kind of shadows Molly feared most—dark and deep, enough space for someone, monster or man, to hide. But it wasn't the darkness Hwicce feared. Instead, he feared for his little girl.

He moved silently through the space and out into the cargo hold. It remained empty—a fact that bothered him more than he cared to admit. Where did all those crates he and Baker loaded go? Baker hadn't seemed concerned—but then, she'd been distracted by Emiko.

Circling the large space, he listened for the sound. The

ventilation system hummed as expected, punctuated by the standard creaks and groans the old ship made as it unevenly lost heat. Then he heard a scraping followed by a plop—was that what woke him up? He scratched his head as he tried to determine the origin of the sound, but he couldn't pinpoint it.

He went up to the bridge and checked the nav display. They were about three hours out from reaching the gate. The ship's diagnostic screens said the ship functioned within its optimal parameters. Green lights on the pilot's controls indicated autopilot was engaged and operating as it should. Nothing on the bridge appeared out of the ordinary.

With a sigh, he slumped into the captain's chair and gazed out the front window. The metallic orange surface of the gate dominated the view. The rocky world that bound the shimmering rift in space in place was visible to the right, its dull and dark surface difficult to see.

"Wait!"

He blinked rapidly, but the gate remained the same colour—the wrong colour. His gate nav instructor's face surfaced in his mind; his dire warnings reverberated through Hwicce's head.

"It can't be."

He rubbed his face as he glanced down at the nav console to confirm. The *Shimmer* was on a direct course for the wrong side of the gate. Entering the orange side would tear their ship apart.

"Oh, crap."

Either Boris was a navigational idiot, or he'd set them on a doomed path on purpose. He swallowed and stared at the gate as his mind raced through the possibilities.

A flash of light near the ship caught his attention—a shuttle. Using a side console, he zoomed in on it. It was a standard civilian model capable of going through the gates. Yet it lacked the Protectorate required callsign—or distinguishing marks of any kind.

As it accelerated ahead, Hwicce back-calculated its course; it must have been docked with the *Shimmer*. That would explain what he'd heard. The shuttle angled into a low orbit around the anchor world—a course that would slingshot it through the right side of the gate.

Watching the retreating shuttle made his gut churn. It confirmed his earlier suspicion. Boris was up to more than just smuggling. Whatever his grandmother had put him up to had begun. But Hwicce still didn't know what it was.

This time, a biometric lock prevented him from accessing the ship's logs. Hacking that sort of thing was outside his skillset, so he went for the next best thing. Clenching his jaw, he marched to the captain's cabin and banged on the door. Boris didn't answer. After waiting a few minutes, Hwicce tried the door release and found it wasn't locked—yet another red flag.

He took a deep breath and burst into Boris' cabin, then stopped in his tracks. It looked like someone had robbed their captain. Scattered clothing, open drawers, and brushed aside knick-knacks suggested a hasty search. But Boris wasn't there. Hwicce ran a hand through his hair as he studied the mess.

On the other side of the generous cabin, the bathroom door gaped open. Stepping around the mess on the floor, he made his way over. As soon as he entered the small room, the light flickered on, exposing a utilitarian space constructed of stainless steel in need of a good scrubbing.

Sitting on a shelf above the sink, just below the mirror, was a lime green mug from a taco place on Indigo Station. Holding his breath, he picked it up and looked inside. A waft of minty scent hit him. Crusted toothpaste coated the interior—but there was no toothbrush.

He let out an audible exhale. Only one conclusion made sense: Boris had abandoned them. The shuttle had rendezvoused with the *Shimmer* to pick up Boris while his crew slept.

His nostrils flared as his breathing became more ragged. As heat rose in his body, he squeezed the mug. What kind of coward flees in the night? With his full strength, he threw the mug into the shower's far corner. It shattered into a million lime green pieces that scattered across the shower floor.

"What have you gotten us into?"

He strode back to the common room and banged on Emiko's cabin door. A moment later, it slid open a crack, and Emiko stuck her head out.

"Boris left the ship." His tone sounded harsher than he intended.

Emiko cocked her head. "Why in the hell would he do that?"

"I was hoping you might know," he said as he fixed his gaze on the petit woman.

"Give me a moment," she said before withdrawing inside and closing the door.

Hwicce went and woke up Baker. She grumbled at his disruption of her sleep and demanded a moment as well. With a frown, Hwicce sat down at the table in the common room. A few minutes later, both women, now fully dressed, took places at the table across from him.

"I saw a shuttle," Hwicce said. "Then I checked Boris' cabin. He clearly packed in a hurry, but he didn't forget to take his toothbrush."

"Shit!" Emiko put her elbows on the table.

"Fucking hell. What does that mean?" Baker asked, shifting her gaze between Emiko and Hwicce.

"I don't know," Emiko replied. "But if that dickwad snuck out of here in the middle of the night, it can't be good."

"The autopilot is engaged, and we appear to be on a course to the wrong side of the gate." Hwicce ran a hand through his beard. The knot twisting in his gut was telling him that wasn't the only thing that was very, very wrong. There were more puzzle pieces he didn't yet know about.

"Why would he leave?" Baker stood, the legs of the plastic

chair screeching across the deck. She strode over to the coffee machine and began making a pot.

"He's always been an ass, but this seems way out of character for him."

"When I eavesdropped on his conversation with Mrs. Long, she implied something was going to happen." Hwicce leaned back. "I think we can conclude it has begun."

"It's not going to end well—especially for us." Emiko stood. "I'm going to go to the bridge." She strode out of the room.

Baker turned and looked at him. "Sir?"

Hwicce took a deep breath. "Let's do a full sweep of the ship. Maybe there's a clue hidden somewhere that'll shed light on what's going on."

"Right." She cast a sidelong glance at the percolating coffee.

"Start aft, and I'll go forward," Hwicce said, falling back on his military tone. "And don't forget the *Shimmer* is less than legitimate—there'll be smuggler holes."

"Yes, sir." Baker gave a curt nod before heading out of the common room and down the corridor leading towards the stern of the ship.

Turning in the opposite direction, Hwicce went to the cargo bay. He traipsed across the massive space and passed beside the stairs leading up to the bridge. An entire compartment which he'd never been in sat beneath the bridge. A metal bulkhead separated this section from the main part of the cargo bay. A wide set of double doors were the only entry point.

He stopped in front of the doors and tried to slide one open, but they were locked together. Running a hand through his hair, he focused on the keypad at the side. To open it required a numeric code containing an undefined number of digits. Veena would know what his odds were in guessing the right code, but she remained out of reach.

"Of course," he muttered. "Why would Boris make it easy on us?" He didn't have time to futz with codes.

After letting out a long sigh, he jogged past the common room to the engineering workshop. Once there, he grabbed a laser cutter, welding goggles, and thick gloves before jogging back to the doors.

Using the cutter, he fried the door controls by cutting the circuits in half. A cascade of sparks flew out, followed by a puff of acrid smoke. Then the doors lurched, opening a few centimetres. With both hands, he pulled the starboard door the rest of the way open.

Inside, the ceiling was so low, he could reach up and touch it. As he stepped further in, overhead lights came on. He let out a low whistle as the knot in his gut tightened. The crates he and Baker had loaded on board were all stacked up along the forward wall of the compartment.

"This is suspicious." He walked to the closest one while trying to ignore the uneven gravity.

The crate was locked, but this time, he had a laser cutter with him. He cut off the lock and flipped open the lid.

A coldness gripped his core. His mouth fell open, and he took a step back. "Oh, crap!"

He dropped the laser cutter, ignoring it as the cutter rolled under the crate. Clenching his jaw, he sprinted up to the bridge and burst through the door.

"The crates are filled with military-grade explosives."

Emiko looked up from the screen she'd been working on at the nav console and raised an eyebrow. "You found them?"

"In the compartment beneath us." He crossed his arms over his chest and stared down at the small woman. "The crate I opened has been activated—I think we can assume all of them are."

"That doesn't sound good."

"I can de-activate it with the controller," Hwicce said. He paused and ran over the procedure in his head—it had been drilled into him so many times he suspected he could do it blindfolded.

Emiko cocked her head as though she was about to ask a question.

"They're the same as some of the army time explosive kits. I've used them before."

"Okay." She nodded. "How much time do we have?"

"The timer isn't set, meaning they set the crate to detonate on impact." Hwicce tried to force himself to stay calm by taking deep breaths. If only Boris was here, he could get his hands around that weasel's neck. He shook his head and stared out the window.

"Impact with what?" Emiko followed his gaze.

"Hell if I know." He stalked forward, right up to the clear surface. The gate filled more of the view now, but it was still a long way off.

Emiko slipped into the pilot's seat and started fiddling with the displays. "Shit, I can't access. We're locked out of the controls; I couldn't bring up nav or comms either. It looks like we're screwed."

Hwicce turned to face her. "So the *Shimmer* has effectively been converted to a missile, and we're just passengers?"

"Looks that way." She glanced over at the nav console, then back at him. "There's an escape pod. We can get out of here."

Hwicce squeezed his hands into fists, then forced himself to release them. It was morally wrong to just jump ship without understanding what was being set up to happen. "There has to be a reason Mrs. Long wanted Boris to do this."

"Any idea what they have aimed us at?" Emiko shifted over to the nav console and brought up the familiar figure-eight gate schematic.

"No. An explosion wouldn't harm the gate, and I don't see any other ships out there. We've got to stop this..." His words trailed off as he realized he had no idea what to do next.

"What happens if we go through the wrong side of the gate?" Baker asked from the doorway. She'd arrived at some point during his conversation with Emiko.

"The *Shimmer* won't be able to handle the stresses. And if there's a ship coming out at the same time..." Emiko scratched her head and looked out the bridge window.

"Crap! We have to assume they planned this," Hwicce said. "Our course is timed to have the *Shimmer* smash into a ship coming out of the gate—but what ship?"

Chapter Thirty-Four

"We need a new plan," Veena said as she and Nigel left the empty upper observation deck. Letting her mind churn, she walked in silence the rest of the way back to her cabin.

Nigel's projection kept pace with her. "I must inform you that the *Garden Princess* will go through the first gate in less than an hour."

"I didn't get a good look at...whatever that was. Are you sure it was Click?"

"It was the animal the little girl plays with in your comics."

"Click is a fictional alien. Besides, if it were an animal, it'd be the biggest non-human animal around, that said it did seem octopus-like to me."

"Insects were the largest animals the generation ships brought from Earth."

"Everyone learns that in elementary school." Veena stepped into the elevator and pushed the button for the peony deck. The doors silently slid shut. "Maybe it was a machine of some sort? A live-action Click model?"

She ran her hands down her dress. "Maybe made of nanites." The nanites in Molly's bucket-o-stuff could make very realistic animals—but they were all small enough to fit in the palm of her hand, which was the limit of that kind of technology. "Hell, I don't know what we saw."

Other than copying over some documents, they hadn't accomplished much of anything. The elevator arrived on her level, and she headed down the deserted corridor to her cabin. On her approach, the doors slid open, and she passed through without slowing down. The door whooshed closed as she slumped down on the first sofa.

Her gaze fixed on her patterned bedspread, and she started counting the lines, but that didn't help. With a sigh, she pulled out one of Molly's comics. A smile spread across her lips as she flipped open the first page. Even though she'd read it before, the bright colours and utopian world of a child and her alien friend exploring their surroundings still sucked her in.

Buzzing from Gloria's comms device pulled Veena's attention away from the comic book world. She fished the device out of Molly's backpack and answered the call.

"Hey!" Gloria's face appeared, floating in the air above the device. "How's the cruise?"

Veena glanced around her opulent stateroom. "This place is a little over the top—"

"I've got great news," Gloria cut her off. "I found a ride to Indigo Station, so I can meet you there."

A wave of relief swept over Veena. Soon, she wouldn't need to continue on alone.

"Have your contacts given you any more details on where Molly is?"

Gloria pursed her lips. "Not yet, but I'm sure I'll have info by the time we get to Indigo Station."

Veena nodded. They'd find another ship there and set out. She'd be reunited with Molly soon. She grabbed the Click stuffy and hugged it in close—it still smelled like Molly.

"How'd you find a ride?"

Gloria looked to the side, then back at the device. "Sorry, I don't want to disturb anyone here. I pulled in a favour and got a berth on an old survey ship."

A smile spread across Veena's face. "Thank you so much for helping me."

"I'm happy to help. Is there anything else I can do?"

Veena paused for a moment. "It might be a dead-end, but there's someone here who was there when they took Molly. His name is Dr. Greer. First name Jim or James. Can you find out more info on him?"

"Sure thing," Gloria said with a nod. "How're you holding up?"

"Better now. But I'm worried about how Molly's doing, especially since she doesn't even have her favourite stuffy with her." Veena held up Molly's well-worn stuffed octopus. Its once vibrant pink had faded to a slightly greyed hue. She let out a sigh.

"Since you're doing all you can do, why not take some time and distract yourself? I hear there is an awesome spa on that ship."

Veena shook her head. "That's not really my thing."

"How about that decoding puzzle you've been working on?"

"Maybe..." Veena let her words trail off.

Should she tell Gloria about breaking into Dr. Greer's cabin, his oversized luggage, and the possible animal they'd seen? Her thoughts shifted to the files she downloaded from Greer. Looking at those would be a good use of her time—but not the distraction her friend was suggesting for her.

"I should go. There's a party on the lower observation deck for when we pass through our first gate." Veena bit her lip. It was just a little lie—enough to satisfy Gloria.

"Ooh," Parties were Gloria's thing; Veena could picture her friend rubbing her hands together. "I wish I was there with you."

Veena smiled. "I wish you were too," she said without really meaning it. As much as she appreciated her friend's help, a little bit of alone time to think was what she needed right now. If Gloria were there, she'd drag Veena to every party she could.

"Tootle-loo." The projection of Gloria's head vanished.

Veena let out a long exhale and glanced down at Molly's stuffy in her hand. Its enormous eyes were half the charm of the character. Glittery specs reminiscent of starfield filled its dark pupils—she couldn't help but gaze at them.

"You'll be back in Mol's arms soon," she said to the stuffy. She set it down and turned just as the door to her cabin slid open.

In the doorway appeared a real-life version of Click. Vividly coloured with the same oversized eyes. They looked up at her as though uncertain, then their skin flushed pink.

Veena screamed.

"Nigel?" She stood and backed away from the cartoon-come-to-life in the doorway.

He materialized next to her. "Yes, Dr. O...Oh."

She pointed at Click. "What is that?"

On undulating tentacles, Click moved forward, and the door closed behind them. Their skin morphed to yellow, then purple.

"I-I-I-" Nigel stuttered as though stuck in a loop.

Veena frowned; the AI was going to be no help. She took a deep breath and stared at Click. The animal was the same size as the stuffy, and it had yet to do anything threatening. Maybe she could talk to it.

"Who are you?"

Click flushed scarlet before a complex pattern of swirls passed over their skin. For a moment, Veena thought she recognized the patterns. They lifted a single tentacle and pointed at the stuffed version of themself.

"How can you be a character out of a kid's comic book?" She squinted at them as though that might give her a clue if they were organic or a nanite machine.

The animal used two arms to make a very human-like shrug. In a complex dance of multiple limbs, Click moved over to the wall where the AI console was. As though gravity was irrelevant, it moved up the wall and over the console.

Beside her, Nigel vanished. Then he reformed with a blank expression. He turned to Veena, and she backed away. This wasn't the Nigel she knew.

"I-I-I-" continued Nigel.

Click flushed dark blue, then white.

"I...not...not-not..."

Veena circled around her bed until her back was up against the windows. She stared at the door and debated if she should make a run for it.

"I...not...not...hurt you," Nigel said in a monotone.

"Who are you?" Veena glanced back and forth from Nigel to the animal attached to the wall.

"I...I...Click," Nigel said, just as the animal made a loud click.

"Are you from the comic?" she asked, knowing the idea was insane.

"My kind," Nigel said.

"Was it you we saw in Dr. Greer's cabin?" she asked, starting to feel more intrigued than afraid.

"Yes," Nigel said as Click flushed pink again. "You save me."

Veena bit her lip. "Why did Dr. Greer keep you captive?"

"Not knowing," said Nigel, and Click flushed grey. A flurry of symbols made of a whole rainbow of colours form across their skin. "He...he...stole me."

"He stole my daughter too." Veena moved closer to Click. "Where are you from?"

"Seventh World."

She had no idea where that was. "Can you give me Nigel back for a few moments?"

The hologram glitched, and then Nigel's normal expressions returned.

His eyebrows pulled together as he looked around the room. "What happened?"

"Our mystery has been solved." She pointed to where Click still hung on the wall.

"Oh?" Nigel backed away. "What is that?"

"That's Click," Veena said, and Click flashed red, then yellow. "Have you ever heard of Seventh World?"

"I will search the ship's database," he said, then blinked away.

Veena stared at Click. Without suckers on their arms, they weren't quite like the octopi of old Earth, but that was the best description she could come up with.

Nigel returned. "There is no record of a place called Seventh World."

Click flashed grey again.

"We'll figure it out," Veena said, uncertain why she was willing to help Click. They seemed benign—yet she had no way to know that for sure.

"Attention honoured guests," a voice over the ship's comms announced. "We are ten minutes out from passing through the gate to the Beta System. The upper observation deck is now open, and refreshments are being served."

Veena turned away and walked over to the window. Click dropped to the floor and followed. They climbed up on the back of a sofa to see the view.

Outside, the gate now filled over half of the view, blocking out the stars. Its undulating surface looked liquid and seemed lit from within. The aqua glow reflected off the part of the ship's hull that was within view. It was beautiful yet bizarre at the same time—a point made more disturbing by the fact that no human had yet figured out how the gate system worked.

"Do you wish to go to the observation deck?" Nigel asked.

Veena bit her lip. She didn't want to go, but it might provide an opportunity to observe Dr. Greer. Maybe he had accomplices on board. Maybe there'd be a clue where Molly had been taken. She let out a long exhale.

"I think I should," she said. Then she turned to Click. "Will you stay here?"

Click stared at her with their large eyes. Then they nodded and flashed pink.

"I'll come back as soon as I can, then I'll look on the DeepNet for where Seventh World is."

Click's skin brightened to the point they were glowing pink. Veena took that as a positive sign.

Chapter Thirty-Five

Hwicce rubbed a hand over his face as he stared at the arming mechanism on the explosives inside the now open crate. On top, a red light blinked, taunting him. It connected to a detonator buried deep into the explosives. It was a simple enough system that a soldier right out of basic training could be trusted to set it up. And it was robust enough to prevent anyone tampering with it.

"Crap!" He pursed his lips as what he needed to do was tamper with it.

Likely making the same assessment, Baker huffed beside him. "Fucking hell! Tell me you can hack it. Sir."

"We need the controller." He crouched down for a better view even though looking from another angle wouldn't change anything.

Baker crossed her arms over her chest. "Which we don't have."

"We've searched everywhere. I suspect Boris took it with him." Hwicce ran a hand through his hair. "The coward."

From his new angle, the device gave him little information by design. It was military equipment. He had no idea how the shipment had ended up on the mining outpost or how Boris—or perhaps more accurately, Mrs. Long's people—had gotten it.

"You guys better get up here quick," Emiko said over the ship's intercom.

Hwicce and Baker exchanged a look then took off towards the bridge at a sprint.

"Look." Emiko's face was pale as she pointed at the exit side of the gate.

Hwicce stepped closer to the window—and then he saw it. Even though he'd suspected Boris' plan, getting confirmation made his stomach drop. A ship had just emerged from the gate.

He turned back to Emiko. "Can you zoom in on it?"

"Hang on." She bent over her workstation. "It's transmitting an ID." A moment later, a hologram of the ship materialized over Emiko's console, all sleek lines and fancy golden fittings. "It's the *Garden Princess*."

Hwicce circled around the image, studying it from all angles. It was a luxury liner—the kind of ship that shouldn't be allowed to run with a war going on. Better yet, it should have been impounded and converted into a hospital ship.

Baker frowned. "That's a fucking fancy ass ship," she said in a flat tone. "Unless gaudy opulence is now a crime, why try to ram a ship like that?"

Emiko leaned against the console behind her. "My guess is this is an assassination."

"There's a lot of people on that ship," Hwicce said, even though he agreed with her assessment. "Long Enterprises can't have a beef with all of them."

"Probably not, but I doubt they'd blink about random people getting caught in the crossfire," Emiko said. "I bet there's someone on that ship they want to get rid of."

Hwicce let out a long exhale as he remembered what Mrs. Long had said to Boris. "Long Enterprises wants to send a message to the military by assassinating one of their scientists. I bet they're on that ship." He pointed at the glimmering speck on this side of the gate.

"That seems a bit extreme," Emiko said.

"Won't the military just go after Long Enterprises?" Baker turned to the other two. "I mean, even if Long Enterprises is exceptionally well equipped, the military has more toys than them."

"I suspect their target is part of a classified project." Hwicce slumped down into the captain's chair. He wondered if Mrs. Long's 'celebrated scientist' target was the one of the team working on tweaking human genetics—the project that canceled on using her facility on Hamber's Hole.

"So, the military won't be able to make a public fuss over one of their own being targeted," Emiko said. "That wouldn't stop some black ops shit being done."

"No." Baker shifted. "Unless Long Enterprises didn't want anyone to know it was them who pulled the trigger, so to speak."

Hwicce huffed. Endlessly discussing motives wasn't going to save anyone. He stood and ran a hand down his face.

"Sir, what if Boris is planning on sticking this on us?"

Hwicce stared at Baker. She had a point. It was a stretch, but Long Enterprises could claim two disgruntled ex-soldiers with the right skills could've done this. But that was a problem for later.

"Call the *Garden Princess*. We need to warn them." He reached out towards the holographic green hull before staring at the real thing out the window. "There's still time for them to change course."

Emiko went over to another workstation and fiddled with the controls as Hwicce returned to the windows and stared down at the planet passing below. The rocky surface remained as featureless as before.

With a thunk, Emiko slammed her open palm onto the top of the console. Both Hwicce and Baker turned to her. "I can't..." She hit the computer again. "I can't raise them—our comms are offline."

Everyone on the bridge fell so silent, Hwicce could hear the blood surging through his veins. The people on the other ship were completely unaware that their doom was fast approaching. He swallowed and told himself to focus. There had to be something they could do.

He turned to Emiko. "Can you fix the comms?"

She shook her head.

"There's the escape pod," Baker said in a low tone.

Hwicce ran his hand over his face. "We've got to stop the head-on-collision. That ship isn't armoured." His mouth went dry just at the thought of what a transport ship traveling at their speed and full of explosives would do to the liner. No one would survive that.

"I know." Baker hung her head and shoved her hands into her pockets. "I'm just putting options on the table."

He nodded. "Even if we altered course just a little bit..."

"Can't. The autopilot is directing us right at the other ship —and I doubt they'll see us even when we get closer," Emiko said.

A wave of nausea swept through him as his gut tied into more knots. "What?" He turned to Emiko. The *Garden Princess* had to have scanning equipment.

"We won't show up on standard EM scanning devices." Emiko licked her lips and glanced back down at the screen.

"Why not?"

"Um...Boris retrofitted the ship's hull with EM absorbers. We'll show up a little in the visible spectrum, but that's it."

"The planet below us is grey"—Baker pointed at the anchor world outside—"and the *Shimmer's* hull is grey."

Hwicce closed his eyes as the knot in his gut wound tighter. "They'll never see us in time."

"No," Emiko said in a tiny voice.

He let out a ragged exhale. The passengers and crew on the

other ship wouldn't get a warning. The fate of that ship was now in their hands, and his mind had gone blank.

"Okay, there's got to be something else we can do." Baker started pacing. "Maybe we can dump the crates?"

"We can't move them," Hwicce said. "The failsafe has been activated. If we mess with them, the crates will blow."

"Those crates are booby trapped?" Emiko stared at him.

Hwicce nodded and swallowed. "We could just detonate them." He paused, his mouth now dry. Molly and Veena were out there somewhere—and if he did, this his family would never know what happened to him. The knot in his gut twisted. "Then only debris would hit the liner."

"Sir, that's suicide," Baker said, turning to face him.

"You two can get in the escape pod. I'll let you get away before I blow everything." Hwicce looked out at the liner. He just couldn't let all those people die. At least Veena would understand. But Molly...

Baker crossed her arms over her chest. "I reject that plan. We've got to change our course. Can we override the autopilot? If we could get control of a single thruster—"

"They aren't accessible from the inside."

"Then we go for a spacewalk." Baker stopped and put her hands on her hips. "Sir, you and I have done plenty of spacewalks."

"In full battle armour," he said. "Which we don't have."

"The *Shimmer* has atmo suits," Emiko interjected. "But I have a better idea. We blow the atmosphere out of the port side hatch. If we timed it right, we could change the course just enough."

"Wouldn't the autopilot just compensate?" Hwicce crossed his arms over his chest.

"Not if we did it at the last second."

He nodded. "That just might work."

Baker stood between them, looking back and forth. "That's lunacy."

"Stand down." Hwicce put a hand on her shoulder. "It may be a risky plan, but it's the best we've got."

Emiko frowned. "The ships will probably still contact, but it would be a sideswipe."

"And when the forward section blows, the standard hull plating should be able to handle it," Hwicce continued as he paced back and forth.

Emiko nodded.

"That's a fucking crazy plan." Baker crossed her arms over her chest. "We'd only get one shot to get it right."

Hwicce inhaled deeply. The knot in his gut had loosened a tiny bit. "We can do this. We blow the atmosphere, then get in the escape pod."

"We've got 45 minutes until we need to blow the atmosphere. I'm going to pack my shit." Emiko headed off the bridge.

"Baker," he said before she could follow Emiko.

"Sir?"

"I need you to check the supplies on the escape pod. I have no idea where we'll end up or how long we'll be there."

"I don't want to be crammed in a tin can," she said with wide eyes. "Small spaces aren't my thing. It'll drive me nuts."

She'd never admitted any kind of fear to him before. He paused. In the last few days, he'd learned more about her than in their year of fighting together. Baker was much more complex than he'd imagined.

"I'm certain we won't be in the pod too long—entire fleets are going to be sent out to rescue the rich folk on the liner. Someone will pick us up by mistake."

She smiled. "I'm going to hold you to that." She turned and walked away. "Sir!"

Forty minutes later, the *Garden Princess* filled most of their forward view. The gold-ringed portholes peppering the green hull were now visible with the naked eye. Hwicce took a deep breath as he mentally went through their plan. It wasn't a great plan, but it was the best they could do under the circumstances.

All three of them wore space suits taken from the *Shimmer's* stores. His was a few centimetres too short in the torso, meaning it pulled uncomfortably over his shoulders and crotch. Wearing it for any length of time was going to result in chafing where he'd rather not chafe, but he needed the bubble of atmosphere. Breathing was more important than not chaffing—at least that was what he told himself every time he stood up too tall.

He'd already stashed his few belongings in the escape pod. The pod had been designed for a full ship compliment of eight, which much relieved Baker. It wasn't nearly as cramped as it could have been. She was standing by in the pod—ready to release it as soon as he and Emiko made it on board. The port side door would have to be opened manually, and since it was an airlock, it would require both of them, one on each door.

With a deep breath, he turned away from the massive ship bearing down on them and left the bridge for the last time. He headed to the airlock and found Emiko waiting for him there. Her eyes were wide behind her helmet's visor.

"You ready for this?" he asked.

"Hell no. But I don't see a better option."

"Then let's get this done." He clipped on a safety line to his suit's belt and attached it to a ring welded to the wall. Then he made sure Emiko was equally secure.

"We'll have a two-minute window," Emiko said, checking the wall console just outside the small airlock. The inside airlock door stood open but would automatically close the instant he opened the outside one.

The airflow in his atmo suit made his nose itch—an annoying feature of the low-end suit. His combat armour never left him feeling that way. While twitching his nose to try and deal with the itch, he stood up straight and was rewarded by the crotch seam digging in further.

"Are we in the window?" He tried to sound confident as he adjusted his posture back to slightly stooped. Shifting slightly forward, he stared through the door's window.

The glistening green hull looked almost close enough to touch.

"Hang on." She wedged a metal toolbox into the bottom of the inside door frame.

"You think that'll hold?"

Emiko shrugged and looked down at the toolbox. "It's what I have." She returned her attention to the computer screen. "Open in thirty seconds."

"Right." Hwicce took another glance out the window. He thought he could see faces in the portholes now. A bead of sweat dripped down his forehead. Time seemed to tick slower than ever. He took a deep breath and tried not to think about what was going to happen once he and Emiko joined Baker in the escape pod.

"Now!" Emiko said.

Hwicce spun the ring open. Once released from its cogs, the door flew open, pushed by the atmosphere within the *Shimmer*. He felt the tug against his safety line as the escaping air tried to pull him into the vacuum outside.

With the air went small objects, including someone's tooth-brush (but not Boris'), the salt shaker from the galley, an atrocious amount of lint, and even someone's lime green hoodie. Less than a minute later, the wind subsided, and Hwicce was able to unclip his safety line.

Out the now open door, the *Garden Princess* loomed closer than ever. He couldn't tell if their course had shifted or not. But they'd done all they could do. He and Emiko headed deeper into the ship towards the escape pod.

"Ready to go, Sir?" Baker asked as soon as he'd closed the hatch.

Emiko continued forward to the pod's controls, where she strapped herself to the seat.

Hwicce took the nearest seat and strapped himself in—the little escape pod didn't have gravity plating. "Let's get out of here."

"Releasing pod in..." Emiko's tone remained firm and competent. "3... 2... 1."

A clunk reverberated through the small craft. Then it lurched to the side, and he felt heavier than usual. Through the little porthole beside him, the *Shimmer* filled the view—but it was shrinking fast.

Soon, he could make out the larger hull of the *Garden Princess* beyond. He let out a sigh as he realized they'd been successful. The *Shimmer's* course was no longer aiming directly for the luxury liner—venting the atmosphere had changed their ship's trajectory. He hoped it would be enough.

Thrusters flared on the *Garden Princess*; presumably, they'd just spotted the *Shimmer*. The behemoth began to turn. For a moment, Hwicce thought the ships might actually miss each other, then a cascade of sparks billowed out as the two hulls contacted.

Pieces of the two ships flaked away as the *Shimmer* left a deep gouge in the *Garden Princess*, leaving rows of luxury cabins exposed to the vacuum of space. Then the explosives in the hull of the *Shimmer* detonated. The flash of light forced him to look away.

Moments later, the blast wave hit the escape pod.

Chapter Thirty-Six

Since it sat on a platform overlooking the rest of the lower observation deck, Veena took a seat at the bar. Although she'd programmed it to fit her perfectly, her green nanite dress chafed her right armpit. She shifted the smooth fabric, but that didn't help.

"A cocktail for the lady," the barkeeper said as he slid a green-hued beverage in front of her. He moved on to another patron before she could say thanks.

With a shrug, she picked up the glass and turned towards the view outside. The shimmering surface of the gate seemed close enough to touch now. It encompassed the entire view. As she watched the undulating surface, she took a sip.

The well-aged greenie moss liqueur burned on the way down. Warmth radiated out from her stomach, and she was left with a slightly sour after taste. As she took another sip, she scanned the crowd lounging on the level below.

Even though Nigel had told her Greer would be present, she inhaled sharply when she spotted him. He sat with a group of six, sipping an amber liquid out of a tumbler. His wine-toned suit fit him perfectly and tastefully clashed with his amber and green ascot. Greer made a comment to the others, and his entire party laughed.

The interior lights dimmed as a countdown began. The *Garden Princess* was about to pass through the gate. At zero, the forward most windows plunged through, creating a ripple across the gate's surface. Inside, a mostly translucent aqua wave advanced across the observation deck. Conversations became muted.

As the shimmering front passed over Veena, the air became dry, and a pungent resin scent washed over her. Prickles ran across her skin, causing goosebumps to rise.

The world became disjointed and off-kilter as though she'd put on kaleidoscope goggles. Extra colours laced across the space like a translucent web. She glanced at her empty hand. An aqua glow surrounded her fingers, and as she moved her hand, it followed a nanosecond behind as a glittery wake. Nausea threatened to empty her stomach. She swallowed and closed her eyes—she'd passed through gates before and knew what to expect.

Abruptly, the weird sensations stopped. She opened her eyes just as a different solar system complete with twin suns and a nearby anchor world blinked into view outside the windows.

Taking a deep breath, Veena resumed observing Greer as he mingled with his associates while finishing her drink. From the expressions on their faces, the conversation had taken on a more serious tone. She wished she could hear what they were saying, but Nigel hadn't been willing to arrange that. For a piece of code, he was surprisingly moral.

Greer and his party all scrambled to their feet to stare out the window as the jovial nature of their gathering descended into worried whispers. Veena stood to find what had caught their attention.

A dark mass moved over the surface of the anchor world. It was the same colour as the planet, making it very difficult to see.

Veena did some calculations in her head, and her jaw dropped. The yet unidentified mass was coming right at them.

She tilted her head as she tried to identify the object. A moon in low orbit? A trick of the light? A blast of the ship's alarm shattered her curiosity.

The deck beneath her tilted faster than the gravity could compensate for. She lost her footing, tumbling over the rail separating the raised platform she stood on and the deck below. Right hip down, she landed on the plush carpet. Her unfinished cocktail tumbled from her hand and spilled. All around her, the unsecured chairs slid.

Veena's breath caught in her throat as she realized what was happening. The object she'd seen was on a collision course with them. A behemoth made for luxury travel, the *Garden Princess* lacked maneuverability. The abrupt course change reeked of desperation.

A sour taste formed in her mouth as she pushed herself up to kneeling while holding onto the nearest couch, bolted to the deck, for support.

Others soon came to the same conclusion she had. As people's panic rose, some screamed and ran from the observation deck. The object was close enough now that she could identify it—it was a ship, an old freighter. But why was it approaching the wrong side of the gate?

Veena steadied herself and glanced over to Greer. His hand rested on the window now, and the firm set to his jaw suggested he was trying to stare down the approaching ship.

Ignoring her fear, she crawled closer. Veena leaned her back against a sofa to eavesdrop.

"Get down to the crates." Greer's tone was sharp. "We need to get them loaded in one of the escape pods."

"There won't be time," one of his associates answered.

"Bloody hell! Just load crate 15-C then. I can't afford to lose those samples." Greer slapped the window. "We'll charter new transport at Hamber's Hole."

"Yes, sir." His two associates ran off.

"Nigel 183," Greer called, and a holographic steward with the same form as Veena's appeared. "Secure an escape pod for my people."

"Already done." The hologram spoke in an emotionless tone. "Shall I show you the way?"

"First, I need to retrieve something from my cabin."

"Attention guests, this is the captain speaking," an androgynous voice came over the ship's PA system. The message and the ongoing alarm prevented Veena from hearing any more from Greer.

As the captain explained that a collision was imminent, Veena peaked out from her hiding space just in time to see Greer's back as he strode away. No doubt he was heading to his cabin to collect Click.

She glanced outside at the approaching ship and bit her lip. Atmosphere vented out a side door, and the ship began to change course. It wasn't going to be a head-on collision, but they would still make contact.

"Who rams a passenger liner?" she whispered.

"Dr. Oswiu, please come with me to safety," her Nigel said as he materialized beside her. His eyes were wide as though he felt fear. "You have been assigned a seat in escape pod B-28."

"First, we need to get Click."

Nigel nodded. "Your cabin is in the safe zone. We can take temporary shelter there."

She turned and stared at the hologram. He was trembling. All around, other stewards shepherded their charges off the observation deck.

"Can the ship survive this impact?" she asked as the deck bucked beneath her. For a second time, she fell to her knees.

She looked out the window and watched as the dark ship cut into the *Garden Princess*. Its last-minute change in course meant it delivered a glancing blow, but the impact still made the whole ship vibrate and shutter.

"Emergency bulkheads will hold long enough for the captain to make the right call," Nigel said. "We need to get to safety now."

Veena tried to get to her feet, but the moving deck made it impossible. She crawled after Nigel instead.

A flash of orange appeared outside the windows, followed by a deep rumble resonating through the ship. Veena propelled herself up to her feet and ran.

Chapter Thirty-Seven

Veena charged into her cabin, then stopped and put her hands on her hips. Nigel stopped beside her.

"First, we download your code."

"Ummmm...mmmmm...." Nigel was wringing his hands together again in his glitchy way. "There...may not be time."

"How do I access your code?" She picked up her datapad.

"You need to focus on your escape." Nigel continued rubbing his hands together.

Veena glared at the AI. "I promised."

He nodded. "Fine. I'll move to the cabin's memory," he said, walking over to the wall console. A moment later, he tapped it. "I'm here."

"Okay." She sat on the couch and synced her scroll to the cabin's memory. The AI files were huge—downloading them would take time. She bit her lip. She'd promised, and there was something about her Nigel she found endearing—he'd been an excellent ally, and she needed allies. She took a deep breath and, with a swipe, started the file transfer.

The door to her stateroom slid open, and Greer stood in the open doorway. Veena gasped.

"My steward recorded what you did." Greer's nostrils

flared, and his lips pressed together as he studied her. Wrinkles marred his perfect suit, and his hair hung over his eyes, having escaped from the thick coat of gel. He raised his right hand and pointed at her. "You stole my specimen."

As intimidating as the scientist was, he had taken her daughter. Veena stood, pulling herself up as tall as she could, and stalked towards him.

"You took my daughter." She raised her chin and glared. "And I will not stop until I get her back."

Greer clenched his jaw and scowled back. "That girl—Subject 34—may be the key to everything. Now, where is my specimen?" He advanced far enough into her cabin that the door slid closed behind him.

"Where is Molly?" She held her ground, eyes fixed on Greer.

"If you want the girl to be returned to you after I've completed my research, I suggest you comply with my request now." He advanced forward until he was only a hand's width from her face.

Veena maintained eye contact as the ship jerked again. "Where is she?"

Gravity vanished. Everything not secured floated away from the floor, including both Veena and Greer.

Greer's ascot came loose as he drifted back towards the door. One paisley end of silk rose and momentarily blocked his face. Veena took that time to glance down at her datapad—Nigel's download registered 57% complete.

"All passengers are to put on their spacesuits at this time," a voice over the PA system advised in an overly calm tone.

"I don't have time for this." Greer pulled out a small gun from his waistband and pointed it at her. "I need the alien, and I know you took it."

Veena released the datapad, leaving it tethered to the wall. She pushed off, back further into her cabin, trying to find something to use as a weapon. At least moving made her a harder target to hit.

All at once, gravity returned, dumping Veena onto her bed. Greer wasn't so lucky. He hit the deck and lost his grip on the gun. The weapon skittered towards the foot of the bed.

Veena raced towards it and snatched it up. Just as she pointed it at Greer, gravity evaporated a second time. Her momentum drove her forward and into her opponent. Moving together, they impacted the closed door.

He grabbed the gun and shoved her away. She tumbled through the air and hit the corner of the passageway to the bathroom hard enough to drive all the air from her lungs. She bounced back and into the sitting area, gasping to breathe.

With the wind knocked out of her, she struggled to control her movement and failed. She tumbled onto the sofa, bounced off a desk, then smacked up against the window.

"You kept it contained, right?" Greer floated forward into the room.

Veena continued to gasp for breath. She feared the sharp pain in her side meant she'd broken a rib.

Gravity returned, and they both fell to the ground. With a flash of red, Click emerged from the spacesuit storage cupboard and snatched the gun with a single tentacle. Keeping the weapon clear of their body, they skittered under the bed and disappeared from view.

"Bloody hell! You let that thing free?" Greer glared at her as he stood. "You foolish woman. Do you understand what you've done? We'll never catch it now."

Veena said nothing.

"All passengers are to proceed to their designated escape pods," the voice over the PA announced without an ounce of emotion. "We will be abandoning ship."

"Fuck it. I hope you go down with the ship." He turned and left the room.

Veena closed her eyes and steadied herself. When she

opened them again, Click sat on the bed, staring at her. They flashed orange and dropped the weapon on the bedspread.

"We need to get out of here," she said, gathering up Molly's comics and stuffed Click. She grabbed her few belongings, stuffing everything into her backpack. As fast as she could, she changed back into her cargo pants and shirt before packing the green nano-dress. Molly's bucket-of-stuff went in last. She looked at the gun for a moment—it was a low-powered laser model with enough punch for one or two shots before recharging. She stuffed it in the bag too.

She went over to her datapad and checked the progress. The AI was only 79% downloaded.

"Shit." She ran a hand over her ponytail and took a deep breath. She turned to Click. "There are two spacesuits. Why don't you get into the helmet of one."

Click flashed green, then purple swirls moved across their skin. They let out a series of clicks.

"I wish I could translate that."

Click darted forward and landed on her datapad. They wrapped their limbs around the portable computer while a single tentacle landed on the wall console.

"What the…" Nigel appeared next to Veena. He looked around. "You need to get to your escape pod." Then his face went blank.

"I have the AI," he said, yet Veena knew it was Click speaking through him.

Veena let out a long exhale then nodded. The little alien was proving to be a good ally. "Right. Now let's get out of here."

With a flash of pink, Click skittered along the wall towards the first suit. They crawled into the helmet. Veena put her backpack into the torso and sealed the suit. The nanites shrank the suit down to an appropriate size for the contents.

She put her helmet on and let the nanites form the suit around her. She checked the oxygen levels in both suits, then grabbed the one containing Click under her arm. She didn't know how Click was doing it, but the Nigel projection remained. His face resumed his normal expression.

"This way. We must hurry," he said, waving her towards the door. It slid open, exposing flashing red lights beyond.

After attaching a safety line to the other suit, Veena hoisted it under her arm. It was heavy, but she wasn't leaving it behind. She followed Nigel into the corridor. The corridor was empty. The other passengers must have already made it to their escape pods. She swallowed back the fear that she'd waited too long and ran.

She came out into the open garden at the centre of the ship —it was no longer a peaceful retreat. Fire billowed from a level down below, and someone had turned the waterfall off. Smoke billowed up, blocking the far side from view.

"Which way, Nigel?" She stopped at the rail.

"Recalculating," he said.

An explosion from the corridor on the opposite side blasted the railing and most of the balcony away. As the twisted metal fell, it dawned on Veena she was in a very bad place if the gravity failed again.

"I no longer have access to the ship's network." He sounded horrified.

"Right." Veena turned and sprinted back down the hallway she'd just exited. If her memory was correct, there was an emergency staircase at the far end.

A crack sounded behind her, but she didn't dare look. Then gravity and all the lights cut out. She floated free of the floor. As she rotated, she should have seen the corridor behind her—yet it wasn't there.

Shimmering pieces of ship debris reflected the light from the two suns. The view was almost festive—except now she was floating in space.

"Nigel?" she called, rotating to see the hologram, but he was gone.

In the distance, thrusters from escape pods flared, moving

away from the wreckage. She pushed herself out of the severed corridor towards open space. Maybe someone would spot her and stop. She swallowed back fear as best she could, telling herself that the fancy liner would have fancy escape pods with airlocks.

Her momentum sent her out of the main hull of the ship at the point it had been torn in half. Tears welled up as she saw that not everyone had gotten their suits on in time. Several bodies, already frozen, floated by with surprised expressions on their faces. Looking at them made her shiver.

As she cleared more of the wreckage, she was rewarded with a view of the anchor planet. What was left of the dark ship that had collided with them was tumbling towards the planet's atmosphere-less surface. It hit, and an explosion flashed. Then she couldn't make out the details anymore.

She went back to studying the surrounding debris. A large chunk of the forward part of the ship she'd just escaped from was also falling towards the planet at a rapid rate, making her glad she'd gotten out.

"Now what?"

Chapter Thirty-Eight

Orin's chin dropped at the view before them. The psychedelic chaos of the gate gave way to wreckage extending in all directions.

Beside him, the colour drained from Gloria's face. "Oh shit. The *Garden Princess* is gone!"

"What the hell happened here?" Orin's mouth went dry as his gaze wandered around the three-dimensional wreckage of the liner.

"Veena..." Gloria's words trailed off, and for once, she remained silent.

Orin projected the readings from the *Buttercup's* sensor array onto the windshield to make sense of the debris field. He leaned forward in his seat as though that would give him a better view.

A proximity alarm went off. Tumbling through space, a massive green slap of hull crossed their path. The letter 'P' painted in gold covered one side.

Gripping the controls tighter, Orin held his breath and jerked the ship to port. The hunk of hull passed within a few metres beneath them. Exhaling, he kept his eyes on the view outside the windshield.

Moments later, he had to dodge again around a nondescript

hunk of metal, then around a frozen carcass of a tree. All the while, the proximity alarm kept blaring warnings, the sound boring into his head and making it pound.

At least the debris field was expanding, creating bigger spaces to navigate through with every passing moment. He maneuvered the ship into the nearest void he could find. The alarms abated, leaving an uncomfortable silence fitting a mortuary. Only then did he take a moment to study the sensor readouts.

Buttercup's AI determined that there was enough debris for two ships, meaning there had been a collision. The resulting wreckage was now spread over a sphere of space almost a hundred kilometres in diameter.

"Getting through this is going to be tough." He scratched his head as he stared at the debris field.

"Veena was on that ship." Gloria put a hand over her mouth. "Along with thousands of others."

He let out a long exhale. "I'm picking up alerts from multiple escape pods." He turned their comms to the rescue frequency, and suddenly, the cockpit was filled with voices. "It sounds like most everyone got off in time."

A frozen corpse tumbled across their field of view to punctuate his words.

"Except that guy," Gloria said, pointing at the silver-haired man in a dark suit as he drifted out of view.

The proximity alarm went off again, pulling Orin's attention to the space around the ship. "I need you to monitor the debris."

"Right." Gloria started adjusting the sensor arrays and projecting composite outputs onto the windshield. She cocked her head as more voices joined the chatter on the comms channel. "It sounds like ships from Hamber's Hole are on their way to pick up escape pods."

In formation, the escape pods moved to the other side of the debris field. Probably as part of a pre-programmed feature to amass them together for easy retrieval. Fortunately, the miners of Hamber's Hole had been quick to send help—the rag-tag group of industrial ships must have raced out as soon as they had received the first distress call.

Orin licked his lips. Since the fire, the air on *Buttercup* had become so dry. He zoomed part of his display in on the escape pods. Each one was the same green as the ship and painted with gold numbers.

"There's nothing like a matched set of escape pods," Gloria said.

"I hope Veena's safe on one of them."

"Oh. Wait." Gloria stood and headed aft. A few moments later, she returned. "Veena has one of these with her. I can just call her." She held up a device.

Orin recognized it. The device was a military comms device —the kind that required a high security clearance just to fiddle with. "Why do you both have those? They're supposed to be reserved for military use." His earlier suspicions of Gloria's motives resurfaced.

Gloria grimaced and looked at her device. "Um...well..." She shrugged.

"Never mind." He shook his head. "It's probably best I don't know." He'd get to the bottom of why she had that gear later.

Gloria nodded.

"See if she'll answer a call." Orin returned his attention to the scene outside the ship.

Gloria tried three times, but Veena didn't answer. "Maybe she doesn't have it with her."

Orin didn't come all this way to fail now. He needed to know which escape pod Veena was on, so he could follow. "The crew of the *Garden Princess* would ensure their passengers all had on spacesuits."

Gloria stared blankly at him.

"If she had it in her pocket, then had to put on her spacesuit..."

"Right. She wouldn't be able to answer then." Gloria scratched her head. "I can try to track the signal."

Orin watched pieces of debris drift by as he thought about Gloria's comms device. Those things were never available to any of the civilians on his code-breaking team—neither Gloria nor Veena had the security clearance to get them. So, where did they come from?

"Got it." Gloria flashed him a winning smile. "I've got a location. Let's hope Veena has the other device on her."

She swiped the location onto the main heads-up display on the windshield. A green circle with a triangle inside pointed them to a location deep within the debris field.

"Oh, shit. She's not in one of the escape pods." Orin's head started pounding a little bit harder until it felt like a spike was being driven into his skull.

"Remember the spacesuit," Gloria said.

"Huh?"

"You said she'd be in a spacesuit. So all we need to do is fly over there and pick her up."

"Yes." Orin's headache began to abate—there was hope. Angling *Buttercup's* nose towards the spot, they slowly accelerated. The debris field had spread out enough that passing through it wasn't nearly as hair-raising as before.

As they approached the location of the green triangle, he slowed to a crawl. He turned on the ship's searchlight and swung it back and forth as they approached. A glint caught his attention, and he brought *Buttercup* in close with their lights on full.

"Oh!" Gloria clamped a hand over her mouth.

Just outside their windshield floated another corpse—another man dressed in a shiny suit wearing a surprised expression on his face.

"He doesn't have a spacesuit." Orin frowned.

Gloria turned towards him. "You said they'd all put on their spacesuits. Now we've seen two people who didn't."

"Veena would follow the crew's instructions. I'm sure she's safe in a suit." He gritted his teeth together and marked the corpse's position. There wasn't time to retrieve it, but he could forward the position on to the rescuers.

For twenty minutes, they scanned the debris field, finding more trees floating through space, opulent furniture, and even fancy luggage trailing colourful clothes. Orin was grateful that they didn't find any more corpses. However, even with Gloria's makeshift tracking device, they hadn't found Veena yet. Tension coursed through him as he willed Veena to be found. She had to be out here somewhere.

"There." Gloria cut off his thoughts.

Orin focused the searchlight in the direction Gloria pointed. A human shape revolved amongst the ship pieces. He slowly exhaled. It had to be her. At as slow of a speed as he could, he maneuvered *Buttercup* towards the person.

As they got closer, the shape resolved into a person in a green *Garden Princess* space suit. For a moment, he thought it was two people. The first person was holding onto another suit, but there were no legs and arms. What was in the second suit?

As the searchlight bounced off the helmet's faceplate, the person waved.

Gloria bounced up in her seat and clapped her hands. "There she is!"

Chapter Thirty-Nine

The escape pod tumbled at an accelerating rate, making Hwicce grateful he hadn't found time to eat. He tried to make out the view outside the craft, but it alternated between the rocky expanse of the anchor world and the expanding field of debris at the foot of the gate's exit. Beads of sweat formed on his brow as nausea took hold.

"Can you stop this?" he shouted to Emiko. Upfront, she frantically worked at the pod's controls.

"Working on it," she shouted back.

Hwicce closed his eyes and let his helmet rest against the back of his seat—an action that made him feel worse. He tried to glance Baker's way, but that wasn't good either. A sour taste formed in his mouth as he overheated. His suit's fans were not helping. He swallowed.

"I've got bad news," Emiko said. "The anchor planet's gravity has us and is pulling us in."

Hwicce swallowed again. He wanted to mop the sweat off his face, but the helmet prevented that. It was getting more and more difficult to focus on the escape pod's peril. "Crap."

"We're losing altitude fast."

"Slingshot," Baker said.

Emiko twisted around. "What?"

But Hwicce understood what Baker meant. Any help would arrive too late; they needed to take action. "Speed us up, and we can slingshot around the planet."

"We only have enough fuel for one burn." Emiko sounded uncertain. "Any landing after that will be a crash landing."

"It's our best chance." Hwicce did his best to keep the sound of his own fear out of his tone. "Otherwise, we're going to crash on the anchor world."

Beside him, Baker grabbed on tighter to the armrests of her seat. "Just fucking do it!"

"Hang on," Emiko said.

A moment later, acceleration shoved Hwicce back into his seat. His head became too heavy to hold up, leaving him pinned against the headrest. The escape pod vibrated, and the thrusters groaned. His teeth rattled, forcing him to clench his jaw. After what felt like forever, the craft began to steady.

"How's it looking up there?" he called out to Emiko.

"Well..." She turned and looked at him, an awkward feat in her spacesuit. "I think we're going to miss the planet."

"Brilliant." Hwicce realized that his weight had reduced to that of almost no gravity. He let out a ragged exhale and closed his eyes.

"Oh shit," Emiko said a few minutes later.

Hwicce's eyes popped back open. "What's happening?"

"We're heading straight for the gate's entrance." Up front, she continued working the controls.

Why couldn't they get a break? Hwicce sighed and rotated his shoulders to see out his window. With every passing moment, the undulating aqua surface of the gate grew larger. Emiko was right—they were headed straight for it.

He shifted again to look at Emiko. "Is this escape pod rated for going through a gate?"

"Hell no." Emiko turned his way, her face pale behind the

clear surface of her helmet. "It'll rip us apart and spew us out in a million pieces."

"That doesn't sound good," he said, unbuckling his restraints.

"Stay the hell in your seat," Baker ordered from her seat across the aisle. "Sir."

He paused, frowned, then buckled himself back in. "You got a brilliant plan?"

"It's too late to do anything. We have no choice but to go through that gate," Emiko said.

Silence stretched out between the three of them. Emiko was right; they were just passengers now. Hwicce closed his eyes and tried to come up with options. If the three of them jumped ship—they'd still have enough momentum to end up passing through the gate. Or maybe they'd get lucky and the pod would hold together.

"Okay. How long until we go through?" He leaned his head back in his seat and tried to focus on the problem.

"We got fifteen seconds," Emiko said. "Or so." The craft shook and shimmied. "At least we're out of the debris field."

"How much fuel is left?"

"Just fumes."

The undulating surface of the gate was so close, it filled Hwicce's view. If he didn't know better, he would have thought it was an ocean's surface. He wracked his brain for facts about the gate system—unfortunately, humans knew little, and he knew less than that.

"What's the difference between a rated ship and an unrated one?" he asked. "Assuming both are spaceworthy."

"Hell if I know," Emiko said without looking his way.

He turned to Baker, and she shrugged.

The glistening interface between normal space and the world behind the gate loomed before them. Images of their escape pod being ripped apart flashed through his mind as a knot formed in his neck.

"Brace yourselves." He tried to think positive thoughts. "We'll get through this."

"You're fucking crazy," Baker said. "Sir."

The nose of the escape pod plunged in. Like a rising liquid, the interface passed through the craft as though they were flooding. Emiko vanished from view. Advancing through the cabin, the shimmering front continued. The first row of seats vanished beneath it, and it kept coming.

Hwicce held his breath as it reached him. A wave of ice raced along his skin as he passed through the interface—he'd never felt that when he'd gone through on other ships. But then, he'd never seen such an absolute divide between the gate and normal space on the inside of a hull before. Perhaps that's what being 'rated' for gate travel really meant. He shivered.

When he couldn't hold his breath any longer, he let out a long exhale and opened his eyes. He blinked a few times to make sense of what he saw.

Distorted now, the interior of the escape pod no longer followed the rules of physics he knew. Some parts were weirdly distended, while other parts appeared shrunk. Even though Baker was just over an arm's length away, she seemed to be across a void. Ahead, Emiko seemed to be twice her normal size.

Taking another deep breath to remain calm, Hwicce raised his hands. He held them still, yet his fingers kept twisting and bending in ways that defied what his joints should do.

With each breath, the air morphed. At first, it was more viscous, forcing him to gulp with every breath. Strangely, it tasted of cherries. A moment later, the air became cedar flavoured and so thin, he had to pant to get enough oxygen. But the escape pod remained in one piece.

He opened his mouth to speak, but his words came out as gibberish. Ahead, Emiko turned to face him. Through her faceplate, he could tell she was talking too, but all he could hear was a buzzing sound.

The buzzing sound increased to a painful level as the air seemed to get thicker and thicker. His vision started to narrow, and his thoughts seemed to slow. A worry that he might pass out drifted up, and for some reason, he found that funny.

The surrounding colours shifted—in one moment, shades of magenta dominated the inside of the pod, then it flipped to slime green, and everything around him seemed coated in fuzz.

In a flash, it was over. The world returned to normal.

"Whoa," Baker said. "That was not..." Her words trailed off.

Emiko turned around in her seat. "What you expected?"

"Hell no. That was like I'd eaten the wrong mushrooms." She gave both of them a slight smile. "But we made it."

Hwicce nodded, his mouth dry. "You two okay?"

"Yes, sir!" Baker sounded surprisingly happy.

"I'm good." Emiko turned back to the controls. "Well, shit."

"What?" He unbuckled his seatbelt, grateful Baker didn't chastise him this time, and headed forward.

"We got dumped out over one-hundred million klicks from the gate."

"No way." He sat down and confirmed her calculations—she was right.

Dead ahead, an orb girdled in a thick band of green filled their view, and it was approaching fast. Their course was taking them directly to a planet.

"So which delightful hell hole do we get to crash on?" Baker asked.

Emiko turned back to the escape pod's minimalist controls. "Looks like we're heading right for Smaragdos, only inhabited world in the Charlie System."

"The greenie homeworld?" Baker unbuckled and propelled herself forward until she was beside Emiko. "Well, that's somewhat better than drifting through space for all eternity." Her tone was flat.

"Smaragdos has an oxygenated atmosphere. Anywhere we

land, we'll be able to breathe without suits." Hwicce didn't dare mention that the plants and fungi covering the world weren't edible.

"Don't the greenies have very specific rules about visitors?" Baker leaned over Emiko's shoulder to get a better view.

"Yeah, we'll likely be arrested," Emiko said.

"Well, this just gets better and better." Baker stretched to her full height and let herself float back into the main part of the pod.

Hwicce sighed as he stared out the window. Smaragdos wasn't an ideal landing place, but the anchor planet was far behind them. Only the green-tinged one was within reach.

"How long until we arrive?" he asked.

"Um." Emiko turned back to her controls. "We picked up a lot of speed, so maybe eight hours."

Hwicce checked the atmosphere within the craft—there was plenty of air to breathe. He removed his helmet and took a deep breath. The air tasted fresh enough. Then he realized both Baker and Emiko were staring at him.

"What?"

"Just waiting to see if the air killed you, sir." Baker took off her helmet. "Seems okay."

Emiko removed her helmet as well. With a wide grin on her face, she stared at Hwicce. "I was sure going through the gate was going to kill us all."

"I just hope we gave those rich bastards on the cruise ship enough time to evacuate." Hwicce pulled himself closer to one of the port side windows and looked out.

"So, who brought the dice?"

"You can't play dice without gravity, silly," Emiko reminded Baker.

"Then what the fuck are we going to do?"

Chapter Forty

Veena felt like she'd been drifting in space for days—although there was no way it could have been that long. The spacesuit from the *Emerald Princess* fit perfectly, yet it lacked a diagnostic screen, so she had no idea how much oxygen she had. Nigel had told her, but she couldn't remember now.

Where was her rescue? She tightened her hands into fists and willed a knight in shining armour to appear and whisk her away. After a moment, she burst out laughing at her futile and ridiculous attempt. She forced her limbs to relax.

"Someone will come," she whispered.

The debris field around her created a festive show of light—almost as pretty as the meteor showers back on New Haven. Most of the smaller ship detritus reflected the light from the system's star, glinting and shimmering as they drifted outwards. The bigger pieces tumbled in chaotic patterns, but none appeared to be moving her way. She was safe for now.

"Alright, Veena, focus." She licked her lips as she tried to come up with something she could do.

First, she checked the safety line connecting her to the other spacesuit. She pulled it close and rotated it. Through the clear faceplate of the helmet, Click stared back at her. Their tentacles were wrapped around their body in an uncomfortable-looking contortion so they could fit into the helmet. They flashed lemon yellow, then sky blue. Veena had no idea what that meant—other than proof Click was alive.

Her nose itched as she tucked the other suit back under her arm. She wrinkled her nose and surveyed her surroundings. Every way she rotated, the debris field appeared the same.

"Now what?"

From behind a larger piece of painted hull plating, a bright light pointed her way. The source moved towards her in a deliberate way—it couldn't be a randomly floating hunk of debris. She tried to keep calm, but every ounce of her hoped the light meant rescue.

"Here! I'm here!" She raised her free arm and waved.

The light continued to approach, shining too bright for her to see the source. When it pulled up beside her, she saw it was a small survey vessel painted a jaunty yellow. She couldn't help smiling. She rotated Click so they could see the ship too.

At a slow pace, the ship maneuvered until its open airlock door was within reach. Taking that as an invitation, Veena grabbed hold of the door frame and pulled herself inside. After confirming the other suit was in too, she closed the door and cycled the air.

As soon as the light by the inside door flashed green, it swung open, and Gloria rushed through. Her grin ran almost from ear to ear.

At seeing her friend, Veena smiled so hard her face hurt. She rushed forward and gave Gloria a bear hug. Gloria laughed.

"Thank you for finding us...me." Veena pulled away and set the second suit down at her feet.

"What? Did you think I'd let you down in your time of need?"

"Of course not—"

"You can take off the helmet now," Gloria said, cutting her off.

Veena removed her helmet and filled her lungs. The air wasn't any fresher than her suit, and it left her with a faint charred aftertaste, but she could reach her face again. With a still gloved hand, she scratched her nose.

"Are you okay?"

Veena hugged her friend a second time. "I'm more than okay. How'd you find me?"

"Remember that comms device I gave you?"

Veena scratched her head as she glanced back at the second suit with Molly's backpack stashed inside. "Yeah."

"I wrote a tracking program, and we used it to find you."

"We?" Veena stepped through the airlock door and looked forward. Her breath caught in her throat.

Orin stood between the workshop/lab outside the airlock and what looked like living quarters further forward. He appeared as rumpled as ever, but his eyes were clear. His forehead wrinkled as he met Veena's gaze. He opened his mouth as if to say something, then closed it again.

Veena sharply inhaled and looked back to Gloria. Her heart was pounding now.

"Why is Orin here?"

Gloria shrugged. "It's his ship. I kinda forced him to give me a ride."

"I saw you on Jupiter Station." Veena turned towards her former boss. She didn't know what to think at finding out he was the knight in shining armour who'd rescued her. "You were following me."

"I...I didn't see you there, but yes, I was following you." He ran a hand over his face. "Taking Molly from you was wrong. I fought against it, but I could have done more." He stared down at his feet. "I want to help you get her back."

Veena's heart continued pounding as she glared at him—more accurately at the top of his balding head. "You knew they were going to take Molly before they did?"

"Yes."

Before Veena could speak, Gloria stepped between them. "Look, the three of us are going to work together to get Molly back."

Veena looked at her friend and let out a long breath. Part of her wanted to pummel him for allowing Molly to be taken, while another part accepted that he'd been caught up in this too. Could she trust Orin? She swallowed. At least she could count on Gloria. She nodded. "I need to get out of this suit."

Gloria smiled. "While you do that, I'm going to make some tea and Orin..." She glanced his way. "Is going to hang out in the cockpit."

He nodded and turned away.

"Thanks," she said.

"I'll put the water on." Gloria headed forward as well.

Alone at last, Veena went over and removed the helmet on the second suit. Click skittered out, swivelling their entire body to look around. They were nearly transparent now.

Nigel appeared. He stared at the wall, turned then stared at the airlock door. His brows pulled together as he scratched his head. "This is not the *Garden Princess*."

"No, the *Garden Princess* was destroyed." Veena removed the rest of her suit and jammed the nanites into the helmet.

"Pity." Nigel went to the outside door and peered through the window. "The *Garden Princess* was the only place I'd ever existed."

"You exist in my scroll now," she said as she checked the device. "Although, I think Click is the one transmitting you." She looked at Click, and they flushed pink.

"Right." Nigel glanced down at the octopus-like creature.

"I'll figure out a better solution for you."

He nodded, then frowned. "Now what do I do?"

"I think it's best if the two of you stay out of sight. I've got a gut feeling that this rescue isn't exactly what it seems."

"Is something nefarious going on?" Nigel peeked into the main part of the ship.

"My old boss is here, and he just told me he knew they were going to take Molly."

Nigel turned to face her. "That bastard!"

"Yeah." Veena ran a hand over her head, grateful she could. Nothing seemed to add up, but she couldn't figure out what the problem was.

Nigel glanced down at Click, then back to Veena. "We will remain incognito."

"You don't need to stay in the airlock; just stay out of sight."

Click flushed a pale blue then returned to their nearly transparent colouring.

Veena nodded to her strange companions before grabbing Molly's backpack and heading into the main living area of the ship. Gloria had already made the tea and was sitting at the table, waiting. She smiled as Veena entered and pushed a steaming mug her way.

After putting the backpack on the ground, Veena sat and took a sip.

"You must have had quite the ordeal."

"Yeah." Veena yawned—the day's excitement was catching up with her. "I guess I picked the wrong ship." She realized she hadn't picked the ship at all—Theo65 had.

Gloria glanced down at Molly's backpack. "Did you save your datapad?"

"Yeah, it's in there." Veena took another sip. "Along with the stuffy Molly can't sleep without."

"If I didn't say it before, I'll say it now. I'm so sorry Mol's out there alone."

"Thanks for being such a great friend." Veena glanced towards the closed door that must lead to the cockpit. "How did you end up with Orin?"

As Gloria told the story of how she pushed her way onto Orin's ship, Veena studied the space. For such an old ship, it was in good shape.

Something in Gloria's story caught her attention. "Wait. Orin said he just happened to be going to Indigo Station?"

Gloria nodded. "That's what he said."

"Did he say why?"

"No."

"That's a pretty big coincidence." Veena ran a hand over her head and down her ponytail.

Gloria leaned in closer. "Do you suspect him of something?"

Veena met Gloria's gaze. "His presence is just another piece of the puzzle. General Swa either organized or called the group that took Molly."

"It appears that way." Gloria finished her tea.

"Do you think Orin was part of that too?" Orin had always been kind to her, just a closet alcoholic trying to get by in the aftermath of the bombing of New Haven. But had that just been a front? Veena swallowed.

Gloria cocked her head. "It wouldn't surprise me."

"But why? I don't get what his motive for going above and beyond his normal role could be." Veena licked her lips. "He's always seemed so broken, so unfocused. Even if following me was Swa's priority, why would she send him?"

"He does seem to be barely holding it together," Gloria said. "But it could just be an act. Maybe, he's been playing us all along."

"Maybe...maybe the rumours about him losing his wife in the bombing of New Haven aren't true." Veena leaned back in her chair. "I've never even seen a picture of her."

"He's never mentioned her to me," Gloria said.

"What do we do now?" Veena glanced at the door to the cockpit.

Gloria stood and put the teacups in the sink. "You're the genius."

Veena felt heat flush across her face. "Cryptology was my

hobby before I got pulled into working for the military, that's all."

With a smile, Gloria returned to her seat. "You do have a knack for it. I trust you're just as good at coming up with plans."

Veena snorted. "If Orin is working for Swa, we might need to commandeer the ship."

"That could work. I can fly this beast if necessary."

Veena stared at her friend. "You've never mentioned anything about being a pilot."

Gloria shrugged.

The door to the cockpit slid open, and both women fell silent. Orin took one step into the common room. "Um, I think it's best I sleep on the bridge," he said, looking back and forth from Veena to Gloria. He licked his lips. "I just got to clear out my stuff."

Veena nodded and said nothing. Orin vanished into the sleeping cabin and, a few minutes later, re-emerged with a full-looking duffle bag and an armload of yellow bedding.

"I changed the sheets for you."

"Thank you," Veena said while looking at her hands.

Orin pursed his lips and paused as though ready to say more. But without a word, he went back into the cockpit, and the door slid shut behind him. As soon as he was out of sight, Veena slumped back in her seat and yawned.

"You should grab some shut-eye. We can come up with a cunning plan tomorrow," Gloria said as she leaned against the kitchen counter.

"Good idea." Veena stood and went to the sleeping cabin door; it slid open. She took a deep breath and turned to Gloria. "Thank you for coming for me. You've been a great friend."

Gloria grinned. "No problem. Us code-breakers gotta stick together. Now get your ass to bed."

Laughing, Veena entered the small cabin, and the door slid shut behind her. There was barely enough room to move between the two sets of bunk beds bolted to the walls. From the jumbled pile of stuff on the aft top bunk, Veena assumed that was the one Gloria had claimed.

Veena sat on the bottom forward bunk, removed her boots, and lay back. It wasn't the over-the-top luxury of her cabin on the *Garden Princess*, but it felt more honest somehow. She pulled the heavy curtain closed, separating her bunk from the rest of the space. Exhausted, she fell right to sleep.

Chapter Forty-One

As they plunged deeper into Smaragdos' atmosphere, the escape pod's vibrations increased in intensity. It got to the point Hwicce thought his teeth might vibrate out of his head. He grabbed onto the armrests and tried to force himself to breathe deeply. Emiko had everything under control; they would survive the landing.

His thoughts drifted to Veena. How she was out there somewhere, alone and trying to get Molly back. He needed to survive and pull his family back together. He closed his eyes as a wave of nausea swept over him. He was certain the pod was about to break apart. Veena may never know he died trying to get back to her.

"Hey, sir," Baker called from across the aisle.

He opened his eyes but didn't even try to turn her way—the helmet combined with the seatbelt would make that near impossible. "What?"

"Look outside. We're on fire." Her voice held excitement, not panic.

Hwicce groaned but shifted his torso slightly so he could see out the front windshield. Emiko blocked most of the view, but the red-orange glow as the outside of the escape pod heated in the atmosphere was unmistakable.

"How's the pod holding up?" he asked, swallowing back excess saliva. Vomiting in a spacesuit would be nasty.

"The heat shielding is doing its job." Emiko didn't turn away from the front windshield. "And the onboard computer has taken over for our landing."

"Is that a good idea?"

"This model of escape pod has a parachute," Emiko said. "The computer will know the optimum time to deploy it."

"Huh." Hwicce closed his eyes—that was the best news he'd had all day. "You could have told me that earlier."

"We're still going to hit the ground hard," she said. "But at a survivable speed."

"Isn't Smaragdos covered in moss?" Baker asked. "Like a big cushy pillow?"

Hwicce tried to dredge up what he knew about the greenie homeworld. In the initial terraforming attempt, old Earth plants hadn't thrived, which is why the colonists took the extreme step of engineering chlorophyll into their skin—that meant they could directly use energy from their star. They had made themselves smaller too in an attempt at efficiency. But neither fact told him anything about surviving a landing in a glorified lawn dart.

"I've seen pictures," Emiko said. "Moss is the best way to describe it, yet it doesn't give the native fauna justice. Forest of moss might be better."

"A thicker cushion on landing is better." Baker sounded like she was enjoying herself.

Hwicce groaned. "Are we going to land anywhere near a settlement?"

Emiko fell quiet for a moment, presumably looking at the craft's minimalist nav display. "Yeah, we should land within ten klicks of one of their bigger towns. But they aren't known to be welcoming to strangers."

"If they don't like strangers around, perhaps they'll be quick to help us get off-world." Hwicce squeezed his eyes closed as the vibrations increased again. He had to clench his jaw to keep his teeth from rattling.

"Chute opening in 5... 4... 3... 2... 1..."

The escape pod decelerated with a crack, and Hwicce found himself facing straight down. The nose of their little craft now pointed to the ground.

"What the hell happened?" Hwicce was tempted to release his seat belt, but he'd fall onto Emiko if he did.

"We're okay," Emiko said. "We're okay."

"Is it supposed to point straight down?"

"Not exactly. But our speed is...."

The escape pod hit the ground with a wet thunk. It didn't even bounce. Hwicce's legs and arms flopped around as the seatbelt kept him in his seat. They were stationary, and everything went silent except for the thundering beat of his heart.

He swallowed and took a deep breath. He wasn't dead.

Opening his eyes, he waited for his eyes to adjust to the dimness. Dark green shadows now replaced the bright light outside. Their escape pod had lost power.

As they were now taking all his weight, the shoulder straps of his seat belt were making it hard to breathe. His arms and legs dangled down, leaving him feeling like a discarded marionette. He tried to get a hold of the seat in front of him as he released his seat belt. His weight dragged him over, and he fell down into Emiko. He scrambled to the side as she moved the other direction.

"Emiko, are you okay?"

"Yeah," Emiko said. She rolled over and put her feet under herself. Baker extended her hand and pulled Emiko to her feet.

"Now what, sir?"

"Hell if I know." He closed his eyes, willing his nausea to go away.

"How's the air?" Emiko asked.

Baker pulled a portable air quality monitor out of a compartment under the nav panel. She activated it and waved it around. "Oxygen is a little high, but it's breathable."

"In that case, helmets off," Hwicce said.

He removed his helmet and put it on the front bulkhead. The air smelled moist but not like the overrun algae tanks back on the *Shimmer*. Instead, it was fresh and alive. It was also warm. He removed his entire suit. Baker and Emiko followed his lead, both now in their usual clothes.

Hwicce climbed up, using the backs of the seats until he was level with the hatch. Through the small round window in the hatch's centre, all he could see was green.

"Do you think opening that's a good idea?" Baker asked as she climbed up beside him.

"We can't stay here forever."

Hwicce glanced down at Emiko. She was at work packing all their food supplies into what he could best describe as sacks. "If you let a torrent of water in here, I don't want to be stuck starving on the surface." She pointed to the hatch. "Remember, the native fauna here isn't edible."

"Okay, we pack, and then I open the hatch."

Baker gave a curt nod, then climbed down to help Emiko. Hwicce followed.

Ten minutes later, they were ready. With his sack converted to an uncomfortable backpack and already on his back, Hwicce opened the hatch.

A thick wave of stench—decaying organic matter—wafted through the escape pod, but no flood of water. He reached out the hatch and touched a soft wall of green.

"Moss." Emiko let out a low whistle. "We're embedded in moss."

"Well...shit." Baker reached forward and grabbed a handful of the stuff. It came away easily in large chunks. "It's as cushy as I'd hoped."

"I guess we're digging our way out of here." Hwicce started grabbing the moss and pulling it inside the escape pod.

"That's going to take some time," Emiko said in a flat tone.

Hwicce ignored her. He took off his backpack and slung the straps over the open hatch. Then he crawled through as far as he could and continued creating a tunnel in the moss with his hands, angling up as best he could. With each handful of moss pulled into the escape pod, the tunnel reached further in. He put his weight on the moss below; it felt like an extra soft mattress, but it held him. He kept on digging—it was slow going.

Baker stuck her head out the hatch after what felt like half an hour. ""Hey, sir. Em's got some soup on. Why don't you take a break? I can keep the digging going."

Hwicce's hands, arms, and shoulders felt numb. He nodded in agreement and shimmied back into the escape pod. He climbed down to where Emiko had set up a portable stove and had a pot of simmering liquid on the go. She sat cross-legged on a mound of moss, stirring. She ladled out a mugful and handed it to him.

Up close, it smelled like enthusiastic mushroom soup, the kind made of more artificial chemicals than actual fungi. His stomach growled.

"Found it in the emergency rations." Emiko served herself a mug.

"Thanks." Hwicce took a deep glug of the soup, then he realized Emiko was staring at him. "What?"

"B said your—"

"B?" Hwicce raised an eyebrow.

"Baker. She doesn't like her first name."

"I had no idea she even had a first name." Hwicce looked over to the hatch. Chunks of moss regularly flew through; Baker was making excellent progress. "Sorry, you were asking something?"

"B said your wife is good with codes." She set her mug down.

Hwicce took a deep breath as images of Veena filled his head. "Good would be inaccurate. She's probably the best there is at it."

"Um." Emiko scratched her head, then hugged her arms around herself. "I..." Her words trailed off.

"Hey," he said in a soft tone. "I'll help you however I can."

Emiko nodded and licked her lips.

"Is there something you need?" Hwicce studied the small woman who'd become Baker's love interest—whether Baker had admitted it yet or not.

"I... there's...information..." Her words trailed off again as she stared down at her mug. In that moment, she appeared vulnerable and extremely young.

"You want Veena to hack into somewhere," finished Hwicce. "I'm sure she'd be willing to help. Where do you want to get into?"

"I was born on Indigo Station, but the records about my family were lost." She kept her gaze on the simmering pot of soup as she spoke.

"I've heard that Indigo Station has a rigid guild system." He took another long sip and emptied the mug. Without asking, Emiko filled it for him.

"Yeah. Without a family connection or money, it proved impossible to get a good job." Emiko met his gaze. "But really, all I want is to know my real last name and have the records to prove it."

"It's not Green?"

"I took that name when I left the station. But without proper records, the best job I could find was on the *Shimmer*. Boris never checked my credentials. I should have taken that as a red flag."

A huge mass of moss bounced out of the hatch and down into the cockpit.

"Hey guys, I'm at the surface," Baker shouted from some-where above.

Hwicce turned to Emiko. "I'm sure Veena will be happy to help you."

"Thank you," she said, then bit her lip.

"Until then, the three of us should stick together. We make a good team." He smiled at her as he downed his second mug of soup. "Let's go see what this world looks like."

Chapter Forty-Two

Veena stood at the bottom of the stairs inside the secret hangar back on the Rock with Major Zane at her side.

"Mom!" shrieked Molly.

Veena spun around until she spotted her girl being held by a woman dressed in grey. Dr. Greer and another woman, also in grey, stood beside her.

"Molly!"

Molly struggled with the woman who held her. "Mom! You found me." She twisted her arm out of the adult's grip and raced over to Veena.

"I'm here," Veena said as she knelt down to hug her daughter.

Thirty metres away, three guards emerged from a side room. They pointed their rifles at Veena as they advanced towards her. But Molly reached Veena first, and she wrapped her arms around the girl, lifting her.

"I thought you wouldn't come," Molly said as she squeezed Veena tightly.

"I will always come for you." Veena forced her voice to sound calm as she glanced around.

"She needs to come with us," Dr. Greer said as he approached. "Let her go, and everyone will be safe."

"No!"

A loud crunch pulled Veena from her dream, and immediately, she was wide awake. Her heart pounded as she debated if she'd really heard something or not. As she rubbed the sleep out of her eyes, the crunching sounded again—something was definitely not right. She rolled out of bed, barely avoiding getting tangled in her bunk's curtain. As she pushed herself up to her feet, she questioned every little sound.

The ship lurched. A split second later, gravity glitched just enough to confirm her suspicion something was wrong.

"Gloria?" Veena looked over at her friend's bunk—it was empty but rumpled as though Gloria had just gotten up. Maybe she'd heard the noise too and was already out investigating.

"Nigel?" she whispered.

"Yes, madam." He appeared next to her.

"Do you know what's going on?"

"Sadly no. I'm not connected to this ship." He froze. His pixels expanded slightly, then returned to his normal form. "There is another ship," Nigel said, but Veena knew it was Click.

"What ship?"

"It has weapons," they said. "I fear they will take me. I... don't want to go back."

"Can you stay hidden?" she asked.

"Will try." Nigel disintegrated into nothing.

Mentally telling herself to stay calm, Veena went up to the cockpit. Inside, Orin slept in the pilot's chair, and Gloria wasn't there. Outside, the debris field and anchor planet remained in view. Nothing on the consoles indicated another ship was in the area.

"Orin," Veena said, hoping he'd wake up without her having to shake him.

"Hmm." He ran a hand over his face. "What's going on?" He turned her way, the whites of his eyes glinting in the low light.

"I think there's a ship nearby."

Orin immediately perked up and started examining the sensor readings. "I don't see—"

In a burst of static, the comms system came to life, cutting Orin off. "Attention *Buttercup*. This is the battle cruiser *Defiant*." WhoeverWhoever was on the other end spoke in a tone that expected compliance.

Orin's eyes went wide. "Oh, shit!" The two of them shared a look, then Orin opened a comms line. "This is Orin Akton, captain of the *Buttercup*. How may I help you?"

"We are pulling your ship in now for inspection. Resistance will not be tolerated. Speak to the deck officer upon arrival." The line went dead.

"Well...crap." Veena frowned.

"I'm sorry." Orin turned to Veena, his forehead wrinkled. "I didn't see them coming."

Veena slid into the co-pilot's seat. "That's because they have stealth technology."

"You don't have the clearance to know about that," he said in a low tone.

"Nevertheless, I do."

"I'll chalk that up to unauthorized water cooler talk and leave it at that."

Veena forced a smile. "Sure."

"As fabulous as *Buttercup* is, it unarmed and slow. I can't fight them off or even evade them, and we're too close to hide."

"I get that."

As though a metal monstrosity was consuming them from behind, the starfield was blotted out by metal paneling. *Defiant's* hangar had swallowed them whole. They had no choice but to face what waited for them on the Protectorate's flagship.

"I have no idea why they are after us. I took leave that was owed me, and I reported that you took an extended leave as well. There's no crime in that." Orin glanced her way and frowned. "Besides, how would they even know you're here?"

"You didn't call them?" She leaned forward to get a better view of the *Defiant's* ribbed interior.

"Hell no," he said, shaking his head. "I meant what I said

about wanting to help. With the *Buttercup* and my contacts, I'd hoped we could get to Molly quicker."

"Truly?" Veena had to admit he'd gone well out of his way to try to help her if this were all true.

"Look, I only want to help, and I regret not stopping them from taking your girl in the first place. She needs you."

Veena bit her lip and looked away. What if Orin really was an ally? He seemed genuine. She took a deep breath as her anger towards him dissipated. Still, it was too much of a coincidence that the *Defiant* found them as soon as she came on board.

Orin returned his attention back to the controls and extended *Buttercup's* landing gear. A moment later, the ship shuttered as it came to rest on the deck. Through the windshield, they watched the massive hangar doors close, locking them inside the *Defiant*.

"They already have Molly. What more could they want?"

"I have no idea." Orin continued shutting down *Buttercup*. "Can you tell Gloria what's going on?"

Veena nodded and headed aft. The gravity felt subtly different, suggesting it now came from the battlecruiser.

"Oh!" Veena stopped on the other side of the cockpit door. "There you are."

Gloria stood in the kitchen impeccably clad in a yellow dress the same shade as *Buttercup*. She smiled when she saw Veena, then shrugged. "I couldn't sleep."

"I was about to wake you anyway. The *Defiant* has pulled us into their main hangar, and we don't know why."

Returning to the sleeping cabin, Veena picked up her datapad and stuffed it in the inside pocket of her jacket before putting on the garment.

The gun she'd acquired from Greer sat on the top of Molly's backpack. She let out a long exhale as she contemplated stashing it in her pocket for defence.

"That would be foolish," she whispered as she tucked the

weapon under her mattress. Grabbing her boots, she went back to the kitchen and took a seat.

"Do you know why our Navy has captured us?" she asked Gloria as she pulled on her boots.

"No." Gloria didn't meet Veena's gaze. "Did you ever decode that project? You know the one that got assigned to me after you left?"

"Sorry, I didn't have a chance." Veena raised an eyebrow. "Wait, do you think that they are here for you?"

"After you left, Swa called to me to her office to emphasize how important that code is." Gloria sighed and slumped down onto the bench seat beside the table.

"That's it, isn't it?"

"I suspect so."

"Why didn't you tell me they were pushing you so hard?"

"I... I..." Gloria's eyes glistened when she finally met Veena's gaze. "I didn't want to admit I couldn't do it."

Veena snorted and rested her elbows on the table. "I couldn't either—and I'd been working on decoding it for years."

Gloria perked up. "Years?"

"A group on the DeepNet approached me with it back when I was still at New Haven University."

"Well, shit. Now I don't feel nearly as dumb."

A loud pounding on the main airlock door reverberated through the ship.

Gloria stood and smoothed out the wrinkles in her dress. "Sounds like our welcome party is ready for us."

"I guess we should go see what they want," Veena said.

Chapter Forty-Three

Chunks of decomposing moss came away in his hands as Hwicce pulled himself out of the last metre of the moss tube. With a far-from-graceful maneuver, he emerged onto the surface like a worm on a rainy day.

As he lay on the spongy ground, he took a deep breath. Then another. The blast of humid air seemed to stick in his lungs, full of smells he couldn't identify. He almost gagged. After rolling onto his back, he stared up. Grey-green clouds covered the sky, creating a uniform blanket over the world. They hung low and ready to dump rain on them at any minute.

"Keep your ass moving. Sir." Baker emerged from the hole behind him. "You don't want me stepping all over you."

With a grunt, Hwicce pushed himself up to standing and took a few steps to get out of her way. Every time he put down a foot, he sunk in up to his ankle. Traversing the spongy ground was going to be a problem—every step they took would require more effort than usual.

Around them, fuzzy masses that couldn't quite be described as trees reached up. The tallest stood twice his height—the moss forest every guidebook of Smaragdos promised.

Without a view of the sky or even far-off topography, navigating through the forest would be a challenge. At least no one was injured, but he had no idea which way to walk to find the greenie settlement.

He turned to the escape pod. Only the aft third of it stuck out of the mossy substrate. They'd been lucky for such a soft landing—a hard surface would've flattened them.

"Check this shit out," Baker said from a few metres away.

Hwicce strode over, his boots making a squelching sound with each step. Baker crouched in front of a series of lemon yellow plants or maybe fungi—he'd never been good at exobiology. Each one stuck up from the ground, thinner at the base and expanding as it went up. At the top, shallow cups of about a hand's width in diameter flared out, each filled with a milky liquid. Baker tapped the side, and a slow-motion wave radiated across the surface.

Emiko walked up beside them. "Remember, we can't consume anything here."

"This is weird shit," Baker said to Emiko, then she shifted to Hwicce. "Sir."

"Do you know if things here are safe to touch?" He gestured to their surroundings.

"Don't know." Taking care not to look up, Emiko squatted down next to Baker. The two of them peered at the yellow plant.

"It's like this liquid is extra viscous—even with what I assume is endless rain." Baker shook the stalk again.

Under the green sky, Emiko's skin looked paler than usual. "It's probably best we wear gloves and avoid touching things."

The white liquid from the plant spilled over and covered Baker's left hand. "Ah shit."

Emiko acted fast and pulled out her water bottle. She poured it out over Baker's hand. "We gotta be careful here. I'm sure you'll be fine, but I don't want anything to happen to you."

"Right. We need gloves," said Hwicce.

The two women turned and stared at him. He swallowed, feeling like he'd interrupted something.

"Are there any gloves in the escape pod?" He glanced over at the hole leading back down to the pod. It had been a tight fit coming up.

Emiko kept her eyes lowered as she stood. "Yeah, I saw a bag of them. I'll go get them."

"You haven't look up at the sky once since we crawled up to the surface," Hwicce said.

Emiko shrugged as her cheeks flushed red.

"You said you grew up on a space station," Baker said as she stood.

"Yeah. Indigo Station."

"Have you ever been on an open planet before?" Hwicce tried to sound kind, but he needed to know his people's limitations.

Emiko glanced at Baker, then bit her lip. "No." Her shoulders heaved as she took a deep breath. "I didn't expect..." She pointed up without looking that way. "Such a big sky."

Hwicce looked up at the surging clouds. They seemed low enough he could reach up and touch them. Compared to other sky's he'd seen, this one didn't seem 'big' to him, but then he'd grown up under an open sky.

"I...I..."

Baker came forward and put a hand on Emiko's shoulder. Emiko covered it with one of her own hands.

"I know better, but without a roof, I feel like I could be sucked into space at any moment."

Hwicce nodded. "It's different being planetside."

"Yeah."

"We need to make a decision," he said. "We can wait in the escape pod and hope the greenies send out a rescue party. Or we can head out and find them." He fixed his gaze on Emiko. "If we leave, we'll most likely end up sleeping under the sky."

"We could send up a flare. Maybe the greenies would send

out a rescue party." Baker stayed next to Emiko as she spoke. "I'm sure they saw us streak across the sky like a damn shooting star."

Still keeping her eyes adverted from the sky, Emiko scratched the back of her head. "I'm not sure they'd go out of their way to help us. And I hate waiting for things to happen."

"So going to them is our best option." Hwicce tried to sound certain.

"At least they're pacifists," Baker said. "So, unlikely to shoot at us. And I bet there's a tarp somewhere in the wreck we could make a tent out of."

"Are you sure you'll be okay out in the open?"

"Yes," Emiko said, pulling herself up to her full height. Even though she still looked paler than usual, she seemed to be keeping it together.

"Good. Let's get our packs and whatever other gear we might need, then we'll set out." He slowly rotated, trying to find something different about the directions.

"Do you have any idea which way we should trek?"

"Nope," Hwicce admitted. "Is it too late to get some nav info from the escape pod?"

Baker went over and kicked the aft thruster on the pod. "This bucket of bolts is dead."

He glanced up at the pea-soup coloured sky and took a deep breath. Then he turned back to the others. "I'm open to suggestions on a course." Hwicce slowly turned around a second time. The environment was so uniform, he couldn't even tell what time of day it was. "We could walk forever out here."

"Start with the high ground," Baker said, pointing to the tail end of the escape pod. "But don't you dare fall off that thing. I don't want to end up pulling your ass out of some hole."

"Right." He jumped up on the pod's hull and made his way to the very top of the part that stuck out of the ground. From there, he could see over the moss forest. In one direction, the terrain sloped down with a gap in the foliage a hundred metres away. The opposite direction slopped up to what appeared to be a more open plateau.

"It seems we have two options." He looked down at the others and explained what he'd seen.

"Uphill," Emiko said. Beside her, Baker nodded.

"Going for the high ground makes sense." He climbed back down. "Let's get our gear and move out."

Chapter Forty-Four

Standing before the airlock door, Veena bit her lip and took a deep breath. The reality that they'd just been captured was overtaking her exhaustion. It was the middle of the night, and all she really wanted to do was to crawl back into her bunk and dream of happy days with Molly and Hwicce.

To her left, Gloria bounced on her toes. For once, her friend had little to say, leaving an uncomfortable silence.

Veena turned to her. "It'll be alright."

"Yeah," was all Gloria said without meeting Veena's gaze.

To her right, Orin stood as motionless as a statue, his face as tight as his fists balled at his side.

"There was no way we could've escaped them," Veena said as she put a hand on his shoulder.

"I should've stayed awake."

"It wouldn't have mattered."

"I..." His word trailed off, and he stared down at his feet. "Let's get this over with."

Veena took a step forward and stared through the little window in the centre of the door. "Well, there they are, patiently waiting." She turned and looked at the others. Neither of the other two met her gaze. "Let's go see what they want."

Veena pulled the door's leaver, and a click sounded from inside the mechanism. She swung the door open and latched it in place.

A testament to parallel lines and glossy whites, the battlecruiser hangar dwarfed *Buttercup*, making the old survey ship seem smaller than it was. On both sides of them, short-range fighters painted the same maroon as Hwicce's battle armour extended off in lines, each parked in a yellow box painted on the deck. Straight ahead, a bulbous window provided a distorted view of the control room. It bustled with activity, a sharp contrast to the stillness of the hangar.

She glanced down at their welcoming party of stern faces and armed soldiers as she extended *Buttercup's* staircase. Unable to think of a reason to delay any more, she stepped down to the deck.

Wearing rust-wine coloured battle armour, a group of soldiers stood in formation a short way off. They weren't pointing their weapons at her, but they appeared at the ready. Veena pulled herself up straight and turned to the unarmoured officer standing there.

"I need to confirm the identification of everyone on board," the officer said. The bobbles on her full dress uniform glinted in the hangar's bright light.

"Why have you detained us?" Veena asked in a neutral tone as Orin exited the ship and stood beside her.

"I'm the captain of this ship." Orin held his chin high as he gestured to the *Buttercup*. Its aged, yellow hull a sharp contrast to the pristine ships in the hangar. "There are only three of us on board."

The officer turned to him. "I need everyone's identification," she said, this time with more force. She held out a portable fingerprint scanner to Orin.

He frowned but put his thumb on the device.

"Orin Atkin." She read from her device. "It says here that

you have taken an extended leave from Rock 13-A5. Is that correct?"

"Yes," he said.

The officer turned to Veena and extended the device. Assuming she had no choice, Veena put her thumb on it.

"Veena Oswiu," the officer read with a frown. "Also on an extended leave from the same department."

Veena hid her surprise that her official record didn't include her escapades before leaving—or even a warrant for her arrest.

"That's correct," Veena answered as Gloria exited the ship and stopped on the other side of her.

The officer repeated the same procedure with Gloria before turning back to Orin. "We will search your ship." Her tone left no room for doubt.

"Go ahead." Orin stepped further away from the stairs.

Two unarmoured soldiers went inside while Veena did her best to keep her expression neutral. Click was in there. She had to trust the little alien could keep themselves hidden.

"Come with me." The officer turned and strode away towards a corridor leading off from the hangar.

After a quick glance to Orin, Veena ran a few paces to catch up with the officer. Orin and Gloria fell into step beside her just as they passed the air-tight doors at the hangar's bulkhead. On the other side, an empty corridor greeted them as though an order had been sent out to keep the ship's crew away.

Veena counted each turn the officer made as she took them further into the bowels of the *Defiant.* Hwicce had travelled on this ship. He'd tried to explain to her how like a maze the interior was. At the time, she'd assumed he'd exaggerated. As they made the seventh turn down yet another hallway, she realized how right he'd been.

Their eighth turn took them down a narrower corridor with doors lining each side. A plaque on each door started with a 'J' then three digits. Beyond that, there was no indication what was behind the doors.

At J-731, the officer stopped and put her thumb on the pad beside the door. It slid open, revealing a small room that was somewhere between a lounge and jail cell.

"Wait here," she said as she stood aside.

"Why are we here?" Veena asked.

The officer frowned at her. "An explanation will be provided once my soldiers finish searching your ship."

"But—" Veena's words were cut off as Orin grabbed her elbow and pulled her into the room.

"Captain Von's operating on someone else's orders," he said as the door slid shut behind them.

Veena turned to him. "You know her?"

"The *Defiant* visited the Rock a number of times." He shrugged. "So, I've met Von. She always comes off as rather harsh, and she's a huge stickler for the rules."

"What's she going to do with us?"

"We've done nothing wrong," Orin said. "Once they complete their search, they'll let us go."

Veena went to the door and hit the release button—the door didn't open. "No surprise." She frowned.

"They're not going to let us just wander around," Gloria said.

"I know, but I had to check." Veena shifted her gaze to Orin. "You sure they'll just let us go?"

Orin's forehead wrinkled once again as he shook his head. "No, I'm not sure at all."

"Now what?" Gloria flopped onto one of the sofas that lined the walls. "I could do with more shut-eye."

In response, Veena yawned. "I feel like I could sleep for a week."

Beside the door, a small kitchenette was built into the wall. A shiny carafe sat on the counter beside three mugs, each with the ship's crest etched into them. The crew of the *Defiant* had known exactly how many of them there were on *Buttercup*—a realization that didn't sit right with Veena.

She turned and looked at Orin and Gloria. Orin had taken a seat on the other sofa. Both of them seemed lost in their own thoughts. Veena bit her lip as she considered the possibility one of them had been in contact with the *Defiant*. That seemed impossible. Gloria had been a friend for years, and Orin had seemed so genuine when he'd explained why he'd come after here. Yet...

She filled two mugs with what turned out to be coffee and handed one to Gloria then Orin. After pouring one for herself, she took a seat.

"I went after Molly before they got her off the Rock. I'm surprised that I didn't get arrested as soon as they identified me."

"Just play it cool," Gloria said, holding her mug in both hands. "I'm sure they'll let us go."

"Hmmm." Orin set his mug down on the coffee table before crossing his arms over his chest. He scrunched up his face as though in deep thought. "If there was an arrest warrant for you, it should've come up. At the very least, you entered an area of the Rock you didn't have clearance to be in. Then you took off from the facility. I'm surprised there wasn't one."

"Yeah, me too." Veena took a sip. The coffee wasn't good—military coffee never was—but it was better than the mint tea on *Buttercup*. She slouched back into the sofa. "So why didn't they just arrest me?"

An hour later, after Veena had 132 sips of the bad coffee, three soldiers marched into the room without even bothering to knock. They stood at the soldiers' arrival.

Orin took a step towards them. "Surely you've done a full search of my ship by now, and I know there was nothing to find. So, when can we leave?"

The soldier with corporal's chevrons made a face like he'd

smelled something off. "We're not here to answer your questions."

"Then why are you here?" Veena asked.

He moved out of the way as the privates behind him came forward and dumped out a large bag he'd been carrying. Veena's eyes followed Molly's backpack as it tumbled out and onto the floor. Two other dull coloured bags fell out on top of it. Without a word, the soldiers retreated, and the door slid shut behind them.

Orin stared at the door. "Well, that was weird."

Veena ran her hand over her head and down her ponytail. "Since I left the Rock, everything has been weird."

Gloria said nothing, ignored her bag, and sat back down.

Veena picked up Mol's backpack and returned to the sofa. She checked the backpack's contents—all her stuff was there, including her datapad with the copied documents from Greer, Molly's bucket-o-stuff, and the stack of *Bubble and Click* comics. Even her green nanite dress was stuffed in the bottom.

She scratched her head and looked at Orin. "Why bring us our stuff?"

He picked up his own bag off the floor and sat down beside her. "I assume they went through everything." He unzipped his bag and started going through the contents. "They can't hold us without placing charges."

Just then, the door slid open, and Captain Von walked in. "Gloria Norton, please come with me," she said, her face as stern as before.

Gloria stood and looked at Veena and Orin. She shrugged, then turned and followed Von out of the room.

Veena let out a long exhale. "Something weird is going on."

Orin pursed his lips together before looking at her. "Gloria said the two of you were traveling to Indigo Station."

"She helped me get off the Rock. Then, she found me again on Jupiter Station, but I lost track of her in the crowd." Veena pulled out Molly's Click stuffy and stroked its well-worn face.

She longed to hug Mol so much, tears started to form. She counted her breaths in an effort to stay calm.

"I meant what I said earlier," Orin said after a long silence. "I intend to help you get Molly back."

She glanced up at him. His earnest expression made her want to believe him. Maybe she could. She wiped a tear away. Next, she pulled out Molly's bucket-o-stuff.

"Hey, I just got one of those for my nephews." Orin took the bucket into his hands. "I hear they're a great toy." He opened the lid and looked inside.

"Yeah." Veena took another deep breath. "Molly loves making it form little animals. She has programmed quite a menagerie."

Orin handed the bucket back to her. Veena gazed inside, picturing the chaos Molly made with the animals. Little rhinos running across their floor to flocks of bats gliding from bed to bed. She sniffed, then took out a ball of nanites as big as her palm.

She longed to see the animals again—if she released the nanites, they'd go through the last sequence Mol had programmed. Telling herself she'd have time later, she shoved the handful of nanites into her pocket.

"I kinda wasn't thinking straight when I packed." Veena put the bucket-o-stuff back in the bag. Inside, her hand brushed up against the comms device Gloria had given her—the kind she shouldn't have been able to get her hands on as a civilian cryptographer.

"What?" Orin asked, bringing Veena's focus back to the moment.

"This." She held it up for Orin to see.

He let out a low whistle. "I'd forgotten the two of you had those. I'm surprised Von didn't have them confiscated. Do you know where Gloria got them?"

"I didn't ask." Frowning, Veena turned it over in her hand. Occam's razor told her that the simplest solution was probably the right one. What if Gloria simply had access to them? That would mean Gloria was more than a cryptographer.

"We used it to find you in the debris field."

Veena's mind raced as she turned the comms device on. What if it was Gloria's job to keep tabs on her?

"I have a suspicion," she said as she picked up her datapad and connected the two devices.

"You won't be able to do that," Orin said.

"I know." She looked back down to her datapad and used a chunk of DeepNet code she'd been keeping on a secret memory partition to break into the comms device. She let out a long exhale when the two devices synced.

Orin shifted closer to her so he could see the screen as well. "You got in."

"This one is only linked to Gloria's. I wonder...." Veena messaged Gloria.

A beep sounded from Gloria's bag—the other device. Orin retrieved it and handed it to her. He sat beside her and watched her work.

"I had no idea your skills extended to this kind of thing," he said in a whisper as though the room might be listening—which could very well be the case.

"I doubt putting hacking on my resume would be wise." She broke into Gloria's device the same way she'd hacked her own. Unlike her device, Gloria's was not limited—she could call anywhere.

Orin pursed his lips together. "I should tell you that Swa knows about your skills."

Veena shrugged as she brought up a list of Gloria's past calls.

Scratching his head, Orin stared at the list. "She's been regularly calling someone."

"She made a call just before you picked me up." Veena put her finger under the timestamp of the last call; her finger trembled as the implication hit her. "Gloria made a call moments before *Defiant* reeled us in."

"She betrayed us." Orin's tone was flat. "I'd had my suspicions about her. T should have--"

Just then, the door opened, cutting Orin off. Von entered—without Gloria.

"Dr. Oswiu, come with me."

Veena glanced at Orin and bit her lip. He frowned but said nothing. What could he say? He was in as deep as her, and neither of them could command anyone here. Gloria had sold them out.

In what felt like slow motion, Veena handed her datapad to Orin and stood. She felt sick to her stomach. Her friend had betrayed them. Gloria pretended to be helping, pretended to care... Veena swallowed and met Von's gaze.

"Let's go."

She followed Captain Von from the room towards whatever Gloria had set her up for.

Chapter Forty-Five

Drenched in sweat, Hwicce did his best to mop the moisture from his face. Now that they'd been on the ground a few hours, the humid air tasted like greenie moss liqueur—pungent and overwhelmingly earthy. He glanced up at the sky for the millionth time; it remained cloaked in uniformly grey-green clouds.

He couldn't help but let out a sigh. Trudging through the moss and fungi forest took more effort than he'd expected. With each step, his boot sunk into the moist substrate and forced him to pull it out again. The squelch with each footfall grated on him—and there was nowhere dry to sit and rest for a minute.

Traversing Smaragdos was proving to be a difficult slog, but what choice did they have? He put his head down and continued on.

"This fucking sucks," Baker muttered behind him. If she complained, it had to be bad.

He stopped and let the two women catch up. Baker's face glistened with sweat while Emiko's shone red with exertion—they both looked exhausted. "I'm out of brilliant ideas." He frowned. "If we can find a dry patch, we could put down the tarp and take a break."

"We're almost to the high ground." Emiko's positivity was clearly forced. "I'm sure of it."

Hwicce slowly turned. The fuzzy analogues of trees blocked out any view, and the sky remained as unvarying as ever. With the soft ground and thick vegetation, he couldn't tell if they were slogging up or down.

"Right then," he said. "We best keep going."

"As an aside, are there any predators here?" Baker asked. "Like big-ass bugs or dinosaurs?"

"Just bacteria." Emiko continued past them, heading towards one of the many fungal formations—this one included thin white pillars topped with hand-sized translucent red domes.

Baker ran a few paces and caught up with Emiko as she reached the fungus. "They might digest me faster than a pride of lions."

Emiko snorted as she gave the fungi a wide berth. "Mythical beasts can't hurt us."

With another sigh, Hwicce followed.

Just when he'd had enough of the mucky terrain, the saturated ground gave way to lichen-coated rock punctuated with occasional stands of moss. The upward slope became much more pronounced. Emiko was right—they'd reached the high ground. Walking on it was a delight. If the rocky terrain continued, they'd cover much more ground.

After another ten minutes of walking, the 'trees' shrunk in size enough they could see over them. In the distance, the ground only rose another ten metres or so. Then the plateau extended as far as they could see. Here and there, more vividly coloured fungi formations reached upwards, some twice their height.

Taking care not to step on it, Baker stopped to study a pink and green fungus that spread across the rock like an abstract shag carpet. "There's some weird shit on this world."

"At least it's easier to walk on firm ground." Hwicce trudged on towards the summit. The two women followed.

Few patches of rock remained bare—where there wasn't moss, fractal patterns of lichens created a low carpet regularly punctuated by the weird fungal structures. Hwicce continued on, telling himself this had to be the right direction. It made sense that a human settlement would be on solid ground.

At the summit, they stopped and ate a ration bar each. As Baker and Emiko relaxed on an extra fluffy patch of moss whispering into each other's ears, Hwicce surveyed the landscape. The moss forest extended in all directions until it met the low-hanging clouds. Occasional brightly coloured spires of fungi jutted up from the blanket of olive greens.

"Wait, there." He pointed to a variance in the landscape a kilometre in the distance. Baker and Emiko jumped to their feet and rushed to his side. "Those brown domes could be houses."

Baker nodded. "Greenies live in round homes."

Emiko slung her backpack back over her shoulders. "Let's go see." She set off toward the brown domes. Hwicce and Emiko followed.

They soon encountered the squelchy ground again, slowing them down. It took them two hours to walk the kilometre. By the time they could see the domes rising above the moss trees, twilight had begun devouring the light.

Hwicce forged ahead through the final thicket of moss. As he emerged on the other side, he could finally tell what the domes were. He stopped in his tracks and hung his head. The domes were just mushrooms caps—not a village.

"Aw, crap." Baker stopped beside him. "Hours of walking and this is all we get?"

To make matters worse, the clouds finally released the moisture. A torrent of rain pattered down.

"At least they're shelter," Emiko said as she ran for the nearest one. Hwicce and Baker followed.

As the darkness became complete, the three of them sat with their backs against the mushroom's stalk. Emiko was right, the fungus kept the rain off them, and fortunately, it wasn't cold. But the rain didn't let up, saturating the ground to the point that pools of water formed, submerging the moss. Hwicce stared out at the growing puddles, grateful the mushroom had sprouted out of a mound slightly higher than the surroundings.

"I'm starving." Baker rubbed a hand on her stomach. "Wish there was a taco stand nearby."

"Extra spicy crickets?" Emiko leaned closer to Baker.

"With a good dollop of hot sauce on top."

Hwicce's stomach started to grumble—their rationed protein bars had barely dented his hunger. "Are you sure we can't eat the vegetation?"

"I'm sure," Emiko said. "Why would the greenies have taken such a drastic measure of altering their genetics if they could just go into the woods and harvest a salad?"

Hwicce leaned his head back against the mushroom stalk. "Right."

"But on the plus side, if we die out here, nothing will feed on us. We'd give the bacteria around here quite the tummy ache."

"On that note, how'd we miss the village?" Hwicce scratched his head. "We should have seen it from the high ground."

Baker rubbed her hands together. "Greenies are secretive. Maybe their village is hidden away somewhere nearby."

"There could be lights." Emiko pushed herself up to her feet and stepped out into the rain. The mushroom they'd chosen as shelter sat at the edge of the patch, a few metres away from a drop-off.

"See anything?" Baker asked.

Hwicce leaned forward. Maybe Emiko was on to something. He stood and pulled out his knife. "We need to get higher to see any lights."

Baker stared up at him. "You want to go back to the high ground?"

"Nah, I suspect we'd just end up spending the night wadding through soaked moss." He stepped out into the rain and stared up at the mushroom cap. Big drops of water splashed onto his face. "But I bet up there would give me a better view."

"You think it will hold you?" Baker stood by his side.

"We got to try something." He reached up and could just touch the edge of the cap. "I'll need you to give me a boost."

Going into a crouch, Baker laced her fingers together to make a foothold. "I'm ready when you are."

With his knife in his right hand, Hwicce placed a foot on Baker's hands and his left hand on her shoulder. She stood, lifting him up. He stabbed his knife into the mushroom as high up as he could reach, keeping the blade parallel to the edge. With both hands, he grabbed onto the handle and hauled himself up.

Near the edge, the mushroom cap was almost flat and textured enough to provide some grip. He rolled to his side, and the cap dipped under his weight. Holding his breath, he crawled towards the centre based on the assumption the cap would be stronger there.

At the top, he took a deep breath just as the intensity of the rain increased. Water-soaked through his clothes. The sooner they could get off this planet, the better.

He stood. The dark landscape extended out, combining with the sky into obscurity. To make matters worse, the relentless precipitation made it difficult to see.

"You okay up there, sir?" Baker's voice came up from the darkness.

"Yeah." A gust deposited foul-tasting rain into his mouth, he spat it out. "I'm done with this weather-bitten world."

"See the village?"

Taking his time, he rotated and scanned their surroundings. Part of him tried to will the village's lights into view—but it didn't work. His limbs felt heavier as he concluded there was nothing to see. It might have been a mistake to leave the escape pod. At least there, they could've closed the hatch and stayed dry. Plus, what if the greenies had found it already?

He sighed and stepped toward the edge. Something beneath him popped, and the mushroom cap tilted.

"Hey, sir, I think you should get down from there," Baker said from somewhere below.

He opened his mouth to respond just as the stalk gave way. The mushroom cap bent sideways. Scrambling, he tried to get his footing. The stalk below made a ripping sound. Before he could jump clear, he and the cap fell.

At first, he landed on a bed of moss. The ground beneath him was soft, and for a split second, he thought everything would be okay. Then the top layer of the moss started sliding, taking him down the slope.

"Sir!" Baker shouted from somewhere above him now.

He flailed around, trying to find something to grab on to, but there was nothing. He was a passenger now.

The slope steepened, and the landslide of moss accelerated. He tumbled faster and faster. His right shoulder smacked against the slick rock. Twisting, he tried to grab on. His fingers dug in, and his motion stopped. Panting, he pulled himself up to a kneeling position and looked up the way he'd come.

The mushroom cap hit him mid-chest. With a whoosh, it pushed the air out of him, and he lost his grip. The ground beneath him gave way, and he fell into darkness.

With a jarring impact, he hit water. His body plunged deep down, and in the darkness, he couldn't determine which way was up. He gulped down water that tasted like over-brewed tea before he could stop himself. Keeping his eyes open, he used his hands and feet to propel himself forward.

In the distance, he thought he saw a dim light. Even though his body screamed for more oxygen, he kicked with all the power he could muster towards the light. It had to be the surface. His time was running out—only his army training kept his welling panic at bay. If he died here, Veena would never know what happened to him.

He kicked again and propelled himself headfirst into a stone wall. A hexagonal pattern on the wall emitted a faint glow; it wasn't the surface. His vision began narrowing. He needed air now.

As the sound of his heartbeat thrashed in his ears, he pushed off from the glowing wall. Like a torpedo, he charged through the water in a direction he hoped was up.

Water began surging past him, pulling him in another direction. He tried to swim against the flow, but his energy was gone. The water took him, and his world went dark.

Chapter Forty-Six

While suppressing her mounting fear, Veena followed Captain Von through another series of gleaming hallways. In silence, they passed door after door—all closed with cryptic numeric plaques to identify the rooms beyond. A confusing maze didn't start to describe the *Defiant's* layout. Veena didn't bother asking her escort where they were going, as Von's rigid stance suggested obedience was the only option.

Everyone they passed wore a uniform, and every one of them stopped what they were doing and acknowledged their captain as they passed. Veena recognized more fear than respect in the sailors' and soldiers' gaze. She swallowed, staying one pace behind Von.

Finally, they stopped before a set of glossy double doors. As they whooshed open, Von gestured Veena through. Her breathing accelerated as she stepped inside.

At first, all Veena saw were more gleaming surfaces and sharp lines in tune with the rest of the ship. Before her, a monolith of a desk sat empty. The only seat in the room was a white and chrome one behind the desk. Behind it extended a wall of floor-to-ceiling windows exposing the darkness of space beyond.

"Your husband served on this ship," a familiar voice said.

Veena touched her hand to her throat as General Swa emerged from a side door. The indigo of Swa's dress uniform shone vividly under the bright lights, the rich colour a perfect foil to the glinting gold embellishments. The sharp click of her boots echoed off the hard surfaces of the room as she marched past Veena and sat behind her desk.

She shivered as she tried to reason why Swa had called her in. What game was Swa playing?

"The same husband who gave up his commission to run off with one of his subordinates."

Veena said nothing as Swa glared at her. Swa's words were laced with manipulation, and Veena wasn't going to fall for it. She still didn't know why Hwicce had vanished with a subordinate, but he would explain himself. She pulled herself up to her full height. She didn't need to accept Swa's innuendo—her relationship with Hwicce was none of that woman's business.

"You made a terrible choice with that one." Swa smirked. "Then you walked off the job." She snapped her fingers. "Just like that, you're unemployed and all alone."

"Where's Molly?" Veena stared into Swa's eyes and gritted her teeth. She was done playing Swa's game.

"She's safe." Swa leaned back in her chair. "We took her for her own good."

"You kidnapped her." Veena marched forward and put both hands on Swa's desk. "I demand you return her to me."

"Hmm." Swa rotated to the bank of windows and stared out at the view beyond. "Here's the thing." She paused for effect. "That girl has a genetic defect that could destroy us…or be put to good use. My people are making sure that she puts it to good use."

Heat rose in Veena's body, and her heart began hammering in tune with her anger. Swa just justified kidnapping her child by suggesting Molly was a tool instead of a little girl—a little girl who needed her mother. She stood tall again and clenched her fists at her sides. Nothing would stop her from getting Molly back.

"But..." Swa turned back and made eye contact. "There is a way to get the two of you back together. But first, you need to do something for me."

Veena crossed her arms over her chest. "And what's that?"

"You were given some unique text to decode just before leaving Rock 13-A5."

"Yes." Why everyone kept asking her to work on that code? What were they expecting it to be? Where did it come from? Even Gloria... She was sick of everyone asking her about it. What good would understanding that ancient alien text be? Her mind went to Click—clearly, the aliens were still around.

"If you decode it, I'll make sure we reunite you and your daughter." Swa stood and came around her desk, stopping next to Veena.

For a split second, Veena contemplated punching Swa. But other than a moment of satisfaction, that kind of aggression would get her no closer to Molly. She took a deep breath and played along.

"Really?"

Swa leaned against her desk. "My superiors are against it, but I could arrange it."

Veena raised an eyebrow. She didn't trust General Swa one bit. But she'd decode that text—then she'd understand what everyone was fussing was about. And it might provide her with leverage. In that moment, a plan started coming together in her mind.

"I'll need Orin's help with the decoding work."

"Fine." Swa walked back around her desk as though their conversation was over.

"I also need something in writing that you'll keep up your end of our bargain." Veena remained certain that Swa was playing her, but now she had a plan of her own and needed to buy some time. She put her hand on the blob of nanites in her pocket—Molly would get her toy back soon.

"I'll have my assistant draft something up," Swa said with a dismissive nod. "Now Captain Von will show you back to your room." With Swa's words, the doors opened, and Von entered wearing her usual scowl.

Veena followed Von back through the maze of corridors to the room she'd been in before. Orin stood and faced the door as soon as it opened. Veena stepped in, and the door slid shut behind her. Captain Von stayed outside.

"We're being played," Veena said as she walked to where Molly's backpack sat on the couch and rummaged inside.

She pulled out one of the *Bubble and Click* comics and flipped to a mostly white page. With Molly's glitter pen, she wrote. Orin came closer to look at the page.

I'm sure they are monitoring us.

"General Swa is here," she said aloud.

Orin nodded. "Really? She must have moved up in the hierarchy. She always seemed the ambitious type."

"She promised she'd reunite me with Molly if I decoded a message," Veena said. "The one you gave me just before I left."

"I remember that one. None of our normal algorithms could make any sense of it." Orin sat.

Veena took a seat beside him and wrote. *Gloria kept pushing me to work on it—I should have suspected her of being a spy.* "I have a couple of ideas. Maybe we could work on them together."

"I agree," he said, pointing to Veena's words. "Now let's look at this code from another angle."

Veena picked up her datapad and brought up the code. "I can arrange the symbols into groups of six." She slipped to the next screen where she'd already done that. "It's almost as if these groups are just one symbol rotated in six different directions."

"Interesting." Orin bent down over Veena's screen. "How do we get out of here?" he whispered and pointed to a cluster of symbols.

The lights in the room glitched, strobing for a moment, then went out. Emergency lights came on, casting the space in a dim glow.

"Did something happen to the ship?" Orin rubbed his chin and gazed up at the light fixtures above.

Veena cocked her head. "I don't—"

In a cascade of coalescing pinpricks of light, Nigel materialized in the middle of the room. His back faced them, and he now wore a ship officer's uniform.

"Hello?" Nigel's voice warbled. He slowly turned around and grinned when he saw Veena. "Ah ha! There you are."

Orin jumped to his feet and approached the hologram. "Who—"

Veena stood and put a hand on Orin's arm. "Don't worry about him. He's the AI steward I brought with me when I escaped the *Garden Princess*."

"You saved a hunk of code?" Orin turned to look at her. "While the ship you were on disintegrated around you?"

"And that's not all of it," she said, then she addressed Nigel. "Click shut down the cameras and microphones in here, right?"

"That's affirmative. My tentacled friend has proven to be an excellent hacker. They now have control of this ship."

"Click?" Orin raised an eyebrow and held up one of the *Bubble and Click* comics.

Veena nodded. "That pretty much explains it."

Orin's eyebrows pulled together as he continued to stare.

"I'll explain when we get back to the ship." Veena turned to Nigel. "Nigel, what's the escape plan?"

"Click has asked me to guide the three of you." Nigel looked around. "Where is your other companion?"

Just the thought of Gloria's betrayal made heat rise in her chest. "Turns out she's the one who called the battlecruiser. So we'll be leaving her behind."

"Right-o." Nigel adjusted his uniform. "Click says we should be on our way."

Veena packed Molly's backpack, cramming the bucket-o-stuff on the top. She slung it over her shoulders. Orin did the same with his bag.

"This is getting weird. I trust you'll provide a detailed explanation when we get back on the *Buttercup*," he said, keeping his gaze fixed on the hologram.

"I'll tell you everything. I promise." They followed Nigel out into the hall, leaving the military comms devices on the sofa.

Chapter Forty-Seven

Just as Veena stepped into the corridor, a group of the ship's crew with engineer markings on their uniforms raced by. She jumped out of the way and bit her lip.

"Oh dear," Nigel said beside her.

"What?"

His eyes were wide when he met her gaze. "One of the engineers went right through me."

"They seemed focused," Orin said, coming up behind them. "Probably on dealing with the lights—neither Swa nor Von is going to be kind about that."

"Let's get moving," Veena said. "Nigel, you need to take the lead."

"Right-o." Nigel adjusted his uniform and marched in the opposite direction than the engineers. Although his programmed gait was perfect for a Victorian gentleman, it seemed very wrong for an officer. Hoping no one noticed, Veena fell into step a pace behind him. Orin followed close behind.

After turning down three different corridors, Orin asked, "You know where we are going, right?"

"Yes, sir. Click has mapped a path with the least number of probable interactions with the *Defiant's* crew." Nigel turned another corner, and they came face-to-face with a group of armoured soldiers.

"Stop," the first one said.

Veena froze, and Orin walked into her.

The soldier pointed at them. "Where are you taking the civilians?"

"I've been ordered to return them to the hangar bay," Nigel said, and Veena was grateful he didn't glitch. As long as the soldier didn't try to touch the holographic projection of the AI, they might be okay.

"You can't go this way. There's been a report of excess carbon monoxide in the cabins between bulkheads A-115 and A-116. Take them down the port side corridor instead."

"Right," Nigel said, turning and looking at Veena and Orin. "Follow me."

They headed back the way they'd come. As soon as they were out of earshot of the soldiers, Veena said, "Did Click arrange for the carbon monoxide sensors to go off?"

"Maybe?" Nigel stopped and rubbed his hands together. He glitched, and his fingers passed through each other. "Click's mind... it's...not what I expected."

"Okay, focus, Nigel. Are you in contact with them now?" Veena met his gaze.

The overhead lights flicked on to their normal intensity.

"Oh, shit." Orin stared up. "This doesn't look good."

Veena looked both ways down the corridor they were in. Other than the numbers on the doors, nothing indicated where they were.

"Click is gone." Nigel's whole body glitched. "The Overwatch AI's are sweeping the system."

"Get your code back to *Buttercup*. We'll be along shortly." Veena bit her lip.

Nigel winked out, leaving her and Orin alone somewhere in the maze of the battlecruiser.

Orin went to the nearest door and hit the release button.

When it didn't open, he sighed. "Without a military escort, people are going to question where we're going."

"Yeah." Veena ran a hand over her head and grabbed her ponytail. She tried the door on her side of the hall. That one didn't open either.

The overhead lights flickered for a moment, then a door up ahead slid open.

"Did your alien friend do that?"

While running her palms down the side of her pants, Veena approached the open door. "I don't know. But I hope so."

Inside was an enlisted crew cabin with eight bunks built into the walls on either side of the door. Between the bunks were lockers. Holding her breath, Veena took a pace in and looked around. No one was there. The only face was her own reflected back from the mirror on the far wall.

"Uniforms," Orin said as he entered the space behind her. "Let's find some uniforms."

"Right." Veena went to the nearest locker and opened it up. The screen inside the door activated, showing two smiling women on a beach. A little boy ran between them. Veena swallowed. Uniforms were military property; she wasn't actually stealing from one of the women in the footage.

After dropping Molly's backpack and her jacket onto the deck, she pulled out the indigo corporal's uniform and studied it. Engineering department regalia glinted in the cabin's light. With a sigh, she sat on the lower bunk and took off her boots. Then she pulled off her pants and started putting on the stolen uniform.

"These are all women's uniforms," Orin said as he finished looking in the last locker. "I'm going to have to stay dressed as I am."

"Okay, then I'll be escorting you. If we're stopped, I'll do the talking." After buttoning up the uniform jacket, she ran her hands down the fabric. "These are real fabric without nanites. Wait, Mol's nanites." She picked up her jacket, pulled the blob from the bucket-o-stuff, and stashed it in the front pocket of her uniform.

She stepped over to the full-length mirror, and her breath caught in her throat. She hardly recognized herself.

"You look like a soldier," said Orin.

Veena twisted her ponytail into a bun and smoothed down the stray hairs. The uniform was a bit baggy, but Orin was right —she now looked like she belonged on the *Defiant*.

"We need to keep moving." She shoved Molly's backpack and her clothing into a duffle bag. Orin added his bag, then slung the duffle over his shoulder.

"Lead the way, Corporal."

Veena pulled herself up tall then stepped out into the hallway. She turned right and started walking. Around the next corner, they came out into a larger corridor. A pair of engineers were at work on an open circuitry panel across the way. She steadied herself and marched over.

"I just joined the ship," she said.

One of the engineers stopped worked in stared at her.

"I don't think we've met," he said. "What department are you in?"

"Sorry, but I'm in a bit of a rush. I was told to report to the hangar. Can you point me in the right direction?"

He frowned, his eyes moving from her to Orin, then back to her. "Who's your supervisor?"

A breath caught in Veena's throat as her mind began to race. "Look, Admiral Swa wants me in the hangar to inspect the confiscated survey vessel. I don't want to get on her bad side, and I'm sure you don't as well. Which way do I go?"

"Hmm...yeah, we don't want to piss off Swa. Head that way." He pointed down the corridor. "Turn to starboard before the engine rooms."

"Thanks."

Holding her back straight, Veena started walking in the direction he indicated. Orin fell into step beside her.

"Hey," the engineer said behind them.

Veena and Orin turned.

"Why don't you have a toolkit with you?"

"Umm...well... that's a long story..." Veena swallowed. "But I gotta go." She turned and headed towards the hangar bay. A shiver curled up her spine. It was almost as though she could feel the engineer's eyes on her back.

Orin leaned towards her. "I think we're okay."

Veena let out a long exhale. "Cloak and daggers shit was never my thing. I was afraid he'd see me trembling."

"You did better than I would."

A set of double doors led off the corridor up ahead. Veena realized she even recognized where she was—just outside the hangar.

"We're here."

The doors slid open, and a group of armoured soldiers marched into the corridor. The first one pointed at them.

"Dr. Oswiu, stop right there." Augmented by her armour, the soldier's voice boomed out overly loud.

"Oh no!" Orin's voice was barely a whisper.

The two of them froze. As her heart began to race, Veena glanced around at the unlabelled doors lining the other side of the corridor. Between them and the soldiers, a door slid open, and the scent of frying onions wafted out.

"This way." Veena grabbed Orin's hand and dragged him through the door.

Inside was a kitchen full of cooks preparing the next meal. They looked up from the pots and cutting boards as Veena and Orin sprinted past.

"This way, madam," Nigel said as he materialized in front of her. He turned into the main part of the cafeteria.

"Fire! Fire! Fire!" one of the cooks shouted behind them.

Veena turned as dark smoke billowed out of an overhead vent. The acrid smoke started spreading out. "Oh, shit! Did Click do this?"

"Stop! I'm authorized to shoot," a soldier behind them shouted.

"Come on." This time Orin grabbed her hand and dragged her after Nigel.

The three of them wove their way around the empty tables that filled the cafeteria. Smoke filled the space fast, but Veena knew that wouldn't stop the armoured soldier—their heads-up display in their faceplate would keep track of their location. And their helmet would filter their air.

An overhead alarm went off so loud it rattled Veena's teeth. The three of them kept moving towards the far exit of the cafeteria.

"I said STOP!" the soldier following shouted over the sound of the alarm. "Or I will shoot!"

The door was right ahead of them; they were almost there. Veena darted forward. A concentrated bolt of green light crossed the room, burning a hole into the doorframe. As Veena focused on the hole, Orin let go of her hand. He fell to the ground between two tables.

"Oh, shit!" Veena bent over him as she realized the laser had passed through him. "Where are you hit?"

"Put your hands up," demanded the soldier as she advanced across the room—the tables were not spaced far enough apart for someone in full armour, forcing her to shimmy sideways to pass.

"I'm okay," Orin said, but his pale face said otherwise. He rolled onto his side and pushed himself back up to his feet.

"But where are you hit?" Veena took the duffle bag and slung it over her shoulder.

"It grazed my right arm." He glanced back at the soldier as he cradled his right arm with his left.

Veena frowned, trying to see where he'd been hit.

"There's no time. We've got to keep moving."

"Right." Veena turned and ran towards the door. The duffle

bag bounced on her back with each step, but she kept going. Orin stayed close behind her.

They passed out into the hall just as a firefighting crew decked out in full gear and pulling multiple hoses entered the cafeteria from the other direction.

"This way," someone in full firefighting gear said as he pointed to another set of doors.

As Veena and Orin headed that way, other escaping crew members crowded in on them. The group pushed out of the smoke-filled air and into a common room full of medics.

Veena took a deep breath, filling her lungs with clear air. The door they'd come through was now sealed—and the soldier chasing them was nowhere in sight. She stopped the nearest medic.

"I need to return him"—she pointed at Orin—"back to his ship. What's the quickest way to the hangar?"

"The main concourse is shut down, but you can cut through flight control," he said, pointing to an open door across the room.

"Thanks." Veena put a hand on Orin's shoulder, and the two of them headed that way.

Chapter Forty-Eight

A coughing fit brought Hwicce back to consciousness. He turned to his side and choked up a surprising amount of water that tasted of burnt tea. As he rolled onto his back, memories of his fall through the darkness flooded into his mind.

For a moment, he was drowning again with a honeycomb of glowing lights blocking his way. Veena reached out to him from the other side, her fingertips nearly reaching his. In a flash, a field of stars stretched out between them. He gasped. The sound of his racing heartbeat brought his thoughts back to the present.

He took a deep breath and opened his eyes. Blackness surrounded him. He squeezed his eyes closed for a moment, then opened them again. Everything remained black—the kind of inky abyss that felt inhabited by something sinister. The darkness started pressing in on him, and his breathing sped up to ragged pants. He shivered.

"Get a grip," he said to himself as the familiar knot in his gut tightened even more. "You're not afraid of the dark."

With his left hand, he touched the ground. His fingertips slid over the slime-coated rock beneath him—he'd have to be careful not to lose his footing. From somewhere close by, water flowed, filling the air with spray and a cacophony of sound. Ending up in the water again probably wouldn't end well for him.

"Baker," he called out in a tone barely above a whisper. His throat was dry as though the water had sucked all moisture out of him. It was unlikely she'd be within hearing range, but he had to try. He licked his lips and shouted, "Baker?"

But the moving water absorbed his words. No one would be able to hear his calls. He pushed down the panic welling inside him and took several long, slow breaths.

He checked his belt for the flashlight. A moan escaped his lips when he realized he didn't even have his belt anymore. He had no flashlight, no knife, not even a ration bar. Rubbing his upper arms, his mind raced. He wasn't going to last long in the dark. A shiver ran up his spine.

"What the hell do I do now?"

He thought back to his survival training. It had been an unpleasant two weeks shivering on an ice world in a spacesuit—an experience that didn't seem to apply to his current situation.

"Baker?" he called again. "I know you won't let me down. You never have."

Baker would've started looking for him the instant the mushroom cap plunged into the cave. She'd stop at nothing to find him.

"All I need to do is stay alive until you found me."

After reaching up to make sure he wouldn't hit his head, he shifted to sitting cross-legged on the ground.

"Promise me something," Veena said, rolling over in bed next to him. Her dark liquorice curls cascaded over her neck and cheek. Her dark eyes glinted with mischief as she.

He blinked; Veena wasn't here. He'd failed to get in touch with her after quitting the army. He buried his head in his hands and groaned.

"I was too hasty—I should've sent you a message before quitting." He swallowed. "As Baker would say, I made a dumbass move. I should have..."

By now, she had to have assumed he'd abandoned her and Molly—or worse, that he was dead and never coming back to her. Hell, he could end up dead, and she'd never know.

"Veena, I love you. I should have tried harder to reach you."

With a sigh, he lay down on his back again. His body ached from the fall, but he didn't think he'd broken anything. The surrounding darkness seemed thick, as though it were alive, waiting for him. He closed his eyes and pictured being in bed with Veena the morning he shipped out from New Haven.

He pictured every detail, from the warm glow of Veena's skin to how the light streamed through the windows. It was the last time he'd been on New Haven—that world now gone, bombed into oblivion.

"What do you want me to promise?" he asked the woman in his imagination.

Veena's eyes met his. "Always come back to me and Mol."

"I promise." He leaned forward and kissed Veena's forehead.

She pushed him over onto his back and slid on top of him. "If you break your promise, I'll hunt you down."

The sound of little feet running down the hall drew both their attention. The door burst open and Molly ran in, grinning from ear to ear. Her hair and eyes were just like her mother's, but her smile was her own. She held up her worn stuffed animal.

"Click decided you're going to make banana oatmeal for breakfast."

"They have?" Hwicce smiled as Veena slid off him. He shivered now that her warmth was gone. He'd made the oatmeal that day, and he'd hugged Veena and Molly for the last time.

He took a deep breath and opened his eyes. Lounging in his memories wouldn't help him keep his promise. He sat up.

Staying on all fours, he began exploring his surroundings. He found the water's edge a few paces away. As he dipped his hand into the flowing water, he shivered. In the dark, he couldn't determine how big the water mass was. Would the rain above cause it to rise? The thought of rising water levels was too much, and he pushed it from his mind.

Turning his back on the water's edge, he crawled until he reached a rock wall. Standing, he followed the rock wall by keeping one hand on it. It seemed he was in an alcove about thirty paces long. Beneath the layer of algae or other growth, the walls seemed too regular to be natural—it was like someone had cut a cavern out of the rock. But he couldn't find an exit other than the water.

He sat with his back against the wall, facing the water. At least it wasn't cold—hypothermia wouldn't be what killed him. There was plenty of water, so dehydration wasn't an issue, assuming the water was safe to drink. If he stayed put, he was facing starvation unless Baker managed to find him.

With a yawn, he slid down to the ground. He had time. A nap would help him think better. Even though he lay on a rock, his exhaustion soon caught up to him, and he dozed off. The darkness of the cavern was soon replaced by his last breakfast with his family.

Chapter Forty-Nine

Veena let out a long exhale when they entered the hangar. *Buttercup* sat where it had been before, the yellow of its hull reflecting the oversaturated lights and casting a warm glow on the deck around it.

She smiled as she headed towards the ship. They were almost away. A few paces from *Buttercup's* airlock door, she paused, and Orin stopped beside her. She ran a hand down her ponytail and bit her lip as she glanced towards the hangar door. A chill ran up her spine.

Nigel materialized at the bottom of the stairs. "We must get out of here right away,"

"Agreed." Veena nodded and turned towards their ship. "I don't want to stay a moment longer than necessary."

Nigel bowed his head, then vanished.

"Let me take the bag," Orin said, and Veena handed him the duffle. He winced when he took the load but didn't complain. "Lock up out here, and I'll warm up the ship." He disappeared inside. "I'm with your computerized friend. We need to get out of here while we can."

Veena pulled herself up tall and looked him in the eye. She'd misjudged her former boss; he'd proven a solid ally. "Let's get the hell out of here," she said with all the confidence she could muster.

After giving her a curt nod, Orin rushed inside, leaving Veena alone. A stronger prickling sensation crawled up her neck, and her mouth went dry. She swallowed as she slowly rotated.

Gloria stood halfway between her and the entrance to the hanger. She now wore the Protectorate's military indigo. With a scowl on her face, she stared at Veena.

Veena curled her lip as she fixated on Gloria's outfit. A sour taste formed in her mouth.

"Were you part of the plan to snatch Molly from the beginning? Or just a spy keeping tabs on the civilian decoders?" Veena let out a long exhale. She'd trusted this woman, even considered her a friend.

"Look, it wasn't supposed to turn out this way." Gloria advanced.

Veena clenched her fists at her sides. "You turned us in— betrayed us."

"My actions were about loyalty to the Protectorate." Gloria frowned. "I didn't mean for anyone to get hurt, but sometimes that's necessary."

"I thought..." Veena's words trailed off, and she pressed her lips together. She'd believed Gloria wanted to help her get Molly back. She'd trusted her promise of help without questioning the other woman's motives.

"It was never personal."

"You helped them take my child."

"For the greater good."

"You pretended to be my friend. You tried to trick me into decoding that"—Veena gritted her teeth together—"...that... fucking piece of code."

"Look, there's still a way out for you—a way to be reunited with Molly." Gloria licked her lips. "Just finish decoding that message, and Swa will be good to her word and reunite you with your little girl."

"Like you were good to your word?"

The two women stared at each other. Gloria's expression went cold—like she'd put on a mask. She huffed and raised her right arm, levelling a stun gun towards Veena's chest. "You and your spawn are a risk to everyone's safety. Letting you run free was a mistake."

Veena's heart rate accelerated, and she took a step back. The veneer of friendship had been stripped away. She didn't recognize this woman anymore. Gloria had played her.

In her peripheral vision, *Buttercup's* yellow hull beckoned her —a safe haven if only she could reach it. But the three steps it would take her would give Gloria more than enough time to shoot her.

"Even your husband proved to be a traitor." Gloria moved a pace closer and sneered. "I wish I could just kill you now and end the mess you've made. But I follow my orders."

"It's that encoded message, isn't it?" Veena tried to keep her hands from trembling.

"That message isn't human. There's something out there other than us humans, something other, something dangerous. You need to decode that message. Humans—no, the Protectorate—must get the upper hand."

Veena put her hand into the pocket of her stolen uniform. The glob of Molly's nanites was still there. They felt warm and rubbery—inviting, even. She squeezed the mass to activate them, then she pulled them out of her pocket. The nanites followed their pre-programmed routine to disassemble and reform into a flock of mythical birds. The thumb-sized blue and red birds took flight, flapping their wings like the birds in the old vids.

"What the—" Gloria's gaze moved upwards as she watched the birds ascend.

Veena charged forward, dropping her shoulder at the last

minute. She crashed into Gloria, and the two women fell to the deck. The stungun skirted away.

Behind her, *Buttercup's* engines whined as they warmed up. How much time did Orin need?

Gloria took advantage of Veena's distraction and grabbed onto her left wrist, using it as leverage to roll Veena face down onto the deck. With a smooth motion, Gloria rolled on top of Veena.

Veena tried to wiggle free but failed. For the first time, she regretted not making Hwicce teach her more unarmed combat. Gloria clearly had combat training—another thing that didn't fit with the woman Veena thought she knew. Gloria brought her other arm around Veena's neck and squeezed.

The chokehold cut Veena's air off. Her vision narrowed until all she could see was the patch of deck right in front of her. One of the tiny red birds flew into view. She reached out and touched it. The nanites reformed into a glossy black spider marked with a red hourglass. It skittered towards her, crawling over her hand and up her arm.

"What the hell!" Gloria shouted as the arachnid walked over her. She loosened her grip and batted at the formed nanites.

Using Gloria's distraction, Veena arched up onto her heels and twisted, shoving Gloria off her. Veena rolled in the opposite direction, stopping in a push-up position. Before she could stand, Gloria grabbed onto her left ankle.

The first step leading into *Buttercup* was centimetres from her face. She was almost free. Veena kicked with her right foot, contacting Gloria in the face.

Somehow Gloria held on, pulling Veena away from the step. She slid easily on the slick deck.

"I won't be a pawn," Veena said as she twisted and looked at her opponent.

Crimson blood now dripped from Gloria's nose. She ignored it as she continued to pull Veena away from *Buttercup*.

Veena looked past Gloria and towards the hangar doors—a

group of armoured soldiers was advancing. She was running out of time. She lashed out with a second kick, this time contacting Gloria's shoulder.

Gloria released her grip, and Veena launched herself onto her feet and sprinted up the steps.

"Remember, we still have Molly," Gloria taunted just before Veena pulled in the stairs and slammed the outside door shut.

As soon as the door sealed, the *Buttercup* lifted off. Orin accelerated fast enough that Veena stumbled and lost her footing. She slumped down on the deck and put her head in her hands. They weren't any closer to getting Molly back, and she'd just lost someone she thought was a friend.

Nigel materialized before her. He crouched down and sat beside her. His expression of concern looked real. "Are you alright?"

She took a deep breath and looked at the hologram. "I'm fine," she lied.

Pushing herself back up to her feet, she left the airlock. Click sat on the floor just inside the common room. They flashed red, then orange.

"Click says they are happy we've escaped," Nigel said from behind her.

Veena nodded as she stared at the little alien—the one Greer wanted for some reason. She let out a long exhale and slumped down at the kitchen table.

Molly, Click, and the alien code all went together somehow, and she needed to figure out how to get her girl back.

"You okay?" shouted Orin from the cockpit.

Click jumped up on the table in front of her as Nigel took the seat across from her. As she looked at them, she realized she now knew who she could trust.

"I think things will be okay," she said loud enough Orin could hear. She nodded and continued more quietly, "We can figure this everything out and get Molly back."

Epilogue

Dr. Greer frowned at the holographic image before him. A projection of General Swa's head hung in the air over his desk. The annoying woman's virtual presence had already ruined his day—the army made him deal with her way too often. He'd barely made it back to his lab after an assassination attempt. He needed to be left alone if they wanted him to make progress.

"My work here is important, and I need to get back to it," he said as if he was the one with the rank.

Swa pursed her lips, her face taking on a pinched expression. "Don't forget your place, Doctor. You aren't as valuable as you think you are."

"My work is outside military hierarchy." He raised his chin. "Without me, you'll never isolate the right genetic marker."

"Without me, your supplies will be cut off." Swa narrowed her eyes as she stared at him. "You are so far off the loop, no one would ever find you."

Greer exhaled through his nose while maintaining his rigid posture. Swa was an annoyance he had no choice but to deal with.

"Your loss of the alien is a black mark against you."

Greer forced himself to stay still—he hadn't realized Swa

even knew about the alien. "When your people retrieve the alien, I need it back. It doesn't matter if it's alive."

Swa cocked her head. "Why do you need the alien?"

"Its blood holds markers that may help my work."

She nodded as though the answer satisfied her. "I have intelligence relevant to Molly Oswiu."

"You mean Subject 34?" It always irritated him when others insisted his subjects had names. They'd proven their lack of humanity long before they were brought to him. Deliberate or not, genetic tweaks could make humans into something other—something less than human, something more useful as a tool than anything else.

"Is that what you call her now?" Swa sneered at him.

"What's the news?"

"Both of 'Subject 34's' parents have dropped out of sight," Swa said. "The mother has escaped. And the father is out there somewhere. I suspect they'll be hunting for their girl—maybe together."

He snorted. "They don't have the resources to locate me or Subject 34 here. Hell, you just used my lab's remoteness as a threat against me."

"The girl's parents are motivated." Swa looked him in the eye. "I wouldn't be surprised if they find a way."

He saw Swa's tactic for what it was: she wanted to meddle in his affairs. Perhaps even keep tabs on him. But if she wanted him to craft a Protectorate super soldier to counter those their enemy fielded at the battle of Candy Cane Lane, she needed to leave him alone.

He frowned. "I'll double security." A thought came to him, and he almost smiled. "When you catch Subject 34's mother, bring her to me."

"She needs to finish decoding the alien message first."

"She can do that here."

"Fine," Swa said. "I'll put my full resources to work hunting for the parents. I'll update you as required."

"Fine." He reached forward and turned the holograph off.

Greer stared out his office window. Yellows swirled around reds in an endless storm dancing across the gas giant that hung over the horizon of his moon. The radiation emitted would make his facility near invisible. From orbit, his little corner of the system would remain hidden—on the off chance anyone even found this system.

No worlds nearby were candidates for terraforming. Just piles of rocks, some with iron rain and others with land scorched by tidal fires. Even the water world here was covered by ice. No, they wouldn't find him here.

He stood and walked to the pens that held his experiments. Passing the cell-like rooms, he examined each of his subjects through the clear wall at the end. Most stood and stared at him as he passed by.

All of them were descended from the tweaks made prior to the Protectorate's enactment of the GenEn protocols. He stopped and stared at one of his greenies. The woman stared right back, her green skin pale under the artificial lights.

At most, the tweaks made his subjects slightly more able to survive on their adopted worlds. The ability to photosynthesize nourishment from light wouldn't create a super-soldier.

Moving on, he stared at the Rokan soldier Swa had acquired for him. The soldier didn't stare back; the lab light would be too bright for his darkness-adapted eyes. He'd hoped for one of their purple cloaks—the ones rumoured to have telepathic abilities. Instead, he'd been given an ordinary soldier barely more than an adolescent. He frowned. The Rokan offered him little.

He continued on to the one subject who held promise.

At the end of the hall, he stopped and looked inside the cell. Curled up, Subject 34 slept on her narrow cot.

He knocked on the window.

She stretched out and turned towards him. "Is there a message from my mom?" she asked—the same question she asked every time. "She needs to bring my Click stuffy."

"Not yet," he lied. It was better if his subjects still thought he was going to let them rejoin society—and that people off this moon still cared about them.

Subject 34 stood and walked over to the clear wall. "When?"

"Soon. I promise." He smiled.

Subject 34 clenched her fists and stared him in the eye. The barrier between them vibrated. "My mom and dad are coming for me."

"Of course they are, my dear." Greer did his best to keep his excitement off his face. This little girl was exactly the subject he needed.

The story continues in…
The Alien Algorthm
Book 2 of the Encoded Orbits Trilogy

Thanks for reading!

Molly is still out there.

If you've made it this far, you know Veena isn't the type to quit — but she's running out of leads, running from the law, and her husband is stuck in a cave on a planet of inedible moss. Things are about to get worse before they get better.

The hunt for Molly continues in *The Alien Algorithm*.

Veena stumbles onto an alien technology that might be her best shot at getting her daughter back — if she can figure out how to use it before a bounty hunter catches up with her. Meanwhile, Hwicce is marooned with a group of reclusive, deeply unwelcoming Luddites, and Veena only knows roughly where he is. Roughly.

From a secret underground city to a run-down space station to a glittering archipelago of floating islands, the race is on.

[Get The Alien Algorithm →https://books2read.com/ TheAlienAlgorithm**]**

Thanks for reading!

And if you'd like to hear about new releases and the occasional free short story, you can join my newsletter at jeannettebe-dard.com.

About the Author

By day I'm a scientist, by night I write science fiction. I have hard drives clogged with ideas and outlines—sometimes they dissolve into ones and zeros, but sometimes they coalesce to form an entire novel. My stories are filled with action and adventure where something always blows up, usually in the first fifty pages.

You can connect with me here: https://jeannettebedard.com/

Also by Jeannette Bedard

ENCODED ORBITS

Fractured Orbits

The Alien Algorithm

Subject 34

THE SETTLER CHRONICLES

Day 115 on an Alien World

Far Side of the Moon

Abandoned Ships, Hijacked Minds

The Alien Artifact

Acknowledgments

In no particular order I'd like to thank: Christine, Alana, and Amy for being kind enough to provide feedback on early drafts.

To Jeff Elkins and Tom Holbrook—their feedback made this book so much better.

To Gavin for giving me time to write and enduring hearing me talk about it.

www.ingramcontent.com/pod-product-compliance
Lightning Source LLC
Chambersburg PA
CBHW020949030726
47496CB00005B/1424